"You Don't Know Anything About Me," Faith Protested

"Don't you think you're taking a big chance in asking a stranger to be your partner?"

"I know you're in the oil business, so you know what you'd be getting into. And I've got a gut feeling I'm near a strike."

"I don't invest money on gut feelings. That *is* what you're interested in, isn't it? My money—presuming I have any."

"I'm interested in a backer, and investing money is part of the business. Well, what do you say? When do you think you can get back to me on this?"

"Within a couple of days. Maybe sooner."

It was a crazy proposition, she realized as he left. But there was something about the man, the same thing that had prompted her to think at their first meeting, what's a nice guy like you doing in a place like this?

ELAINE CAMP
Vein of Gold

Silhouette Special Edition

Originally Published by Silhouette Books
division of
Harlequin Enterprises Ltd.

To Robby and Stony,
for showing me what friendship is all about
and for proving that distance
can't sever the ties that bind us.

It is in men as in soils,
where sometimes there is a vein of gold,
which the owner knows not of.
Jonathan Swift

*First published in Great Britain 1986
by Silhouette Books, 15–16 Brook's Mews, London W1A 1DR*

© Deborah E. Camp 1986

Silhouette, Silhouette Special and Colophon are Trade Marks
of Harlequin Enterprises B.V.

ISBN 0 373 09285 7

23–0586

*Printed and bound in Great Britain by
Cox & Wyman Ltd, Reading*

ELAINE CAMP

dreamed for many years of becoming a writer. Once she'd tried it, she quickly became successful, perhaps because of her reporter's eye, which gives her a special advantage in observing human relationships.

Other Silhouette Books by Elaine Camp

Silhouette Desire

Love Letters
Hook, Line and Sinker

Silhouette Special Edition

For Love or Money
In a Pirate's Arms
Just Another Pretty Face

*For further information about
Silhouette Books please write to:*

Jane Nicholls
Silhouette Books
PO Box 236
Thornton Road
Croydon
Surrey CR9 3RU

Chapter One

What's a great looking guy like you doing in a place like this? Faith Hutton wondered as she idly examined Houston Traynor's numerous attributes while his attention was arrested by the land lease she had handed him.

He was by far the best-looking Texan she had negotiated with since she'd become a landman for PATCO Petroleum Company. Most of the oilmen she'd met were forty or over, but Houston was in his late twenties or early thirties. The other oilmen were married with children, but this Texan was single. The others were playful and full of hot air, but this one was shy and mannerly. He was different, all right. Delightfully different, she mentally tacked on.

Tearing her gaze away from him long enough to glance around the spacious fifth-wheel trailer he called home, Faith noted that it was tidy with a homespun charm. Colorful throw pillows were artfully arranged, an intricate patchwork quilt was draped over the back of a rocking chair and pots of African violets and grape ivy filled the window ledges. A desk in one corner of the living room was the only allowance to clutter. Papers, pens and ledgers spilled across the desk top, and an electric typewriter was piled high with magazines and newspapers.

Faith looked back at Houston and found the horizontal scar under his full lower lip absolutely fascinating. Whoever had stitched it had done a poor job. She could see where two or three of the sutures had been, now little vertical lines of scar tissue. Other than that, he was attractive in an understated way. His looks didn't bowl a woman over, but sort of sneaked up on her, Faith mused. In fact, she was just now noticing his light blond hair, which was combed straight back from his wide, lined forehead, and the tawny color of his eyes as he read the land lease agreement. His lips pulled back in a quick grimace to reveal straight white teeth, which could only mean that he didn't chew tobacco. Thank heavens! Faith thought with a roll of her azure eyes. Tobacco chewing was one habit she abhorred, and it had kept her from accepting invitations from otherwise desirable Texas men.

Realizing that she was daydreaming on company time, she forced her thoughts back to business, telling herself that her job had become so mundane she was reduced to rapt fascination over any little thing. How long could the company waste her talents? She wasn't a landman; she was a petroleum geologist!

Houston lifted his gaze from the lease agreement, letting it flutter from his lean fingers to the kitchen table. He relaxed in the ladder-backed chair and released his breath in a slow sigh. Faith lifted her brows in expectation and waited for him to agree to the terms. He seemed to be a no-nonsense man, so she probably wouldn't have to endure the nit-picking and jovial banter she had tolerated from others.

He'd sign the lease and she could be on her way back to the Pecos branch office.

"As you can see, it's a fair contract," she said, reciting her standard hurry-up-and-sign-it dictum. "All it needs is your signature on the dotted line."

"It's fair, all right," he drawled in true Texan fashion. "Mighty fair."

"Good. Do you have a pen?" she asked, reaching for her purse. "If not, I have one in here."

"I'm not signing it, ma'am."

Unperturbed, she folded her arms on the table and met his level gaze. So she had been wrong about him, she mused. He wanted to argue, after all. So be it. She arched a brow, displaying mild curiosity. "Oh? And why not, Mr. Traynor?"

"Because I'm not interested in leasing my land to PATCO again." He pushed the lease across the table toward her. "Thanks all the same."

She ignored the lease, refusing to pick it up. "Has another company approached you? If that's the case, we can—"

"No, that's not it." He tugged at the white and tan handkerchief tied around his wide neck. "I'm not leasing it to anybody."

"What are you planning to do with it?"

One side of his mouth slanted up in a bashful grin. "Begging your pardon, ma'am, but that's none of your business."

Momentarily knocked off guard by his attractive smile, Faith looked away from him to gather her thoughts. "Are you going to graze cattle on it? You can still do that and let PATCO continue drilling. Your neighbors, the MacQuays, have been doing just that for years."

"I'm not a cattleman," he stated simply, then glanced toward the kitchen counter. "Could I offer you a cup of coffee? It's instant, but it's tasty."

"No, thank you," Faith said, quickly taking stock of the situation. A simple land lease renewal had suddenly hit the skids, and she was determined not to return to PATCO empty-handed. "Has PATCO done something that didn't meet with your approval? Debris can be a problem, but the contract calls for us to clean up after ourselves—"

"You've been real good about that," he interrupted. "I've got no quarrel with PATCO. I just don't want to lease the land again."

"Well, then what is it, Mr. Traynor?" she asked, squaring her shoulders as she tried to present a confident air. What did he want her to do? she wondered. Did he want her to beg him to sign the blasted lease? "I'm sure we can compromise. I think we're close to striking oil. All we need is a few more months and you'll be raking in the profits. We both want that, don't we?"

"I want to thank you for your time, ma'am." He stood up, towering over her.

Faith blinked up at him, dumbfounded by his sudden dismissal. "Let me leave the lease here and I'll get back to you—"

"No need for that." He picked up the lease and placed it firmly in her hand. "Take it with you. I'm not signing it." He cupped her elbow in one large hand and pulled her up from the chair. "You drive carefully back to Pecos."

"Mr. Traynor," Faith jerked her elbow free and faced him. "What am I going to tell the company? There must be a reason why you're not signing the lease."

He strode to the front door and opened it. "I don't know what to tell them other than the truth, Miss Hutton."

"And what *is* the truth?" Faith asked, picking up her purse and clutching the unsigned lease in her other hand as she walked to the door.

"That I wouldn't sign it," he said with infuriating simplicity. "That's all they need to know." He placed a hand to the small of her back in a pretense of helping her down the outside steps, but Faith knew that she was getting the bum's rush a lá Houston Traynor.

Once down the steps, she turned back to face him. "Mr. Traynor, please reconsider. I don't understand why you would pass up such an offer unless you've had a better one."

He smiled and touched the fingers of one hand to his forehead in a jaunty salute. "Nice meeting you, Miss Hutton. Bye now." He closed the door firmly and locked it.

Faith wrenched open her car door, settled into the bucket seat and started the car. What's with him? she wondered angrily. Who did he think he was, practically ordering her off his property? She steered the car along the rutted dirt road, and the oil rig in question flashed past. How was she going to explain this to her boss? Samson Applegate expected her to return with a renewal, not a refusal.

She turned off onto a gravel road that led to Asa MacQuay's land. Mac had sold Houston the property, so maybe he knew what Houston was up to. If she could find out what Houston Traynor planned to do with the land, then she could negotiate with him. His evasiveness left her defenseless.

Mac leased his property to PATCO, and it had made him a wealthy man. One of the biggest land owners in Loving County, Texas, Mac was reported to have more money than he knew what to do with. His land was rich in oil, which left him plenty of time to fool around with his cattle and not worry about fluctuating beef prices. Faith had worked with Mac before and she liked him. He'd shoot straight, she told herself. Mac never beat around the bush about anything.

Houston Traynor could take a lesson from Mac, she thought, recalling the comments she'd heard about Houston in the nearby town of Mentone. Of course, nothing was *near* anything in this wide open, flat, western part of Texas, but Mentone was a community pool in a region that otherwise supported no more than a sprinkling of humanity.

A few people in Mentone had referred to Houston as a loner, a hermit who kept to himself and didn't encourage friendships.

"He's a strange one," the waitress in Mentone's coffee shop had told Faith. "With his looks, he could have women falling all over him, but he hardly ever comes into town, and when he does, he runs a few errands and scoots back to his place without exchanging more than a few 'how-you-doings' with anyone."

"Maybe he's just shy," Faith had suggested, drawing a frown from the waitress.

"Maybe," she had replied. "And maybe he's just a solitary man who likes it that way."

Asa MacQuay's sprawling ranch house came into view in the distance, and Faith pulled her thoughts back to the present. Mac had known Houston Traynor since Traynor was a boy, so if anyone would know why Traynor had suddenly decided not to renew his land lease with PATCO, Mac would. She pressed down on the accelerator and the Mustang shot forward until the house was no longer a period among the exclamation points of oil rigs. The house faced east, and a low garage to the north of it sheltered a fleet of fancy cars—Lincolns, Mercedes and an early-model Thunderbird that sat next to a custom-built, midnight-blue pickup truck. Faith parked her Mustang in front of the house, got out and rang the doorbell.

A doe-eyed woman answered the door and spoke English with a Mexican accent.

"Is Mac in?" Faith asked. "I'm Faith Hutton from PATCO."

"Come in, please," the maid said, stepping back, then closing the door behind Faith. "Please wait in here. I'll get Señor Mac."

"Thank you." Faith entered the formal living room and sat in one of the wing-backed chairs that flanked the marble fireplace. The ticking of the grandfather clock was deafening in the quiet room.

"Faith?"

Faith turned toward the melodic voice and smiled when she saw Mac's wife. "Bonita Kaye! It's been ages since I've seen you." She stood up and received Bonita Kaye's robust hug. "How have you been?"

"Fit as a fiddle," Bonita Kaye said with a jovial burst of laughter. "What have you done to your hair?"

"Nothing," Faith said, touching the golden-blond hair that had been tamed into a loose bundle on the crown of her head.

"You haven't cut it, have you?"

"No."

"Good," Bonita Kaye said, stepping back to give Faith a thorough once-over. "If I had hair like yours, I'd always wear it loose. It's a shame to pin it up. I used to have hair that fell past my waist." She pushed at the white bangs of her Dutch-girl haircut. "That was a long time ago when my hair was strawberry blond."

"I imagine it was lovely," Faith noted, examining Bonita Kaye's shining blue eyes and smooth complexion. She had probably been a real beauty in her prime, Faith thought. Her attention was diverted by Mac's arrival. "Hello, Mac. I hope I haven't come at a bad time."

"It's never a bad time for me to see you, honey." Mac reached out and grasped her hand firmly before letting go.

A lean man with mischievous blue eyes, thick white hair and a full white mustache, Mac was dressed in his usual faded jeans, denim shirt and scuffed boots. The only concessions to his wealth were the gold and diamond rings on his liver-spotted fingers.

"How about a drink?" We've got some homemade apple cider," he offered, his eyes twinkling with a merriment that was an intricate part of his nature.

"You won't have to twist my arm," Faith said, letting Bonita Kaye guide her from the living room to the den at the back of the house where she spotted a new picture on the paneled wall. "Is that you new grandchild?" she asked, pointing to the photograph of a chubby-cheeked baby.

"It sure is. That's our fifth one. Junior and Chrissie named her Bonnie Christine. Isn't she the cutest thing you've ever laid your eyes on?"

"She's beautiful," Faith agreed, glancing at the other photographs. "Have you seen any of your children recently?"

"Not since Christmas," Mac answered. "None of them feel about Texas the way me and Bonita Kaye do. They were glad to move and not too thrilled about coming back for visits."

Faith smiled sympathetically and sat on the comfortable couch as the maid entered the den and placed a tray of apple cider on the coffee table. The five MacQuay offspring had scattered to Phoenix, Los Angeles, Seattle, Des Moines and Nashville. What would happen with the MacQuay spread when Mac and Bonita Kaye were gone? Faith wondered a little sadly. Would the children sell it and allow it to be broken up into a patchwork of land tracts?

"What brings you out this way?" Mac asked, handing a glass of apple cider to Faith.

"Business, of course. I've been talking to Houston Traynor."

"Oh, that Houston!" Bonita Kaye chuckled. "Isn't he a cutup?"

Faith threw Bonita Kaye a bewildered look. Were they talking about the same person? "Well, he wasn't cracking jokes while I was with him. In fact, I found it difficult to talk with him. He was very evasive.''

Mac eased himself into a leather lounger and tasted the cold cider. ''He's a little standoffish with strangers, but once you get to know him he opens up. We're fond of him.''

''We've known Houston since he was six,'' Bonita Kaye chimed in as she sat next to Faith on the couch. ''He's like family to us.'' A beatific smile lit up her cherubic face. ''Like a son.''

''What were you talking to him about?'' Mac asked.

''Renewing his land lease with PATCO, but he wouldn't sign the lease and he wouldn't tell me why.'' Faith drank some of the tart juice, giving Mac a chance to comment. When he didn't, she decided to press. ''Has he had another offer for that land?''

''Not that I know of.'' Mac glanced at Bonita Kaye, and a silent message was passed back and forth. ''Faith, I might as well tell you that Houston plans to drill on that land himself.''

Faith almost choked on the apple cider. She coughed and her eyes watered. ''Drill on it himself?'' she repeated, her voice hoarse and louder than usual. ''Does he have that kind of money?''

''Well, now...'' Mac stared at his hands for a moment in quiet contemplation. ''Houston's finances aren't anybody's business but his own, and if I did know something about them, I wouldn't tell anybody. A man's wallet is best kept in his own hip pocket.''

Feeling justly chastised, Faith felt her color deepen to a rosy hue. Leave it to a Texan to put you in your place politely but firmly, she thought. Most Texans she had met said little, but what they did say carried a lot of weight.

''I know it's none of my business, but drilling for oil is a costly venture. I can't believe that Traynor would be so foolish as to—''

"Houston is anything but foolish," Bonita Kaye cut in sharply, then smiled to take the sting from her words. "If he's drilling, then he's thought it over carefully."

Faith finished the cider and set the glass on the tray in front of her. "I was sent out here to get his lease renewed, and I'm not leaving without his John Hancock. I think I'll go back to his place and try to talk some sense into him."

"You can try," Mac said dubiously, "but you won't change his mind. Bonita Kaye's right. Houston's given this a lot of thought. He's been planning to drill on his land ever since he bought it from me five years ago. He's been saving every penny, and I guess he's got enough pennies now or he wouldn't be spurning that new lease of yours." Mac ran his callused hands down the legs of his worn jeans, and diamonds sparkled on his ring fingers.

"Does he have any experience in drilling for oil?" Faith asked.

"Why, sure! He's a Texan, isn't he?" Mac chuckled and looked at Bonita Kaye to share his joke. "He's been working on rigs since he was a kid. In fact, I think he worked for PATCO for a couple of years, didn't he, honey?"

"I believe so," Bonita Kaye agreed. "But it's been a few years back. The last rig he worked on was Dub Bennet's number four."

"Dub Bennet," Faith repeated with a touch of scorn. "A wildcatter. I bet that's who talked Traynor into this harebrained idea. Dub probably failed to mention that bankruptcy goes hand in hand with most independent ventures."

Mac's smile was slow and wise. "Wildcatters are the only pioneers left."

"They're a rare breed, all right," Bonita Kaye agreed.

"I understand your point of view, Faith, but you can't fault a man for grabbing his dream." Mac rose from the lounger and went to the narrow windows that were draped in yellow sheers.

"Even if it means losing everything?" Faith asked.

"Even then," Mac said softly as he pulled back one of the sheer panels to let the sunlight pour in. "Where's the glory without the risk?"

"Spoken like a true Texas oilman," Faith said, smiling. "PATCO's been good to you, Mac. Why can't Traynor take a lesson from that?"

"If I were Houston's age, I'd probably drill myself," he said, finally turning sideways to look at Faith and Bonita Kaye. "I was in my forties when PATCO approached me about drilling for oil here, but if I'd been in my thirties, things would have been different. Of course, I wasn't an oilman like Houston. I've always been a cattleman who just happened to own land that was full of black gold."

"Working on rigs and drilling your own are two different things," Faith argued, then decided to save her breath. The MacQuays were in Traynor's corner. Whatever Traynor wanted was fine with them. "Thanks for the refreshment, but I've got to run."

"Are you going back to Houston's?" Bonita Kaye asked as she stood up.

"Yes. I'm going to give it one more try before I head back to PATCO."

"Good luck, honey." Bonita Kaye placed an arm around Faith's shoulders. "Come back and see us, you hear?"

"Yes, I will. 'Bye, Mac."

"See you later, Faith. Don't be such a stranger." Mac's smile was at once encouraging and sympathetic. "Good luck with Houston."

Bonita Kaye saw Faith to the door and stood on the threshold until Faith had pulled away from the house.

Traynor was a stubborn, foolish man, Faith thought heatedly. He was obviously suffering from delusions of grandeur. He'd worked among wildcatters long enough to believe that he could amass a fortune all by himself. She'd seen the symptoms before, and she'd seen more than a few wildcatters in bankruptcy court. The least she could do was make Traynor see reason. Besides, Samson would be furious if she returned without Traynor's renewed lease. PATCO believed in this venture. A lot of company money had been sunk into that hole.

Approaching Traynor's land, Faith peered through the dusty windshield and saw Traynor standing outside his trailer. A shallow pan of water and mirror sat atop a tall tool chest. Traynor, bare chested, was pulling a razor through the lather on the lower half of his face. He paused and glanced at her car as she was getting out of it, then turned back to the mirror.

"Did you forget something?" he asked as she approached him.

"I wanted to talk to you about this lease again," Faith answered, stopping beside him.

"I'm not signing it." He dipped the razor into the pan of water, swished it around, then pulled it down his lathered cheek. "You're wasting your time."

Momentarily transfixed by the glide of the razor down his throat, Faith shook free of the spell and forced her thoughts back to the lease. "I just came from the MacQuays. Mac says that you're thinking of drilling for oil by yourself."

The razor slid up his throat and under his chin. "That so?"

"Is it true?" Faith demanded, irritated with his evasiveness.

"Yes." He dunked the razor into the pan again. "Something wrong with that?"

"It's very costly. You could easily lose everything you have, but if you sign this lease, you can avoid any risk of—"

"No, thanks."

"For your own good I think you should reconsider."

The razor lapped up the rest of the lather. Houston dropped it in the pan, whipped a red towel from around his neck and vigorously rubbed his face with it. Faith breathed in the smell of soap and water as her gaze moved nervously over his coppery skin. The tops of his shoulders were pink from a slight sunburn, but the rest of him was the color of brown sugar. His wide chest was lightly covered with dark blond hair that swirled and dipped in a thin straight line to his navel. Her nerve endings fluttered and Faith stepped back from him, alarmingly aware of his potency. He was dangerously masculine, she thought with trepidation, and she warned herself to keep her head on straight and not be sidetracked so easily by his masculine appeal.

"Mr. Traynor, I...I..."

"Yes?" he asked, arching his blond brows. "You're here for my own good?"

"Yes, that's right," Faith said, scrambling to get back on the right track. "I'd hate to see you lose everything you've worked so hard for. Drilling is expensive. The cost per day can go as high as—"

"I wasn't born yesterday, you know," he interrupted in a lazy, honeyed drawl. "I'm aware of the costs, but you have to invest money to make money."

"You'll never make it alone," Faith said, shaking her head with each word. "Within two months you'll be broke and begging PATCO to bail you out."

His eyes lost all semblance of friendliness and his drawling speech sharpened to a terse staccato. "It'll be a cold day in hell when I beg anybody for anything." With an economy of movement that testified to his mounting temper, he poured the water from the pan and gathered up the rest of his toiletries. "Goodbye, ma'am."

"But Mr. Traynor..." Faith reached out for his arm, but he eluded her touch. "Houston, listen to me!"

"If you haven't noticed, Miss Hutton, I'm about this far from losing my patience with you." He brought his thumb and forefinger within a fraction of an inch from each other. "I'm not signing your lease and I don't want your advice, so why don't you hightail it back to Pecos and leave me alone?"

She took a few moments to scrutinize him and decided that he wasn't making idle threats. He was dead serious, and she had overstayed her welcome by a long shot.

"Very well." Faith tipped up her chin with effort, grudgingly acknowledging that she had lost this final round. "Good luck with your project, Mr. Taynor. You'll need it."

He bounded up the steps to his trailer and slammed the door behind him. Faith bit back a heated epithet and got into her car. Gunning the engine, she left Houston Traynor's land in a cloud of dust.

Faith stared at the empty coffeepot and counted to ten. Why was it that the coffeepot in the company canteen was always empty when she wanted a cup? Common courtesy was in short supply around the Pecos office, she thought with a fit of pettiness as she grabbed the pot and took it with her to the small supply room off the main canteen. The men always waited for a woman to make a fresh pot instead of doing it themselves.

It hadn't been one of her best weeks at PATCO, thanks to Houston Traynor's refusal to sign the renewal lease, she thought as she prepared the coffee. Her boss hadn't bothered to hide his disappointment at the news, and Faith knew that Samson had chalked the whole fiasco up to Faith's incompetence. He ridiculed her every chance he got, and this was just one more opportunity to make her feel small and useless. Samson, along with the other chief officers, didn't want her in the company. She reminded them of Terrence Hutton, her father, who had once been the major shareholder and chief executive officer. They hadn't wanted him around, and they certainly didn't want his daughter.

If she had any sense, she would submit her resignation and work for another company, she told herself as she waited for the coffee to brew. But loyalty to the company that should have been hers by inheritance kept her at PATCO even though she was unhappy as a landman. They couldn't keep her down forever, could they? Eventually they would have to promote her because she was a trained geologist and very close to receiving her petroleum engineering accreditation.

Voices in the canteen pulled her from her musings, and she listened closely, recognizing the deep voice of Samson Applegate and the wheezing whisper of Jack Campbell, PATCO's chief executive officer, who was visiting the Pecos branch office.

"So what are you doing about Houston Traynor's lease?" Jack asked.

"I'm sending Cliff Richards out there. He'll come back with Traynor's signature," Samson said with a knowing chuckle.

"Should have sent him out there in the first place," Jack said. "We knew that Traynor wouldn't welcome us. Sending Faith Hutton was a waste of company time."

"Well, she has to do something around here to earn her salary," Samson said with a snicker that made Faith burn with anger.

Faith stepped close to the door, which was slightly ajar. The men's voices were clearer, and she held her breath and hoped she wouldn't be discovered.

"There's no coffee," Samson noted with a sigh. "I'll send my secretary in here to make some."

"Right. Let's go over those projection figures before I head back to Midland."

"You'll let me take you out to dinner tonight before you board the company plane, won't you?"

"Not this time, Samson. I've got a dinner engagement in Midland this evening."

Footsteps sounded, growing fainter as the men moved from the canteen.

"I guess I should talk to Faith about getting tougher in negotiations," Samson said.

Faith opened the door and stepped into the canteen in time to see Jack's indifferent shrug.

"Don't worry about it. She's just here on a pass and that pass is about to expire."

Faith gritted her teeth in fury as Samson's chuckle floated back to her. Here on a pass! The words ricocheted in her mind, and she felt her blood boil. How dare they? Her grandfather had founded this company, and by all rights, she should be sitting in Campbell's office! If her father had only used some common sense instead of—

She cut off the rest of her angry thoughts, telling herself that there wasn't any use in crying about the past. What was done was done. But she didn't have to take this treatment. She was a trained geologist. She could work anywhere. She had her intelligence, her independence and her pride, she told herself as she marched back to her department.

A shiver of apprehension shook her, but she ignored it. A Hutton never stayed where she wasn't welcome or appreciated. She had been wasting away at PATCO, and it was time to cut her losses and hit the unemployment trail. At least she was on firm financial footing, she assured herself. PATCO owed her a month's salary and three weeks of vacation pay. She had a healthy savings account and some stocks and bonds, too.

Armed with this she smiled cheerfully as she sat behind her typewriter and composed a terse, unemotional letter of resignation. When she applied her signature to it, she realized that she felt better about herself than she had since before her father's death five years ago. Five years! The span of time appalled her. Had she been stuck in this rut for five long years? Shaking her head, she realized that she had Houston Traynor to thank for her present predicament. If it hadn't been for his stubborn refusal to sign PATCO's lease, she wouldn't be severing her ties to a company that had been part of her life for as long as she could remember.

She had been trying to do Houston Traynor a favor by discouraging him from wildcatting, but he had inadvertently turned the tables on her so that it was *he* who was doing *her* a favor.

"Thanks, Traynor," she murmured as she stood up and headed for Samson Applegate's plush office on the top floor. "I owe you one."

Chapter Two

Faith maneuvered the sky-blue Mustang into one of the parking spaces in front of the Pecos bank and switched off the engine. Before leaving the car, she covered her most treasured keepsake with a blanket.

Not that anyone would be tempted to steal this square piece of glass, she thought ruefully. A drop of crude oil from PATCO's first gusher rested in the center of the thick glass. Her grandfather, Cain Patton, had passed this bit of memorabilia on to her mother, who had presented it to her father when he had taken control of PATCO. Faith had inherited it after her father's death, and it went everywhere with her.

Glancing in the backseat where she had placed all her other possessions, Faith shook off the beginnings of depression. Don't get maudlin, she warned herself. This isn't the end of the world. Something will come along, something better than what you're leaving behind.

After closing out her checking and savings accounts, she would be free to go anywhere. Dallas would be her first stop, she thought as she grabbed her purse and got out of the car. Years of working in small towns and lonely oil fields had left her yearning for a more sophisticated atmosphere. The mere thought of evenings spent at the ballet or opera made her itch to leave Pecos and head for the bright lights of Dallas.

Faith hurried into the bank, anxious to sever her last ties to PATCO and Pecos. She had been bound to both for too long with nothing to show for it other than a residue of bitterness.

Within a few minutes she had withdrawn her money from the bank and was tucking the cashier's check and travelers' checks into her purse when a familiar voice made her glance up. She smiled when she spotted Houston Traynor emerging from the loan office. From the surly expression on his tanned face, Faith surmised that his negotiations had not gone well.

"Don't take it personally, Houston," the loan officer said as he pumped Houston's hand. "Someday you'll thank me for denying you this second loan."

"And someday you'll kick yourself for not loaning me the money, Joe. I'm telling you that this is a sure thing."

"Houston, you know as well as I do that there's no sure thing in the oil business. It's all risky." The loan officer released Houston's hand, then patted him on the back. "Good luck, Houston. I mean that."

Houston's irritated expression softened. "Thanks, Joe." He turned from the loan officer, and his brown eyes widened when he saw Faith.

She raised a hand in greeting and paused at the double doors as Houston approached her. So he doesn't have enough money for his oil venture, she mused with a smile. No surprise there. She'd known he was getting in over his head. He was dressed for business in a pair of dark trousers, white shirt and striped tie. His golden hair was neatly combed but was still unruly where it covered the tops of his ears and curled over his collar. His cowboy boots were black and shiny with rows of white stitching, and he held a black cowboy hat between his hands. The hat had a beaded band with a cluster of gray and red feathers arranged in the front of it. His Sunday-go-to-meeting hat, no doubt, Faith thought with an inner chuckle.

"Howdy!" He shook her hand, and his was warm and lightly callused. "Small world, isn't it?"

"It is in Pecos," she agreed. "I'm glad I got to see you before I left."

"Left? Where are you going?"

"I don't know. I just know that I'm leaving Pecos. I've resigned from PATCO." She acknowledged the fleeting shock on his face. "That's right. I'm a free agent, so I've closed out my accounts and I'm heading for greener pastures."

"Is that right?" He rubbed his cheek, then touched the scar on his chin. "I stopped by here to float another loan, but the bankers here are more conservative than I'd thought." He squinted one tawny eye and offered a cagey grin. "I've got a great idea."

"Oh? What's that?"

"How would you like to be a partner in a surefire gusher?"

An automatic refusal rose to her lips but died suddenly when Faith encountered the sheen of hope in his earthy eyes. Was he serious? He didn't even know her! He's desperate, she warned herself. All he wants is money, not an active partner.

"This isn't the place to discuss this kind of thing," Houston said, cutting into her seesawing thoughts. "Let me buy you a cup of coffee at that place across the street, and we'll argue the finer points." He cupped her elbow in his hand and guided her from the bank and across the street before Faith could summon a response. "I guess you have another job all lined up, don't you?"

"No, I don't," she admitted, moving away from his gentle hand as she entered the small coffee shop.

A colorful jukebox squatted in one corner and blared a standard country western song about infidelity. A shapely waitress fed quarters into it and punched in a few more favorites. A counter with seven stools took up one side of the narrow cafe, and five booths lined the other long wall. Brahman bull horns adorned another and were hung above a neon-lighted clock and a drugstore calendar. Faith went to the back booth and slid onto the red vinyl seat while Houston sat across the table from her. Glancing at the calendar with its picture of a valentine-shaped box of candy, Faith noted that no one had bothered to tear off the pages since February even though it was well into June.

She surveyed the rest of the tiny space, thinking that this cafe could be found all across the Lone Star state. The words to the song blaring from the jukebox floated into her consciousness and caught her attention.

"What's that song?" she asked, tilting her head to one side to hear the music better over the rumbling voices of the two men seated at the counter a few feet away.

Houston listened for a moment, then grinned. "That's the number one song. Haven't you ever heard it before?"

"No." She shook her head, puzzled and not believing her own ears. "Is he saying what I think he's saying?"

Bringing his grin under control, Houston feigned gravity. "The lyrics are, 'She's so sweet honeybees keep buzzing around her head, and I can't get near her without getting stung.' Gets you right here, doesn't it?" He tapped a fist over his heart and gave in to his smile when she laughed.

"How original," Faith said, still laughing. "Is that really the number one song?"

"Well, it is around here," he amended before acknowledging the waitress. "Good morning, Yvonne."

The pretty, dark-haired woman sighed expansively. "You keep messing up my name, Houston. It's not E-vonne. It's *Why*-vonne."

"Oh, that's right." Houston glanced at Faith with a crafty wink. "An old country boy like me can't pronounce those foreign names."

Faith hid her smile behind her hand and turned her head to stare out the dusty window as Houston ordered two cups of coffee with cream. She faced him again when the waitress had left them.

"Is that a running exchange between you two?"

Houston placed his fancy hat in the seat beside him and loosened his tie. "I keep thinking that one day she might find out that she mispronounces her name, but I guess it's hopeless. She's been *Why*-vonne for so long, she'd never change it."

"Do you know a lot of people in Pecos?" Faith asked, recalling the comments she'd heard about him being an unfriendly recluse.

"I know *of* a lot of people, but I can't say that I have a lot of friends here." He leaned back to let Yvonne place the cups on the table. "Thanks. How's you mother doing?"

"Oh, pretty good." Yvonne gave a quick shrug. "She's still bothered by her arthritis and all, but she gets around okay when she uses her cane."

"That's good to hear. Tell her that I asked about her."

"I will. Can I get you anything else?"

"No, this will do it for now."

"Enjoy." Yvonne glanced at Faith. "Who's your lady friend?"

"I'm sorry," Houston said, sitting straighter. "I clean forgot my manners. *Why*-vonne Strickner, this is Faith

Hutton. She's a...I mean, she used to be a landman with PATCO."

"Nice to make your acquaintance," Yvonne said, smiling. "I think I've seen you around town."

"You probably have," Faith agreed. "Nice to meet you."

"Hey, *Why*-vonne!" One of the cowboys at the counter turned and tapped the waitress on the shoulder. "Where's that menu you promised me an hour ago?"

"Keep your pants on, Luther," Yvonne returned with a saucy flip of her hand. "I've got other customers, you know." She rolled her dark eyes in exasperation before moving with exaggerated lazyness to the counter.

Houston chuckled and sipped the hot coffee. "She's a card, isn't she?"

"Yes." Faith drank her coffee and waited for Houston to break the silence. He made a pretense of stirring more cream into his coffee, tasting it, then adding a spoonful of sugar. Finally he looked at her with serious intent.

"About that partnership I offered..."

"Having second thoughts?" Faith asked, smiling. "I don't blame you, and I'll understand if you withdraw it."

"Oh, I'm not going to withdraw it," he assured her. "I've got to have a partner now that the bank has turned me down and it might as well be you."

Faith averted her gaze, suddenly uncomfortable with the situation. "You don't know anything about me. Don't you think you're taking a big chance asking a stranger to be your partner?"

"I know you're in the oil business, so you know what you'd be getting into." He pushed the cup and saucer to one side and folded his arms on top of the table. "I've got a gut feeling that I'm near a strike."

"I don't invest money on gut feelings," Faith said sternly. "That *is* what you're interested in, isn't it? My money, presuming I have any."

"I'm interested in a backer, and investing money is part of the business. Well, what do you say?"

She finished her coffee, giving herself time to form an answer. Her first thought was that this would be a golden opportunity to thumb her nose at PATCO, but she cautioned herself. Revenge was a poor reason to enter a business—especially a business as risky as a wildcat well. "Tell you what, I'll investigate this opportunity and get back to you. I look before I leap, and I don't know enough about your operation to be able to form an opinion."

"That's fair." He fished a dollar and some change from his pocket and dropped them on the table. "I've got to get back to my place. When do you think you'll be getting back to me on this?"

"Within a couple of days. Maybe sooner."

"Okay." He picked up his hat and nodded toward the street. "Can I walk you to your car?"

"No thanks. You go on. I think I'll have another cup of coffee."

He nodded, stood up and held out one hand. "This is the chance of a lifetime," he said as he shook her hand. "I hope you come along for the ride."

"We'll see. Thanks for the offer." She looked over her shoulder and watched him stride from the cafe, pausing only long enough to wink at Yvonne and put on his hat before he let the door swing closed behind him. Looking out the window, she noticed that he was slightly bow-legged with a long, easy gait that spoke of physical fitness and good health. He got into a battered blue pickup across the street and drove out of sight.

He was like all the other oilmen she had encountered, she thought as she faced front and stared into her empty coffee cup. He was a dreamer, a wild schemer who believed in flimsy things like gut feelings and good luck charms. Just like her father, she thought with a twinge of bitterness.

Terrence Hutton had lived his whole life taking chances and acting on whims. Faith liked to think that she took after her grandfather, who had prided himself on being a level-headed businessman in a corporation founded on risk and luck. Looking for oil might be like searching for a needle in a haystack, but one could still use good sense and back it up with the latest technology.

"Want another cup?" Yvonne asked, moving the pot of coffee closer.

"Yes, please."

"It's good to see Houston out with a nice lady," Yvonne said after filling the cup to the brim. "I used to live in Mentone and I've known Houston since high school."

"Really?" Faith perked up, eager for any information on the man who had offered her a partnership. "I don't know him very well, but..."

"He's a good man," Yvonne stated firmly. "After the accident, he sort of drew into himself and then dropped out of sight, but I can understand that. I don't care what folks around here say about him, I like him and I'm glad he came back to Loving County. That took a lot of guts, I'm here to tell you." She propped one hand on her hip and sighed. "I was fat when I was in high school and everybody made fun of me, but not Houston. He was always nice to me, and I don't forget kindnesses."

"You mentioned an accident," Faith said, grabbing onto that bit of information. "What hap—"

"Yvonne, could you stop flapping your gums and bring me my bacon and eggs?"

Yvonne spun around to face the complaining man at the counter. "You'll catch more flies with honey, Luther," she retorted.

"Don't want any flies. Just want my bacon and eggs," Luther snapped back.

Yvonne flounced down the narrow aisle, her rubber-soled shoes squeaking on the linoleum. She rounded the counter and grabbed the plate of bacon and eggs from the serving window ledge, then placed it in front of Luther.

"There you go, Luther. Now button it up so I can hear this song. It's my favorite."

Luther obeyed, and the song that had amused Faith earlier filled the room. Faith drank the coffee as her thoughts returned to Houston's offer. It wouldn't hurt to check it out, she mused. She had sources at PATCO who would bend the rules and tell her what she needed to know. Glancing out the window, she spotted a pay phone outside the bank. She left the cafe and crossed the street to the phone. After depositing a coin in it and receiving a dial tone, she dialed the PATCO number by memory and waited to be connected with Norman Shaeffer in geology. Norman was one of the few employees left who remembered her grandfather. He had been kind to her after her father had died, and she held him in high regard.

"Norman, this is Faith."

"Faith!" His voice rose an octave, then settled. "Is it true that you've resigned?"

"It's true."

"I hate to hear that. It's not right. This company has never been without a Patton heir."

"Well, it is now." She kept her voice light, refusing to allow the sadness to overtake her.

"What are you going to do?"

"I'm not sure. Norman, haven't you seen the core samples on Houston Traynor's property?"

"Houston Traynor..." He paused for a few seconds. "Oh, right! Out there by MacQuay's property in Loving County."

"That's right."

"Yes, I've seen them. Did you know that we didn't get a renewal on that lease? Cliff Richards said that Traynor ordered him off the property."

"Is that right?" Faith smiled and savored the small victory. "Well, how did the last soil sample look to you?"

"Hold on and let me get that file."

"Okay." She turned to gaze at the bank and the traffic at the drive-in window.

"I'm back," Norman said. "Let's see here...hmm. What do you make of that?"

"What? What is it?" Faith gripped the receiver and spun back around to the telephone, resting her elbows on the ledge and leaning in between the sheltering sheets of Plexiglass.

"It's a shame we lost that lease. These core samples look promising."

"They do?" Excitement shot through her, and she realized that she was seriously considering Houston's offer.

"Sure do. The formation structure is tight, and there's some parallel scratches along the fault plane."

"No kidding?" Faith smiled. "Those parallel marks suggest that something's trapped under there, right?"

"It's a possibility, but this piece of ground is tricky. I was waiting to catch another core sample at the next fifty feet to see how things are going. It's still spitting up salt water."

"It is?" Faith's smile slipped from her lips. Salt water was bad news, but not disastrous. "I was thinking we'd need to drill at least down to thirty-seven hundred feet before we'd hit pay dirt. What are we at now?"

"We're at...twelve hundred or thereabouts. We've lost the lease, Faith, so why are you so interested?"

"The owner has asked me to be his partner."

"You mean you're thinking of wildcatting it?" Norman asked, his voice cracking with disbelief.

"Yes, but I'm just thinking about it. It's not definite."

"Faith, you know better," Norman scolded. "Drilling takes a small fortune, and you could lose everything!"

Faith smiled, feeling as if she had just had her own advice thrown back in her face. "That's the company talking, Norman. As a friend, tell me what you think."

Silence stretched across the phone line for several seconds; then Norman's voice filled the void.

"As a friend, I'd say that if you're going to do something foolish like sink your money into a hole in the ground, then this is a good hole to sink it into. I like what I see on this report. I think Traynor's got himself a vein of gold running through his land."

Faith released her breath in a long sigh. "Thanks, Norm. I know you didn't have to give me this information...."

"I had no business giving you this information," he corrected. "If anyone finds out, I could get axed."

"I know." Faith straightened and drew in a deep breath. "I appreciate your help."

"You're not going to drop out of sight, are you? You know where I live, and I expect to see you from time to time."

"Don't worry. I'll keep in touch."

"Faith, if you invest in this wildcatting venture, your grandfather will turn over in his grave."

Faith laughed. "I'll bet you're right, but I'm only considering it. What I'll probably do is drive into Dallas and show my résumé to a few of the oil companies there."

"That makes better sense. Good luck."

"Thanks again, Norm." She replaced the receiver and went to her car.

Sitting behind the wheel, she reviewed Norman's information and felt that current of excitement sizzle within her again. The sensation was different from what she had experienced when she had worked for PATCO. When oil was struck on a lease she had negotiated, she had been merely relieved, since her position hinged on solid leases that made PATCO money. Oh, no, this was totally different. For the first time she could empathize with the oilmen. She had witnessed the glint of oil fever in their eyes, but now the fever raged through her and made her shiver.

Hold on, she cautioned as she gripped the steering wheel to stabilize herself. She was acting like her father instead of keeping a cool head on her shoulders. If she invested her money, she could lose everything and have to start all over again at the ripe age of twenty-five. The prospect was sobering, but not frightening. During her life she had been both rich and poor, and if she lost her money, it wouldn't be the first time she'd been broke.

She cast her thoughts to brighter prospects. If she did strike oil, it would be a sweet revenge. PATCO had drilled there and lost the lease. Houston Traynor was giving her the chance to take over and reap the benefits, which wouldn't go unnoticed by the PATCO board of directors. She'd go out with a bang instead of a whimper.

Revenge tipped the scales in Houston's favor, and Faith started the car. She'd drive out and tell Houston he had a partner before she could change her mind, she resolved, barely acknowledging the thread of trepidation weaving through her.

Who would have thought that Faith Hutton would invest in a wildcat well? she wondered, smiling at the irony of it. Norman was right. Her grandfather was probably spinning in his grave while her father grinned with delight.

When she arrived at Houston's, PATCO employees were dismantling their equipment under Houston's watchful eye. Recognizing her car, Houston broke away from the activity to open the door and help her out of the Mustang.

"Well, well. I didn't expect you so soon. I hope this doesn't mean you're going to turn down my offer."

"I'm here to discuss your offer," she hedged, deciding to hammer out some details before she gave in to him lock, stock and barrel. "I see that PATCO isn't wasting any time in clearing out."

"No, but I expected that. I'm glad. The sooner they're gone, the sooner I can get to work." He nodded toward his trailer. "Let's go in there where it's cooler."

She entered the neat trailer and sat at the kitchen table. "I'll come to the point, since I know you're busy. I'm considering a partnership."

"Great!" He dropped into one of the other chairs and smiled. "You won't regret it."

"I want to be clear on one point," she continued. "I expect to be an equal partner, not a silent one. I don't want to just invest my money. I want to have a say in every aspect. I want to catch core samples and study them."

"Fine with me," he said, sweeping off his yellow hard hat and placing it on the table. "I'd appreciate your expertise."

"You would?" She stared at him in surprise, having expected some resistance.

"Sure. Mac tells me that you're a geologist."

"That's right. You've talked to Mac about me?"

"Yes, I hope you don't mind."

"No." She regarded him with fresh insight, noticing things in him that she had not seen before. He was more careful than she had imagined, and she was relieved to know that he had investigated her credibility. "I'm just a few credit hours short of getting a degree in petroleum engineering, so I have a solid background in this business."

"I know that." He held out his hand. "Let's shake on it, partner."

Faith stared at his outstretched hand for a few moments, still feeling a measure of apprehension. "You agree to consult me on every phase of this operation?"

"I promise. I'm all for equality."

She smiled and shook his hand. His handshake was firm and decisive, and his eyes held a glint of gentle amusement. Releasing her hand, he leaned back in the chair and let his gaze roam over her face in a lazy perusal that left Faith feeling self-conscious. Her heart kicked into double time, and she was hard-pressed to explain her reaction.

"Don't you think we should draw up some kind of written agreement?" she asked a bit breathlessly.

"My word is my bond, and I assume the same is true for you. If you'd feel better having it all written down, I suppose I could draft some kind of document."

"No." She swallowed hard, realizing that she was turning her back on something she had always held dear. "Get it in writing" had been preached to her since she was a child, so why was she taking this man's word for such a costly agreement? His smile swept aside her misgivings and left her bewildered. What was it about Houston Traynor that made her trust him without question?

"Now that we're partners, I guess I can call you Faith, can't I?" he asked.

"Being partners puts us on a first name basis." She tipped her head to one side in thoughtful contemplation. "Were you born in Houston?"

"How'd you guess?" he teased, his brown eyes alight with mischief. "My mother loved Texas. I only lived in Houston a couple of years before we moved here. How did you get your name?"

"Oh, I don't know. I suppose my parents liked the sound of it."

"So do I." He picked up his hard hat and studied it for a few moments before asking, "Where are you going to live?"

"Live?" She glanced around the trailer in confusion, then realized with a jolt that she had no place to hang her hat. "I don't know. I wonder if I could find a place in Mentone."

"I doubt it. You're welcome to park a trailer here. There's a dealership in Pecos that sells new and used ones."

"I'll look into it." She stood up and moved to the door with Houston at her side. "Everything I own is out there in that Mustang."

"You travel light. That's good," he said as he walked her to her car. "Let me know if I can help you with anything."

"I will." She slipped into the driver's seat, and Houston closed the door. The impact of what she was doing slammed into her, and she laughed. "I can't believe I'm doing this. It's so unlike me."

"Making money is making money, but playing the odds..." He winked and made a clicking sound with his tongue. "That's the spice of life!"

Faith started the engine as the cutting edge of a memory sliced through her. Her father had said that same thing more than once, and look where it had gotten him, she thought with a frown. Was she throwing good money after bad? She glanced at Houston, suddenly aware of a glaring omission.

"Houston, you've never asked me how much money I'm willing to invest."

He placed his hands on the car and leaned closer to speak over the rumble of machinery in the background. "I figured you'd know how much money I'm likely to need and that you wouldn't have offered to be a partner unless you could invest enough to make a difference."

Admiration for him stole through her. She had definitely sold him short, she thought. He lived by more solid things than gut feelings and instinct, thank heavens!

"You're right," she said, shifting the car into gear. "I'll be back soon."

"Drive carefully," he said, stepping back from the car and giving her room to turn it around and head down the rutted road. "I'll be right here waiting for you."

She held his gaze for a few moments longer, then drove slowly along the road. A couple of workers stopped to stare as her car went by, and she hoped they recognized her and passed the gossip on through the channels at PATCO. She wished she could see Samson Applegate's reaction to the news that she had become a partner in a wildcat rig. She just hoped this whole thing didn't blow up in her face.

Houston was more knowledgeable than she had first thought, but he was still very much like her father, and that worried her. She'd have to keep an eye on him and curb his tendency to act instinctively. A careful man wouldn't have offered her a partnership right out of the blue, she reasoned.

She smiled, grateful that Houston wasn't *that* careful.

Chapter Three

Crossing his arms along the top rail of the white fence, Houston surveyed the cattle in the corral. He counted twenty, all well fed and nervous about being penned up.

"Ticks are bad this year, aren't they?" Houston asked, glancing at Mac, who was leaning against the fence beside him.

"Pretty bad. Look at them." Mac's face wrinkled into a grin. "They know they're about to be dipped in pesticide, and they don't like it. Who says that cows are stupid?"

Houston nodded as he watched the cowhands prepare the big bath that they'd run the cows through in a few minutes. "Turkeys are about the dumbest animals I've ever been around. They all have a death wish, if you ask me. They *look* for ways to kill themselves."

"That's right," Mac agreed, his blue eyes twinkling, then narrowing in a cagey scrutiny. "Did you stop by to talk turkey, or is something on your mind?"

Houston sighed and rested his chin on his arms. He'd been at Mac's for two hours and had managed to talk about everything except Faith Hutton. "I've got me a partner, Mac."

"She went for it, did she?" Mac pulled a knife from his pocket and began cleaning his fingernails. "Thought she might."

"When I asked her I had my back against the wall, but now I'm wondering if I did the right thing. I don't know anything about her other than what you've told me—which isn't much—and she *is* a woman."

"She is that, all right." Mac's mustache twitched in amusement. "Best partner I ever had was a woman."

"Who's that?"

Mac's expressive eyes glinted in the sun. "Bonita Kaye. She was working at the bank when I landed in Pecos. I asked her out and...well, I've been living with her ever since. Never met a man I trusted more than I trust Bonita Kaye. And talk about smart? That woman makes me feel downright dense most the time."

"I know the feeling." Houston scowled, remembering Faith's ability to make him feel somehow inadequate. "My new partner is a little high and mighty, wouldn't you say?"

"She's sure of herself, but that's a good trait. High and mighty?" Mac closed the knife and worked it back into the front pocket of his jeans. "She's always been right friendly around me."

"Everyone's friendly around you, Mac." Houston shrugged helplessly. "You said she's a geologist. Why was she a landman for PATCO?"

"Better ask her that." Mac turned around to face the corral and raised his voice over the bawl of the cattle. "Did you know that her granddaddy owned PATCO?"

"No." Houston tilted his head to one side to rest his cheek on his forearms and gave Mac his undivided attention.

"It's named after him. Cain Patton. He was quite a man. Faith's daddy, Terrence Hutton, took over after Cain died, and PATCO passed out of Terrence's hands right before he died."

"I'll be..." Houston straightened from his leisurely slouch. "So she didn't inherit it."

"Nope." Mac ran a hand along his white mustache thoughtfully. "I think she resents that. I would."

As was their custom, the two men lapsed into a comfortable silence as they moved slowly to Houston's truck. As if rehearsed, they sat on the tailgate and dropped more deeply into their own thoughts.

Houston worried about his impulsive decision, weighing the pros and cons but finding no reassurance. He didn't know enough about Faith to have a clue as to whether or not this partnership would work. Was she a nagger or a complainer? He hoped not. Was she tight with a buck? There was nothing worse than having to beg for every dollar. Was she the type who expected instant results? Would she dissolve the partnership in a couple of weeks if they didn't strike something? Surely not, he reasoned. She'd been around the oil business all her life. She must know that drilling took time and couldn't be rushed.

"I don't think you've got anything to worry about," Mac said with a certainty Houston couldn't share. "That offer might have been impulsive on your part, but Faith Hutton's acceptance sure wasn't. That little gal doesn't do anything on a whim. She's like Bonita Kaye that way."

"But working with a woman..." Houston shook his head slowly. "That's what worries me the most."

"It'll be good for you." Mac draped an arm around Houston's shoulders and gave them an affectionate shake.

"You'll get firsthand experience of how a woman's mind works, and boy howdy!" He chuckled with delight. "That's a lesson well learned, son. If you figure that out, then you'll own the keys to unlock all the mysteries of the world."

Houston felt one side of his mouth lift in a reluctant grin. "Maybe you're right."

"Sure I am!" Mac slipped off the tailgate, and his boots kicked up dust as he walked around the truck to open the driver's door. "Where's she going to live?"

"On my property, I think. I told her to buy a trailer," Houston said, joining Mac and sliding onto the truck seat. "You know how long it's been since I've been in close proximity with a woman for any length of time?"

"Too long, son." Mac slammed the door shut and touched the brim of his straw hat in a salute. "Like I said, this'll be good for you."

"Thanks, Mac." Houston started the engine and tried to see things Mac's way. "I guess I'll live through it."

"Working with women can be fun," Mac said above the roar of the engine. "All you gotta do is bend a little, Houston. You'll have to compromise and bite your tongue now and then, but women sure can make it worth your while if you play your cards right."

Hot color washed over Houston's face, and he ducked his head and urged the truck forward. That kind of talk made him uneasy. He didn't want to think about any emotional involvement, because it was out of the question. A woman like Faith Hutton wouldn't give him the time of day, and he knew it. Mac should know better, too.

It didn't take a Romeo to see that Faith Hutton was used to men who wore suits and bought tickets to things like the opera. City life was written all over her, and he wondered how long she'd be able to stand Loving County's isolation.

He'd grown used to it, but it had taken some massive adjustments.

Looking at the rugged, parched land that stretched before him, Houston counted back to the last rainfall he could remember. It had to be almost two years ago. Rain was a miracle in Loving County and the main topic of conversation. Did you get any, how much, wish it would, think it might? The only thing wet around these parts was black and slimy and way underground, and it was worth far more than water.

Would she expect him to entertain her? he wondered. She'd be disappointed if she did. The only entertainment around here was that of your own making. Nobody gave parties or showed movies. The most you could hope for was a friendly game of pool at the game room on Mac's property or maybe a twilight gathering of far-flung neighbors who illuminated the night with the headlights of their pickups and turned on the radios real loud for an impromptu dance under the stars.

No opera. No ballet. No fancy restaurants.

But she knew about this county, he reminded himself. She'd been scouting this area for a couple of years, so she knew there wasn't any social life. But *knowing* of loneliness and boredom and *living* with them day in and day out were two different things. He knew that from painful experience.

It seemed to take longer than usual to reach his patch of earth, and he was glad to see his fifth-wheel trailer in the distance. Smiling, he recalled a rhyme he'd heard since he was a child.

The sun has riz, the sun has set,
And I ain't out of Texas yet!

Leaving the pickup, he went over to the drilling site and felt that familiar stirring of anticipation. Would this be his pot at the end of the rainbow? He rubbed his face vigorously with his hands, trying to release the tension coiling in his body. He'd put his whole life on the line this time. He'd bet it all. If it didn't work...if this hole was dry...

He spun around at the approach of a vehicle, grateful for the interruption. If he thought too much about all he'd risked on this deal, he'd go crazy. Taking a chance was nothing new to him, but this was different. This could ruin him.

Easing down the brim of his cowboy hat, he squinted into the dust and sun at the Mustang pulling a teardrop-shaped trailer behind it. It was Faith, but had she really bought that...that *thing?* Why, it was no bigger than a tool shed!

She stopped the car and scrambled out, a big smile on her face and a proud lift to her chin.

"Good morning!" She came toward him, her jeaned hips swinging confidently and her shoulders squared beneath a navy-blue T-shirt. "I visited that trailer dealer you recommended."

"And you came away with that," Houston noted drolly.

"Yes." She stopped in front of him, then whirled around to admire her purchase. "It's cute, isn't it?"

"It's little, isn't it?"

"It's compact," she corrected, swinging around to face him and delivering a warning scowl. "I don't need much room. The dealer was great. He let me have it for just a few hundred bucks, so it didn't cut into my budget hardly at all. Good deal, huh?"

"Well..." He ran a hand along his jaw as he slowly circled the tiny trailer. It was white on pastel blue, a two-wheeler with one door and two windows, one on each side. He'd go nuts inside it within twenty-four hours and be bouncing off the walls. "Has it got a bathroom and kitchen?"

"Yes." She opened the door and motioned for him to go inside. "Go on. Check it out."

He stepped inside and felt as if he'd filled any extra space. When she entered behind him, he squeezed up against the kitchen counter to give her a little breathing room. The kitchen unit was opposite the door, composed of a small, stainless-steel sink, three feet of countertop, an overhead cabinet, a two-burner stove and a two-shelf refrigerator-freezer. To the right was the living room—generously speaking—with a divan across one end and a table in front of it. To the left a two-seater booth lined one wall and a closet took up the other. He moved to the door at the other end and opened it to stare aghast at the tiny bathroom. It was really a shower stall with a sink in one corner and a drop-down toilet hidden in one wall. He pulled down the toilet bowl and thanked heaven above for the standard unit in his own trailer.

"Don't you love that bathroom?" she asked behind him. "Isn't that toilet bowl wonderful? It's so neat the way it folds up right into the wall and out of the way."

"You'll have to remember to remove your toilet paper and everything else before you take a shower or you'll get them soaked."

"That's no problem."

"These things don't have much water pressure," he said, stowing away the toilet bowl. "They can be a real pain in the neck."

"No problem."

He shook his head in frustration. She was determined to like this thing, so let her! He closed the door and turned around to find her right up against him. She stepped back hastily and bumped into the coffee table.

"Where's your bed?"

Her eyes widened a fraction before she indicated the divan. "That makes out into a bed. Convenient, isn't it?"

He couldn't keep the smile from his mouth any longer. "Don't you think this will be a little like living in a sardine can?"

"No!" She placed her hands on her hips, and her breasts lifted and grabbed his attention. When she noticed that his gaze had moved swiftly from her face to her protruding breasts, she folded her arms across them in obvious defiance.

Houston tore his gaze from her and left the cramped space of the trailer for the wide-open landscape where he could breathe and collect his wits. Damn her! She couldn't blame him for looking! If she didn't want him to look at her breasts, then she shouldn't have offered them up for his inspection!

This isn't going to work out, an inner voice warned. She's going to get under your skin. His blunt fingers absently clawed at his chest before Houston realized what he was doing. He stuck his hands into his pockets to keep from scratching the itch she had started.

"Where should I park my trailer?"

He looked around for a good site, then pointed to a place across from his own. "Right there will be fine. I'll help you unhitch it."

"I can do it," she trilled brightly as she positioned herself behind the steering wheel of the car and hauled the trailer over to the site.

"I can do it," Houston mimicked in a singsong voice. "Miss Independence doesn't need help from any man, especially one who criticizes her cute little sardine can!" He buttoned his lips when she killed the engine and got out of the car to unhitch the trailer. He waited for the inevitable and was overjoyed when it dawned on her that she didn't have anything to place under the front of the trailer to keep it level. Arching an inquisitive brow when her gaze swung around to him, he remained silent. Let her ask. Let her ask him with cream and sugar on top!

"You've got some cement blocks around here, don't you?"

"I think so."

Her blue eyes narrowed to icy slits. "Well, could you get them for me? I need to prop up this end of the trailer."

He tipped his head back, indicating the well site. "There's some over there. I guess you don't need any help with them."

She eyed him with a mixture of anger and amusement as she walked leisurely toward him. "I imagine I could carry those cement blocks by myself and possibly lift the end of that trailer, but I don't think I'd be much use to you flat on my injured back in a hospital bed."

He admired her cockiness and her belief in her ability to lift the end of the trailer by herself, but he didn't share her confidence. "All you have to do is say 'please.'"

She stiffened, and the hint of a smile on her lips vanished. Seconds ticked by while her eyes warred with his. Finally her tense lips moved grudgingly. "Please."

"There you go." He savored the victory for a few moments. "That wasn't so hard, was it?"

"Manners have never been a hardship for me," she tossed over her shoulder as she strode to the scattered cement blocks. This isn't going to work, she told herself. If I have to say "please" and "thank you" for every small favor, it definitely won't work.

Faith wrapped her hands around the ends of one block, sucked in her breath and strained upward. She duck-walked in the direction of the trailer, but Houston intercepted her and took the heavy block from her aching hands.

"Let me," he murmured, holding the block in one hand and moving effortlessly to the trailer.

Fifteen minutes later the trailer was level and Houston was hooking up the water and electricity. Faith sat on the hood of her car, gratefully allowing him plenty of room to work. He dropped to his haunches and peered beneath the trailer, providing her with a spectacular view of his broad back. The denim shirt clung to the wet patches of his skin, reminding Faith of the symmetry of muscle and sinew her eyes had feasted on the other day when he'd been bare to the waist. He swiveled around on the balls of his feet to look at her, and she quickly erased the interest on her face.

"Yes?" she asked.

"Is your propane tank full?"

"Yes, the dealer filled it before I left."

"Good. I'll light your pilot lights if you want."

"That would be good of you."

He disappeared inside the trailer, and Faith propped herself on stiff arms and turned her face up to the relentless sun. She had done some more checking around in Mentone about Houston Traynor but had gleaned little from her informants. The trailer dealer remembered him but had nothing to say other than, "He's a quiet kind of fella." The cashier had only added, "He has such nice eyes, doesn't he?" Faith smiled. Yes, he had nice eyes. Warm brown like cinnamon. Thick eyelashes. Heavy brows. Expressive. Very expressive.

"I guess you know about the water shortage out here." His voice opened her eyes and jerked her into awareness.

"Yes, I know. Water is precious in Loving County."

"Right, so don't waste it."

She smiled sweetly. "I wasn't planning on it. I do intend to bathe, however, if that isn't against your rules."

He looked away from her as if to debate a private issue, then shrugged. "I'll let that one pass. I won't charge you rent for the use of my water and electricity, but you'll have to buy your own propane. I've got a tank over there..." He paused to glance in its direction. "And I'll sell the propane to you at my cost."

"That's very generous, but I'd be more than happy to pay for the electricity and water, too."

"No, that's okay. You're paying for enough already." He propped a booted foot on the fender of her car. "Which brings us to this oil business, I guess. Want to divide duties so we don't trip each other up?"

"That sounds like a good idea." She slid off the hood, leaned against the car and crossed her arms and ankles while her senses appreciated the way he said "oil business." *Awl bidness.* Now *that's* a true Texan, she thought with a fleeting smile. He had a habit of dropping his g's at the end of words, too. Gettin'. Bettin'. Drillin'. His speech was colorful and melodic, rolling easily across her mind.

"I'll file the necessary paperwork for the drilling, if you'll scout around for a rig."

"Great." She smiled, liking the assignment. "I'll start tomorrow if that's okay."

"Fine with me. Remember that we're on a tight budget, so don't get anything real fancy."

"I won't. That reminds me..." She went around to the car and reached inside for her purse. "I have a check for you." She handed it to him and was pleased with his reaction. His radiant smile competed favorably with the brightness of the sun.

"Thanks. That'll go a long way. Tell you what, I'll open a checking account for us in Mentone. That way we can keep our business account separate from our personal accounts. Of course, I'll get some of this in cash for our general operating expenses."

"Good. What shall we call this hole in the ground?" she asked, glancing at the deserted well.

"Let me think...." He gazed up at the sky as if for divine intervention.

"Double H number one?" Faith asked, having already decided on that name this morning.

"Double H?"

"Houston and Hutton, of course."

"Oh, right." A slow smile spread across his face. "That has a nice ring to it." He glanced at his watch. "How about some lunch? I've got some chili I'd be willing to share with you."

"Okay." She fell into step beside him, suddenly aware of the six or seven inches' advantage he had over her. Angling her chin up, she guessed him to be a couple of inches over six feet, maybe as much as four. "I stayed in a motel outside of Mentone last night and didn't bother to eat breakfast this morning. I'm starving."

"I bet you are" He opened the door and let her enter first. "Have a seat and relax." Hanging his hat on a rack beside the door, he headed for the kitchen. "Did you check to see if that air conditioner in your trailer works?"

"Yes. I didn't buy a pig in a poke," she assured him. "It might not suit you, but it suits me fine."

Giving her an apologetic grin, Houston went into the kitchen and opened the refrigerator. "This'll just take a minute to throw together."

"Can I help?"

"No, thanks."

Faith wandered into the kitchen and sat at the table while Houston spooned generous portions of chili into two bowls and placed them in the microwave oven. While the chili heated, he prepared two glasses of ice water and set them on the table. When he placed a bowl of chili before Faith, she sniffed the spicy aroma.

"Does a warning go with this chili?"

He sat across the table from her and draped a napkin across his lap. "It's a mite hot. It's my own special recipe that won me second place two years ago in Terlingua."

"In what?" Faith asked, dipping her spoon into the to-mato-based chili.

"Terlingua. That's where they hold the Wick Fowler Memorial World Championship Chili Cook-Off. Haven't you heard of it?"

"No. Where's Terlingua?"

"West of the Pecos. It's not far from Big Bend National Park."

"I've never been there," Faith admitted.

"No reason why you should have. It's a ghost town. Folks say that Terlingua is the farthest you can go without getting anywhere."

Faith would have rewarded this with a chuckle if her throat hadn't been on fire. She grabbed the water and drank deeply, but the cold liquid gave only minimal relief to her scalded throat. Eyes watering, she glared at the master chef who had concocted this bowl of herbicide.

"I told you it was hot," Houston said with a sly smile. "It goes down easier with each spoonful."

"My taste buds are in shock!" Faith went to the sink to refill her water glass. "They gave you an award for that stuff?"

"Sure did." He sounded uncommonly pleased. "I've improved on the recipe, and I hope to enter the contest again in November. I think I can take first place this year."

"Anyone who survives a bowl of it has a cast-iron stom-ach." She drank the water as she went back to the table and sat down again. Pushing aside the bowl of chili, she ig-nored Houston's show of hurt feelings.

"I thought you were starving," he complained.

"I am, but I'm not suicidal. Do you have anything to eat around here that doesn't melt lead?" Admiration for him consumed her when he spooned a hefty portion of chili into his mouth and didn't even cough when it went down. She shook her head slowly. He was tougher than shoe leather.

"You don't have any manners," he said with grave conviction as he wiped his mouth with the napkin. "I invite you into my home for a bowl of my prize-winning chili and you throw insults in my face. If you want something else to eat, go to your own place and find it."

"That's mannerly of you," she noted with sarcasm. "This partnership might work if we promise not to eat together." Rising from the chair, she took one last drink of cooling water before heading for the door.

Racing across the ten feet that separated their front doors, Faith exploded into her trailer and slammed the door behind her with a force that made the metal walls shake. In a fit of fury she began unpacking and placing her things in the small cupboards and the tiny closet.

There was something about Houston Traynor that got under her skin, she thought as she stuffed her clothes into the closet. Could she help it if his chili made her insides shrivel? What was she supposed to do, pretend that her eyes were watering with unprecedented joy at being allowed to taste such ecstasy? He was lucky she hadn't screamed bloody murder when that spoonful of chili had hit her tongue like a volcano eruption and oozed down her throat with the potency of molten lava.

Her anger spent, she dropped onto the divan in exhaustion. A wry smile curved her lips. Nothing like a mouthful of fire on a hot day in west Texas, she thought with humor as she recalled his pouting expression. He was cute, she decided. In a stangely infuriating way, Houston Traynor was positively endearing.

Looking in the direction of his trailer, she imagined him sitting before his precious bowl of chili, a peeved expression on his rugged face. He'd get over it. All she had to do to get back in his good graces was strike a terrific deal on a drilling rig, and tomorrow she was going to do just that. She knew of a man in Pecos who had several nice rigs for rent. With a little wheeling and dealing she'd be able to lease one and put a smile back on Houston's handsome face.

Chapter Four

I love a joke just as much as the next person, Peewee, but let's get serious about the rental fee on this rig." Faith hitched the strap of her purse higher on her shoulder and calmly confronted the rotund man before her.

Peewee Porter turned his head to the side, and a stream of brown tobacco juice shot between his lips. Faith curled her upper lip in distaste and Peewee grinned, displaying a row of stained dentures.

"Wasn't making any jokes, ma'am," Peewee said, running the back of his hand across his mouth as he talked around the mound of tobacco wedged against his left cheek. "Black Fury here is a fine rig and I won't let her go for peanuts."

Looking past Peewee's wide body, Faith eyed the drilling rig. "How old is it?"

"She's been around awhile," Peewee answered evasively. "But she's still got a lot of years in her. All she needs is a little oil in her joints, and she'll drill her heart out for you.''

"How about a hundred dollars less a day?" Faith said, moving toward the rig and circling it slowly.

"I'll wait for a better suitor." Peewee hooked his thumbs in the straps of his overalls and rocked back on his heels.

Faith turned away from him and looked at the rig again. She didn't want a cable tool rig anyway. A rotary rig would be ideal, but probably too expensive. Glancing at Peewee again, she tried to read past his tranquil expression. Was he firm or calling her bluff? The price per day was too steep, and he must know that. Why was he refusing to compromise? Did he have another interested party?

"Peewee, I've heard around town that you're an honest man," she said, sensing his cautious attention. "In all honesty, you know that you're asking too much money for Black Fury, so why don't we work toward a middle ground on this?"

"I guess it's too much money if you don't have it, but it's a fair offer and I'm sticking to it." A stubborn glint entered his nut-brown eyes before he began draping the tarpaulin back over the rig.

"Peewee!" Exasperation seized her, making her voice rise and break on the second syllable. "Be reasonable!"

He shrugged his shoulders but remained stoically silent. Faith cleared her throat, glared at Peewee's back, then whirled to leave him and Black Fury, but she stopped in her tracks when she saw Houston drive up in his truck. He got out of the battered vehicle and lifted a hand in greeting.

"What are you doing here?" Faith asked, glancing over his red western-cut shirt, jeans and ostrich-skin boots. "I thought you were at the courthouse."

"I was, but I've finished my business there." Houston touched the brim of his brown suede cowboy hat. "Afternoon, Peewee. How's the world treating you today?"

"Can't complain," Peewee answered, coming toward Houston with an outstretched hand. "Put her there, cowboy."

Houston shook Peewee's chubby hand, then glanced at Black Fury. "Nice-looking rig."

"She's a gem," Peewee agreed with a proud grin. "She's hit pay dirt more times than I can count."

"I like the sound of that." Houston flashed a heart-warming grin, then lifted the tarpaulin and examined the rig more closely. "What are you asking for her?"

"Too much," Faith cut in, drawing sharp glares from both men.

"Seven hundred a day," Peewee snapped.

Houston let the corner of the cover drop and turned to face Peewee.

"That's a mite rich for my blood, buddy," Houston admitted. "I sure wish we could strike a bargain on this rig."

Peewee let another stream of tobacco juice fly. "Going to drill on your own land, huh?"

"That's right. I didn't renew that lease with PATCO."

Faith stood to one side as her irritation grew. The two men had shut her out, forgotten that she existed, and she didn't like it one bit. This was her responsibility, not Houston's!

"Takes a lot of money," Peewee noted.

"Sure does, and that's why I'm going to have to walk away from this deal." Houston backed up a step, then stopped and looked at the rig again. "She's just what I want, Peewee. It breaks my heart to lose her."

Faith rolled her eyes upward. Good grief! Houston sounded as if he were losing the woman of his dreams instead of a stupid oil rig! Was Peewee really buying this bit of melodrama? Catching Peewee's sympathetic smile, Faith realized that Peewee Porter was on the verge of tears. She closed her eyes for a moment, warding off a desire to laugh hysterically.

"She's worth that price," Peewee insisted, but his tone was less firm.

"You're right," Houston agreed. "She's worth every penny of it, but I don't have that many pennies." He shrugged, started to turn away, then looked back again as if he couldn't make himself leave. "Peewee, I'm going to make one last offer."

Peewee's hands closed around the shoulder straps of his overalls. "Let's hear it, cowboy."

"Six hundred and one percent override," Houston said crisply.

Faith sprang forward. "Are you cra—" She gritted her teeth when Houston's hand bit into her upper arm so tightly that it made her wince.

Peewee grinned and stuck out his hand. "Deal. She's all yours."

"Well, all right!" Houston laughed and shook on the deal. "I'll pick her up tomorrow."

"That'll be fine. I'll have her ready for you." Peewee slapped him on the back with enough gusto to send Houston forward a step. "Good doing business with you, Houston. I like the way you think."

"Thanks, Peewee."

Faith jerked her arm from Houston's grasp and stomped angrily to her car. She slid onto the seat and stared straight ahead as a slow burn inched up her spine and settled at the base of her neck. When Houston came over and dropped to his haunches beside the car door, she turned to face him. His eyes widened at her murderous expression.

"What's wrong?" he asked innocently.

"Did you or did you not tell me to make a deal on a rig?"

"I did."

"Then why are you sticking your big nose into *my* business?"

He frowned. "It's *our* business, and you can lower your voice. I'm not deaf. I don't know why you're making such a mountain out of a molehill."

"Because I don't like being treated like the 'little woman'!" Faith folded her arms across her breasts and stared blindly ahead. "When I started to add my two cents' worth, you almost broke my arm."

"You're exaggerating...again."

"You had no right to offer him an override without asking me first. I was doing just fine before you came along."

"Looked to me like you were walking away from the deal."

"I was. Peewee was being ridiculous. Besides, I wanted to scout around for a rotary rig."

"Why look for something we can't afford? We're lucky to get that cable tool outfit. It's perfect."

"Who's going to assemble it?"

"Me," he said with stern confidence. "I'm not deaf *or* dumb."

She was close to hurting his feelings, but she didn't care. He had tromped on hers! The city of Pecos spread out before her, and Faith recalled the day she'd run into Houston at the bank. She'd been ready to leave this area, and now she wished she had stuck to her original plan.

"You could have given me the chance to deal on a rotary rig," she murmured.

"What's that?"

"I said that you could have at least given me the chance to make a deal on a rotary rig!"

He winced at her ringing voice. "It would have cost too much money and you know it."

"It's a little late to worry about spending money after promising a one percent override of our future profits to

Peewee. I'd appreciate it if you'd consult me before you promise any more of our money to outsiders."

"Okay, I will." He slapped his hands against his thighs and grinned. "Does that make you happy?"

"It merely eases some of my qualms about this partnership."

"The thing is that Peewee is the kind of man who gets real sentimental about his equipment. He doesn't like to deal with women, either. When I saw you talking to him, I just figured you might need some help."

"I was doing fine." She pierced him with a sharp glare. "It sounds to me as if you're the one who falls in love with machinery." She cleared her throat and mimicked him. "'She's just what I want. It breaks my heart to lose her.' Give me a break!"

Houston grinned, and his chest expanded with pride. "It worked, didn't it?"

"That's a matter of opinion. Peewee would have come around and offered me a better deal than you got us."

"Is that right?"

"Yes, that's right."

His gaze sharpened as if he'd found a chink in her armor. "If you believe that, then I could sell you a stick with one end."

Faith turned her face away from him so that he wouldn't see the smile that crept across her lips. How could she argue effectively with a man who was so disarming? She swallowed the giggle that was threatening to escape and pursed her lips to erase the grin. What's the use, she asked herself. If you can't beat him, join him.

"I guess you're right. After all, it takes one to know one, and after hearing you and Peewee talk about that rig as if it were a beauty queen, I'd say that neither one of you is wrapped too tightly."

His delighted chuckle drew her gaze to his, and an understanding passed between them that sent a tantalizing tingle up Faith's spine. She looked away quickly, feeling that strong tug of attraction again and not liking it one bit.

He's not my type, she thought decisively, and I'm not his. We might make a go of it as business partners, but that's it. Any other kind of relationship would be disastrous. He's a loner and he wants to stay that way. Fine. She didn't want to get tangled up with an impulsive, stubborn, solitary man. She'd gone through that with her father, and she had no desire to repeat the experience.

"How about lunch before we head back to the homestead?" he asked with a congenial smile.

"No, thanks. I've got stuff to do," she said more sharply than she'd intended as she started her car.

His glance was questioning, but he shrugged and stood up. "Fasten your safety belt," he called after her. "And drive carefully!"

She frowned at his reflection in the side mirror and resisted the childish urge to stick out her tongue at him.

Standing a few yards back from the assembled rig, Faith gave an approving nod as Houston threw down his tools and came to stand beside her.

"What do you think?" he asked, wiping his grease-stained hands on a smudged rag.

"It's outdated," Faith mused, still wishing for a rotary rig. "I hope it holds up to the task."

"She'll do the job. I like this kind of rig because it's simple and easy to fix when it breaks." He shoved the rag in the back pocket of his jeans and removed his hard hat. The blond strands along his hairline were wet with perspiration. "Should we start her up?"

Gazing at the horizon where the sun was setting, Faith shook her head. "Better wait until tomorrow. It'll be dark soon."

"Right. First thing tomorrow, partner, we'll be in the oil business!" He grinned and tucked his hard hat under one arm. "Let's get cleaned up, and then you can come over to my place for dinner."

"No, thanks." Faith backed away from him. "I've learned my lesson on that score."

"Aw, shucks." An exaggerated frown pulled at his full lips. "You're still upset over that chili? I promise to fix something you can digest. Won't you give me one last chance to please your persnickety palate?"

She scrutinized him for a few moments before giving in. "Okay. One last chance, so make it good. I'll be over in a couple of hours."

Inside her trailer she stripped off her clothes and stood in front of the air conditioner for several long, luxuriant minutes. In the bathroom she splashed water over her hot face and let rivulets run down her arms. She thought of taking a shower, then decided to wait until morning.

Dressing in a pair of snug khaki shorts and a violet knit top, she crossed the small space to the divan and sat down there to slip on a pair of canvas shoes. Relaxing on the divan, she leafed through a couple of petroleum magazines until she found an article on tricky underground formations, which she read with great interest. An hour later, she threw aside the magazine and ran a brush through her long blond hair before twisting it into a thick braid. She indulged in a few strokes of mascara on her lashes and a splash of mulberry color across her lips before leaving her trailer and walking across the brief expanse of dry earth to Houston's more spacious dwelling.

She knocked, then entered without waiting for a reply. Houston called out from the kitchen for her to join him. He was standing before the microwave, an apron tied around his middle, and he held a casserole dish between his hands.

"Perfect timing," he noted as he placed the dish on the kitchen table. He lifted the cover to release spirals of aromatic steam. "Mmm. Smells delicious."

"Chicken?" Faith asked, looking into the dish. "Chicken and rice!"

"Right. Chicken and rice in a mushroom sauce." He took off the apron and hung it on a peg near the stove. "Does it meet with your approval?"

"Yes." She sat at one place setting and draped a napkin over her lap. "I can digest this without any trouble."

He placed a basket of hot rolls on the table, poured iced tea into two glasses, then took his place across from her. "Dig in," he urged, pushing the casserole dish toward her.

"I'm going to have to return the favor soon and have you over to my place for dinner."

"That's right neighborly of you." He took the dish from her and spooned out a portion of the chicken and rice for himself.

"I guess it's strange having someone living next to you after being out here alone for so long."

"I wouldn't call it strange."

"What would you call it?" she asked.

He cast his gaze upward in thoughtful contemplation for a few moments before answering, "Pleasant."

Faith smiled and tasted the chicken and rice. "This is good!" She reached for one of the warm rolls and buttered it. "Really good."

"Thanks." He swallowed his food before continuing. "Have you lived in cities mostly?"

"Yes, lots of cities." She took another bite of the savory rice and mushrooms. "Dallas, Oklahoma City, Phoenix, Midland." She acknowledged his surprised expression.

"Then there's places like Baghdad, Kuwait, Damascus and Tehran."

"You've been to all those places, too?"

"Yes, and I don't want to go back. We were lucky to get out of Tehran alive."

"Who's 'we'?"

"My father and me. He controlled PATCO before his death, but in the earlier years when my grandfather was still running the company, my father dragged me and my mother all over the globe to learn the oil business. It was a prerequisite if he wanted to inherit the company. My grandfather was a firm believer in handing over the company to someone who knew the oil business inside and out."

"Is your mother still living?"

"No. She passed away when I was sixteen."

"Sorry. I lost my mother when I was ten."

"Really?" She delivered a sad smile. "That's not a very happy thing to have in common, is it?"

"No. Mac told me that your family controlled PATCO."

"Used to control PATCO," she corrected hastily. "My father lost control of the company."

"How did he do that?"

She buttered another roll, debating on how much to tell him, then decided there was no reason to hide anything from him. "He was caught with his hand in the company's hip pocket." She glanced up to catch his reaction, which was less than she had expected. "He embezzled, in other words."

"It was his company," Houston said in defense.

"In a manner of speaking, yes, but PATCO went public twenty years ago. Just because Dad owned the majority of the stock, that didn't give him license to dip into company profits for his own personal use."

"So what happened?"

She sighed wearily. "I don't know exactly. No one ever bothered to fill me in on the specific details, but from what

I could gather on my own, the board of directors confronted him with the evidence, and he lost the company.''

"What a shame.''

The corners of her mouth lifted in a bitter smile as she felt a sadness press behind her eyes. "It left him with nothing. He killed himself later that day.'' She cleared her throat as it tightened with emotion. Feeling Houston's rapt gaze, she met it with as much bravado as she could muster. "It's okay. It happened years ago. I'm over it.''

They grew silent as they finished their dinner. Faith glanced at Houston from time to time, and he seemed lost in his thoughts. When he sighed heavily, she surrendered to her curiosity.

"What are you thinking about?'' she asked, smiling a little. "You look gloomy.''

He pushed his chair away from the table and sprawled lazily in it. "Oh, I was just ruminating.''

"Ruminating,'' Faith repeated. "My grandfather used to say that. What are you ruminating about?''

"How things that happen when you're young can leave permanent scars.'' He turned his head, giving her his profile to study. "It seems like you can bounce back better when you're older, but when you're young it's harder to get past the tragedies. Maybe it's because you don't expect bad things to happen when you're young.''

"When we're young we're filled with delusions.'' She studied his strong profile, letting her gaze wander from his bold nose to his jutting chin as she recalled the accident she'd heard about. Was he thinking about that? Would he tell her about it?

"I don't have any family left other than my sister. Dad died a few years back. Odessa ran away from home right after Mother passed on. Odessa hated Dad. I should have left right after that, but I didn't.''

"You didn't care for your father, either?''

"Couldn't stand him." His tawny eyes flicked over her. "He was a drunk and a bully. He'd work on a rig for a few weeks, start stealing equipment and get fired. We lived in clapboard houses that had newspapers on the walls for wallpaper and no indoor plumbing or electricity. He could've provided a better life for us, but he spent all his money on beer and whores."

Faith averted his gaze, uncomfortable with his honest appraisal of his past. She tried to imagine life with a father like this, but she couldn't. Her father had been an erratic provider, too, but they had never lived in such bleak conditions, and her father had never wasted money on liquor and loose women. He'd squandered money on cars, yachts, hare-brained business ventures and the like, but never on self-destructive vices.

"Odessa was seventeen when she ran away. I was eleven and too young to light out on my own, but I wouldn't have been any worse off if I had. Dad was always too drunk to take care of me, so I fended for myself and suffered the backlash of his reputation. Like father, like son. That's what everybody thought around here." He shook his head. "Well, everyone except for Mac and Bonita Kaye. They were always willing to give me the benefit of the doubt, bless 'em.''

"You haven't seen Odessa since she left?"

"No." He shifted in the chair and faced her again. "That's why I came back. I thought maybe she might look me up. I sure would like to see her again." He began shredding a paper napkin as if he needed something to do with his restless hands. "I tried to find her a few years ago, but I lost her trail in Galveston."

"Where did you go after you left this area?" Faith asked, watching his fingers as they tore off strips of the napkin.

"Lots of places, but mainly west of the Pecos and across the border. I was in the Marines for a few years, and when I got out, I worked on oil rigs here and there."

"I'd heard that the Marines were looking for a few good men." She smiled back at him, glad to have lightened his mood.

"There's some fascinating places around here. Have you ever been in Fort Davis?"

"Yes, but only briefly."

"The courthouse there has a turnstile entrance to keep the stray cattle from wandering in off the street." He chuckled and hooked one elbow over the ladder-backed chair. "The towns are few and far between, but they're all colorful in their own way."

"People around here seem to enjoy the isolation," Faith noted.

"Most of them are delighted to be left alone, and that's why they settled here. You've got to be self-sufficient, tough and independent as hell to like it out here."

"Does that describe you?" Faith asked softly. "Do you like the solitude this place offers?"

"I used to." He began unfolding the napkin. "But when we strike oil, I'm going to pack up and head for the city...*any* city, so long as it's full of friendly people." He held what was left of the napkin between his thumbs and forefingers. "Here, have a heart."

His confession about moving to the city had surprised her, but whatever comments she had been about to make fled from her mind as she stared at the valentine he'd fashioned out of the ordinary napkin. She smiled and took it from him. The large valentine had a cut-out smaller heart in its center.

"How did you do this?" she asked, examining it.

"It's easy." He laughed heartily, and she liked the deep, throaty sound. "You learn to do things like that out here to keep from climbing the walls."

"I thought you liked being by yourself."

"I'm good company, but I've played all the games of solitaire I want to play." He cocked his head to one side. "Do you play cards?"

"A little. I used to play canasta every week with friends."

"Canasta." He frowned slightly. "That's one I've avoided. Ever play poker?"

"A few times. Do you like bridge?"

"Nope." He began clearing the table. "How about crazy eight?"

She laughed and helped him clean off the table. "I haven't played that since I was a kid." She shoved aside two yellow hard hats on the counter and placed a stack of soiled dishes there.

"Oh, that reminds me." He lifted one of the hats and put it on her head, then donned the other one. "Mac stopped by early this morning before you got up and left these for us."

Faith examined his hat, then removed her own to look at the identical black letters—OM—and the oil derricks flanking them. "What does OM stand for?"

"Oil Millionaire."

She grinned and put the hat back on. "It fits."

"And you look like a million dollars in it," he said in a tone that had suddenly become intimate.

A delicious tingle passed through her before she whipped off the hat and turned to the dishwasher. "I'll help you clean up."

"That's okay. I can do it."

"Your independent streak is showing, Mr. Solitaire. Let me help, okay?"

"Okay." He shrugged and rinsed off the dishes, handing them to her so that she could arrange them in the dishwasher.

"I wish I had one of these in my trailer," she said with a wistful sigh.

"Where would you put it?"

"Good point." She added detergent, closed the machine and punched the appropriate button. "All done. This is a wonderful invention." Turning to him, she touched his forearm. "Thanks for a great dinner, Houston. Next time it's on me."

"I'll hold you to that. You're not leaving already, are you?"

"Yes. I hate to eat and run, but..."

"Then don't. Sit a spell with me."

The offer was appealing, but she resisted the urge to sit in one of the comfortable chairs in his living room and enjoy his company. She had expected him to keep her at arm's length and savor his solitude, but he had thrown her a curve. He wanted her company, was even asking her for it, but she felt that they should keep a professional distance.

"No, I really need to get back to my own place. I'm tired, and I want to read an article in the *Oil and Gas Journal* before I turn in."

He seemed genuinely disappointed as he saw her to the door and into the dark outside. He switched on his porch light to illuminate the distance between their trailers.

"See you in the morning, Faith."

"Right. Sleep well!" She closed the door behind her and peeked out the oval of glass. He stood on the threshold for a few moments in silhouette, then finally closed his own door. She saw his shadow pass across the dining room windows before the lights went out, leaving only the one in the living room burning.

Turning around, she tossed aside the hard hat and stared at her cramped living space as her mind replayed the evening's conversation. What he had said about himself conflicted with her earlier assessment of him.

The loner was lonely.

A tender smile curved her lips as she unfolded the heart he'd torn from a paper napkin. She placed it over her own heart, and fondness for him stole through her like sunlight through shadow.

Turning off the shower, Faith stepped from the small room and groaned when she noticed the soaked roll of bathroom tissue.

"Oh, hell!" She removed the wet tissue and dropped it in the equally soggy trash can, remembering Houston's warning about this kind of fiasco. She'd have to train herself to take everything out of the bathroom before she showered, she told herself firmly as she dried off and slipped into her underwear, white T-shirt and blue jean coveralls. Pulling on heavy socks, she stuck her feet into a pair of high-topped, leather work shoes and laced them.

Wearing her new hard hat, she stepped outside into the brilliant sunlight, feeling anticipation stir within her as she started toward the quiet rig.

"Hey, hold up a minute."

She turned to see Houston standing at the backside of her trailer. "What's wrong?"

"This." He pointed to the wet ground beneath her trailer. "See that?"

"Yes. Is something leaking?"

"Yes, your wash water."

She examined the dark patch of earth. "Isn't it supposed to drain out onto the ground?"

"Not if you can help it." He kicked a shallow tub over the wet ground. "You're supposed to catch it and save it."

"What for?" she asked. "Why save dirty water?"

"To wash things with." He ran a hand down his wrinkled shirt, its sleeves rolled up to his elbows. "You don't waste water out here. I thought you understood that."

"I'm not going to wash anything in dirty water!" She placed her fists at her waist and stared at him, daring him to make her.

"You can use this gray water to wash off your car or your trailer. Things get dusty and dirty out here. My rig would be black instead of white if I didn't wash it off from time to time." He ran a forefinger along the side of her own trailer, leaving a streak and showing her the dirt on the end of his finger. "See? Yours is filthy already."

"Okay, okay. You've made your point," she grumbled, turning away from him. Was he *always* right? She hated that in a man. "Let's get to work."

"Water is shipped in here from Midland. If you run out before the next shipment, that's *your* misery."

"I get it. You don't have to beat me over the head to get my attention," she tossed over her shoulder.

"You sure are foul tempered in the mornings, aren't you?"

"Only when I'm greeted with orders and accusations. Let's make some hole." She stopped beside the drill bit, anxious to begin their business venture in earnest.

"Yes, ma'am!" He circled the hulk of machinery before letting her rip.

Black Fury trembled, groaned, shuddered, squeaked and shook the ground before the drill bit finally inched down into the hole PATCO had left. Faith released a nervous laugh. For a minute there, she had half expected Black Fury to crumble into a mass of broken parts.

"That's music to my ears!" Houston shouted above the noise as he hoisted a Lone Star flag up a makeshift flag pole he'd set near the rig.

Faith looked up at the sky-blue, red and white rectangle as it lay limply against the pole. An unfelt breeze stirred it, but not enough to make it flutter. Looking around for Houston, she found that he was opening a bottle of champagne. He stepped close to the hole in the ground and poured the bubbling liquid into it.

"What are you doing?" Faith asked, laughing a little.

"Calling up dinosaurs."

She shook her head, dismissing the superstition. "How's it biting?"

"Good. Real good." His gaze traveled up and down with the red flag tied around the drill stem. "We'll make a good run with this bit."

Faith picked up an oil can and squirted some of the lubricant into a few squeaking joints in the rig. "Black Fury sure makes a lot of noise!"

"Here!" He pushed the champagne bottle into her free hand. "Take a drink."

"It's too early for that stuff."

"You've got to!" His eyes widened in alarm. "It'll bring good luck."

"Come on, Houston. You don't believe in that old black magic, do you?" She studied the grim set of his lips. Good grief! He *did* believe in this mumbo jumbo! "Okay, okay. If it will make you feel better." She took a long drink of the heady champagne, then handed him the bottle.

He finished it off and dropped the empty bottle into a bucket. "We can't help but strike it lucky now." With a jaunty grin, he went around to the other side of the rig to check for any rusty parts. "I knew there was oil under here the first time I saw this land," he shouted to her over the growling machinery.

"How's that?" Faith shouted back.

"From the way the land looked. I could see the structure and it all spelled O-I-L."

"Surface geology?" she asked, disappointed that he would believe in such an unfounded practice.

"That's right." He leaned sideways to look at her through a gap in the rig. "I walked it off, and I knew that PATCO would put their rig right here where we're standing."

Faith shrugged and squirted oil into a creaking joint. She shouldn't be so disappointed in him, she thought, but she was. She'd hoped he'd learned something concrete about the oil business, but it turned out that he relied on flimsy things like surface geology and superstitions. Just like dad, she thought with a worried frown. To hell with core samples, drill stem tests and other proven methods of geology! Who needed that stuff when a man could "see" geology formations and call up dinosaurs by offering them a drink of champagne?

She moved sideways to catch a glimpse of Houston's happy grin. It was a good thing he had her as a partner, she thought, because he didn't know a blessed thing about petroleum geology.

Chapter Five

"Partner, may I go out?"

Faith met Houston's glittering brown eyes over the fan of cards he held in his hands. She glanced at her own four cards, counted up the points and nodded. "By all means!"

Bonita Kaye and Mac released groans as Houston arranged his remaining cards, which helped to meld stacks of aces, queens and sevens. Faith laughed, displaying her lesser point cards.

"We won again!" Still laughing, Faith extended one hand across the card table and shook Houston's. "Way to go, partner!"

"Are you sure you've never played canasta before?" Bonita Kaye asked as she added up her deficit point score.

"Positive. Never thought I'd like it." Houston grinned triumphantly and handed the cards over to Mac. "I guess it's beginner's luck."

"Nonsense," Faith objected. "You've just got a skillful partner, that's all." She sat back in the chair and smiled. "It's been so long since I've played canasta with friends. This is really nice. I'm kind of glad that the rig broke down so that we could get away for a few hours. Thanks for inviting us over tonight."

"It's good that you could fix the rig yourself," Mac said to Houston. "You can start back up in the morning. What's the bad news, Bonita Kaye?"

His wife scowled as she wrote their score on a pad of paper. "We had four wild cards between us, which didn't help any. Our total score for that round was only one hundred and sixty-five. They're ahead of us by three thousand points!"

"We might as well surrender." Mac shrugged good-naturedly and stroked his white mustache. "I know when I'm whipped."

"Fine with me." Bonita Kaye stood up and stretched. "How about some coffee?"

"I'll help you," Faith said, following Bonita Kaye into the kitchen, which was cheerfully decorated in pale blue and sparkling white. "This is a lovely room. I love big kitchens."

"So do I. When we built this house I told Mac that the only thing I really wanted was a nice big kitchen. I hate those cubbyholes in most homes where you have two counters and four feet separating them."

Faith nodded as she leaned against the side-by-side refrigerator. "I'm living in a tiny trailer now. When I bought it I thought it was perfect, but Houston was right. It's so small that I keep running into myself."

Bonita Kaye chuckled and switched on the coffee maker. "Mac told me about it. He said it was the size of a chicken coop."

"It is!" Faith laughed at herself. "I can't believe that I originally thought it was charming. Oh, well! It's only temporary." She gazed out one of the many windows at the star-splashed night. "This has been a wonderful evening."

"Going a little stir-crazy out there in the middle of nothing?" Bonita Kaye's smile was wise and warm.

Faith shrugged helplessly. "I know it's only been two weeks since we brought in the rig and started drilling, but it seems like months."

"My sister-in-law visited us once and just stayed here one day and one night, but I never could get her and my brother to come back for another visit. Finally my sister-in-law told me that Mac and I were welcome to visit her in Corpus Christi any time we wanted, but that she didn't want to come back here. She said, 'Bonita Kaye, the longest summer I ever spent was the day I spent in west Texas.'" Bonita Kaye laughed with Faith, then added, "So I know how this place can get to you if you're not used to it."

"The routine is what drives me nuts," Faith admitted. "We spend the whole day at the rig with Houston fixing this or that broken part while I study soil formations. By sundown we're exhausted, cranky and sick of each other. We go to our separate trailers and have dinner, then fall into our beds. It's the same thing day after day, and that's why this evening out is heaven sent."

"You and Houston are welcome here anytime, honey." Bonita Kaye arranged oatmeal cookies on a platter and set it on a serving tray. "Boredom aside, how are you and Houston getting along?"

"Okay, I guess. We hardly exchange more than a few words during the day. He hums and sings to himself, and I read and peer into my microscope." She paused and smiled. "He has a nice singing voice." Intercepting the matchmaking gleam in Bonita Kaye's blue eyes, Faith added quickly, "But he's not the sort of man I'm used to being with."

"What sort of man are you used to?"

"The more sophisticated kind. Most of the men I've dated are businessmen."

"Houston's a businessman of sorts."

"You know what I mean," Faith said. "The kind of businessman who wears suits and drives foreign cars."

"I don't want you to take offense at this, honey," Bonita Kaye said, "but I think what a man wears or drives is pretty insignificant. Character is more important."

"Yes, you're right." Faith straightened from her lounging position against the refrigerator. "What I'm trying to say is that Houston and I are from two different worlds. We're not cut from the same cloth. It makes for an interesting business partnership, but not a good personal one."

"I don't know if Houston is aware of it—probably not—but he's considered to be quite a catch around these parts." Bonita Kaye smiled, and dimples buried into her cheeks. She set the coffeepot on the tray along with cups, saucers, cream and sugar. "He might not be your type, but he sure has the single women around here swooning and batting their eyelashes." She chuckled, shaking her head in amusement. "My maid melts every time she sees him. The other day she looked out the window and saw him and said, *'Qué paisaje tan hermoso!'*" Bonita Kaye laughed again, then translated, "What beautiful scenery!"

Faith nodded, not having needed the translation since she'd picked up Spanish in the oilfields. "To each his own," she quipped, uneasy with the turn of conversation. Bonita Kaye was turning in a fine performance of the classic matchmaker, Texas style, but Faith didn't need that kind of assistance. "Let me carry that," she said, seizing the silver tray and leading the way from the kitchen to the den.

Houston was relaxing in Mac's leather lounger but rose to his feet when Faith and Bonita Kaye entered the room. He helped Faith place the tray on the table.

"That's heavy. You should have called me and I'd have carried it for you."

Faith threw him a bewildered glare. Since when had he decided that she was a weakling? "Don't worry about it, Houston. After hauling buckets of water all day, this tray is a piece of cake."

"These cookies look good, Bonita Kaye," Houston said, helping himself to a couple. He tasted one and winked his appreciation. "They melt in your mouth."

"How's that rig of Peewee's biting?" Mac asked, taking the cup and saucer Bonita Kaye handed him.

"Pretty good," Houston said, his gaze moving swiftly to Faith as he answered.

Faith delivered a chastising frown. "When it isn't broken down, which is most of the time."

"That so?" Mac asked.

"Nothing major," Houston said, still looking at Faith. "Nothing I can't handle."

Faith lifted one shoulder, dismissing his excuses. "The down-hole pressure will probably blow it clear to Midland."

"No, it won't." Houston's heavy brows met in a frown. "She'll hold up. How much oil you getting out of Mac number six?"

"A hundred and twenty barrels a day," Mac answered.

"And number eight?"

"She's flowing about a hundred and eighty."

Houston smiled and finished off his third cookie. "That's promising. They're the closest to my land. There's just got to be oil down under that cracked ground of mine."

"Sure there is," Mac agreed.

"I've got a feeling about it...right here." Houston tapped his firm stomach. "We're close. I know we're close. My gut tells me so."

"Well, my samples tell me we're several hundred feet from the pay zone," Faith interjected. "Of course, geology is no match for your stomach pains." She smiled sweetly at Houston's piercing glare.

Houston checked his watch and returned the cup and saucer to the tray. "We'd better get going."

Sensing that he was on the verge of biting her head off, Faith stood up and nodded. "Yes, you're right."

"Y'all don't have to run off right now, do you?" Mac asked.

"We've got another long day ahead of us, Mac," Houston explained as he shook Mac's hand. "Thanks for the company tonight."

"It was a great evening," Faith agreed, giving Bonita Kaye an affectionate hug. "Thanks again."

"Y'all come back real soon," Bonita Kaye urged them.

The MacQuays saw them to the door to bid them good night. Faith walked beside Houston to the truck but paused when she saw the light streaming from the windows of the recreation building Mac had built on his property for his own enjoyment and that of his ranch hands.

"How about a game of pool before we go home?" Faith asked, catching sight of a few people inside the building.

Houston looked at the building and the three trucks parked outside it. "Sure, why not?"

They entered the rec room, and the six men and women inside greeted Houston. He introduced her to the three men, all of whom worked on the MacQuay ranch, and their dates. The only one Faith recognized was LaQuita, the Mac-Quays' maid. The dark-haired young woman couldn't keep her eyes off Houston as he and Faith played a game of pool.

Faith discovered that she and Houston were equally matched as pool players. They were both respectable shooters, making more shots than they missed. As Houston lined up a particularly tricky shot, Faith examined his intent expression. His dark blond brows met in concentration and his eyes were a deeper shade of brown than usual. His lashes looked longer, throwing shadows across his cheeks. Her earlier irritation with him faded as she appreciated the firm set of his lips, the graceful strength of his hands and the muscled sinew of his exposed forearms. He missed the shot and cursed softly under his breath.

"My turn," Faith said cheerfully as she leaned over the table and took a bead on the cue ball. "Six ball in the corner pocket."

"Go for it," Houston said behind her.

Faith held her breath, moved the long stick back and forth a few times and steadied herself. Just as she was about to give the white ball a decisive smack, LaQuita's shrill voice scraped across her nerve endings.

"Oh, Houston! Come outside and dance with us!"

The cue stick squeaked against Faith's fingers and tapped the cue ball at a bad angle. The white ball rolled past the six ball, missing it by a good inch.

"Be right there!" Houston called back. "You missed, Faith."

"I know it!" Faith straightened and slammed the stick on the table. "But I was fouled."

"Fouled? How's that?"

"LaQuita screamed at you right before I took my shot."

"You're awful jumpy." He handed the stick back to her and lined up his shot. "Seven and six in the side pocket." He was true to his word. The seven and six rattled into the pocket. "Eight ball in the corner." The eight ball rolled across the table and disappeared. "Game."

Faith replaced her pool stick in the wall rack. "I still say I was fouled."

"Let's go outside and dance."

"Let's go home."

He took one of her hands in his and gave it a tug. "Come on, Grumpy. A dance will do you good."

"Lead the way, Dopey," she shot back, letting him pull her outside where a truck radio blasted a snappy country and western tune. The three couples moved in a two-stepping circle.

"Can you two-step?" Houston asked, pulling her in front of him and grasping her shoulders lightly.

"Can you?"

He grinned and moved her into a lively dance. She placed her hands at his waist and followed his lead effortlessly. When the song ended, LaQuita wasted no time in moving in.

"Can I have the next dance, Houston?" she asked, not bothering to even glance at Faith.

"Well...I..." Houston looked decidedly uncomfortable.

"Go ahead," Faith urged. "I'll sit this one out."

"No way!" Bobby Stockton, LaQuita's date, wrapped a beefy arm around Faith's waist. "I'll dance with you."

Faith resigned herself to the situation, letting Bobby guide her into a slow, shuffling dance. He wasn't nearly as adept as Houston. His wide grin was friendly, and Faith tried to smile back, but she didn't like being held in a viselike grip by a man she'd only met a few minutes ago.

"Bobby, could you give me a little breathing room?" she asked, pressing a hand against his shoulder. "That a boy." She kept a firm hand against him throughout the dance and was infinitely relieved when the last crooning note faded away. Stepping from his embrace, she ran her hands down her sides. "Thanks, Bobby."

"How about another one?"

"I've had enough, thanks." She turned away from his disappointed expression and went over to Houston's pickup to lean against it and watch LaQuita flirt unabashedly with Houston. The woman was really soaking up "the scenery," Faith thought, mildly amused.

"Houston, you dance so good!" LaQuita held on to his forearms and leaned forward. "Would you give me lessons?"

"You don't need lessons," Houston said, obviously uneasy. "Thanks for the dance."

"One more?"

"No, no." He shook his head and tried to shake free of her firm hold.

"Why not?" LaQuita pursed her full lips into a pretty pout.

"Because I was taught to dance with the one I brought." He looked sideways, catching Faith's bemused smile before he motioned for Bobby. "Here's your girl, Bobby!"

LaQuita's hands slipped down Houston's arms and across the backs of his hands in a coquettish gesture. "Another time, Houston, please?"

"Maybe." He turned and hurried to Faith. "Let's go."

"One more dance, Houston?" Faith begged, batting her lashes. "You dance so good!" Ignoring his scowl, she laced her hands behind his neck and adopted a more serious tone. "One more for the road, oilman?"

Humor lit his eyes. "Well, when you put it like that, how can I refuse?" His arms stole around her waist and he back-stepped away from the pickup. "This is an oldie," he said, listening to the instrumental refrain of "Linger Awhile."

Faith tried to recall the words but couldn't. She smiled when Houston's rich baritone provided them.

"'And when you've gone away, each hour will seem like a day. I've got something to tell you, so linger awhile,'" he sang softly near her ear as he moved with her in a western variation of the box-step. He drew back and looked down into her eyes with a boldness that she hadn't expected from him. What had happened to his shyness?

During the past weeks it had been difficult at times to catch his eye; he'd seemed to look everywhere but at her.

Now, however, she had his undivided attention. Faith's own gaze fell away first, and she found herself staring nervously at the scar below his lip.

Permanent scars, she thought, recalling his references to his childhood. He had said that some youthful experiences left permanent scars. Was this one of them?

"How did you get that scar?" she asked before she realized the words were out.

His hands tightened for a moment at her waist. "In a car accident."

"Oh." She looked into his eyes again and confronted the wariness there. "Whoever stitched it up didn't do a very good job."

"Mac's veterinarian stitched it up."

Faith smiled. "That explains it." She looked around, then back at him. "Houston, the song's over."

He stopped in his tracks and grinned when he heard the disc jockey signing off for the evening. "So it is." Glancing at the other couples, he lifted a hand. "Good night, ladies and gents."

"Night, y'all," voices rang out as Houston helped Faith into the pickup.

LaQuita cast Faith a pointed glare as she crossed in front of the pickup with Bobby, but Faith pretended she didn't see it. She remained silent as Houston drove toward what they had begun to refer to as the Double H. The truck bumped over the rough road, bouncing Faith in the seat. She held on to the dash board and looked up at the starry night. The heavens seemed within reach, pressing low on the horizon. She felt at peace with the world, but she was alert to a simmering attraction for the man beside her.

When she had danced with him, she had discovered how wonderful he felt beneath her hands. Was it her imagination, or was his skin warmer than most men's? She had felt the heat of it through the fabric of his shirt. She had longed to let her fingers know the texture of his hair, the shape of his face and the width of his shoulders.

It's just because you're lonely out here, she told herself. Lonely and bored. Any man would...She shook her head as she recalled the *ages* she had spent in Bobby's arms. No, just any man wouldn't have made her react that way. Houston was special, but that was no reason to make more out of her feelings than was actually there. She liked Houston, but that was all there was to it.

"LaQuita seems to have set her sights on you, oilman," she said, anxious to steer herself away from her inner conflicts.

"Oh, that's nothing." He parked the truck and opened the door. "I think she was trying to make Bobby jealous."

"I think she was trying to seduce you, and she didn't give a darn if Bobby was jealous or not." Faith stepped out of the truck and closed the door. She laughed when she saw the dark color staining Houston's cheeks. "I've embarrassed you!"

"No, you haven't. I just think you're all wet. LaQuita must have had a little too much to drink, that's all."

"Really? I didn't know you could get drunk on orange soda." She lifted her brows in an attempt at comic relief. "That's what she was drinking, Houston."

"I thought I saw her with a beer."

"She was bringing it to Bobby."

"Oh." He stuck his hands in the pockets of his jeans and tipped back his head to stare at the Milky Way. "All I know is that she was acting a little crazy."

"Lust does that to some women."

"You're full of it."

"You're blushing."

"And why shouldn't I? We shouldn't be discussing such...such things as..."

"Sex?" She winced when he glared at her. "Sorry. Is that too strong a word for you? How about the birds and the bees? Billing and cooing. Can you handle that?" she goaded, not quite sure why she was intent on making him squirm.

"I can handle it just fine, thanks." He brought his gaze to bear on her, and his hands slipped out of his pockets. "What about you? Can you take it as well as you dish it out?"

"I don't know what you're getting at," she said breathlessly.

"This."

There was a split second when she knew exactly what he was about to do, but she was helpless to stop him. She stiffened when he closed the distance between them with one long-legged stride, and she leaned back when his arm circled her waist, but he pursued her by leaning forward and bending her over his arm. His other hand cupped her chin, holding her face still while his mouth swooped to hers. His lips were firm and unyielding, but softened after a few moments and became probing and gentle.

As abruptly as the kiss had begun, it ended. His hands fell away from her and he stepped back, a cocky grin on his mouth.

"There!"

Faith's equilibrium returned with a jolt. "There what? Was that supposed to have something to do with the birds and the bees?"

The cocky grin vanished. "Are you insulting me?"

"No, I'm just trying to understand what that...little peck was all about. Was I supposed to swoon? It takes more than that to make my head swim. Sorry. Better luck next time." She turned, keeping her own cocky smile at bay, and started for her trailer, her arms swinging confidently at her sides.

As her left arm swung back, lean fingers tightened around her wrist and whirled her around. Faith's breath whistled down her throat before Houston's lips covered hers.

His hands slipped down her arms and around her shoulders, pulling her up to him until her breasts flattened against his chest.

Faith moaned a weak protest, directed more at herself than at him. She had meant to ward him off by a lack of response, but her plan went awry when his mouth softened against hers and his lips parted to take hers in a warm embrace. Through trembling lashes, she caught a glimpse of his closed eyes and determined expression before her eyelids blocked out his face altogether.

His kiss was as furious as a two-alarm fire and just as potentially dangerous. Hands splayed across her back, molding her to his will and searing her flesh through her thin cotton blouse. His tongue was a flame of flicking desire, lashing out and retreating before she could control it. But even though he was kissing her with a raging intensity, there was an underlying gentleness, as if he couldn't manage total brute force. His lips caressed hers, taking more and more with each slight adjustment.

She couldn't recall the last time she had been kissed with such sublime expertise. He likes me, she thought as he ended the kiss and stepped back to hold her at arm's length. He likes me a lot!

"That was better," she admitted. "That one curled my toes."

A reluctant smile touched one corner of his mouth. "You just love to get under my skin, don't you?"

"I wasn't aware that I got under your skin."

"Like a rash," he growled, letting go of her. "Good night, Faith."

She watched, a little dismayed, as he strode to his trailer and slammed the door behind him. Is that all there is? she wondered dejectedly. How could he kiss her like that and leave her?

Shrugging off the rejection, she went inside her own trailer and draped herself on the divan. A saucy smile spread across her lips, and pleasure rose in her like tendrils of steam. Her toes curled in her shoes, and she kicked off the canvas slings.

"Houston, Houston," she whispered, liking the taste of his name on her tongue. "You're not a loner, are you?"

How did he come to deserve that stigma? she wondered. Why did people think he was unfriendly and remote? He was warm and vibrant—a man who had suffered his share of hard knocks but had not become embittered by them.

In a way, he reminded her of her father. A dreamer who yearned for the pot of gold at the end of a distant rainbow. A man who lived by instinct and trust.

She frowned, her good mood dissipating as the parallels became more apparent. No matter how much she had enjoyed it when Houston had displayed his more passionate side, she couldn't allow herself to indulge fully. When that rig out there hit pay dirt, she'd be on her way, and she didn't want to be tied down to another irresponsible dreamer like her father. She couldn't live with uncertainty again. She had loved her father, but she hadn't loved living with him. Life had taught her to look for a man who was level-headed and pragmatic, and Houston didn't meet those requirements.

Chapter Six

Swearing viciously under her breath, Faith tried to wipe the slick soap off her legs and arms with a towel. Failing miserably, she wiggled into her underwear and slipped into a cotton kimono.

"Houston!" She looked out the door and saw him stretched out in the hammock he'd suspended between a scraggly tree and the rig. A straw cowboy hat hid his eyes, but she knew he was awake. "Houston!"

"What?" Faith could hear the irritation in his voice, but it was a tone she had become used to over the past few weeks. The day-to-day routine had created a rut, making for short tempers and sullen dispositions.

"I've run out of water." She hunched her shoulders beneath the clinging material and felt itchy all over. "I ran out in the middle of my shower."

"Surprise, surprise, surprise," he drawled in a Gomer Pyle accent that grated on Faith's nerves. He tipped back the hat and squinted at her. "You use a gallon of it just to brush your teeth!"

"Spare me the lectures on conservation and just fill up my tank, please. I want to wash off this soap."

"The shipment from Midland won't be here for another couple of days," he said, twisting out of the hammock and landing on his feet like a big lazy cat. "If you keep wasting it, we'll run out before then."

Looking past him to the huge holding tank, she sighed wearily. "We've got thousands of gallons in that tank, and—"

"That's for our drilling operation, not for you to use to wash your hair six times a day."

"I don't wash my hair six times a day!" Her voice cracked on the last word, and she struggled to control her temper. "Just fill up my tank so that I can get to work. Do you have to make a federal case out of everything?" She slammed the door and sat on the divan, listening intently and breathing a sigh of gratitude when she heard Houston attach the water hose to her trailer's holding tank.

Heavens, he was hard to live with, she thought as she scratched the soapy film on her arms. Sometimes he was adorable, but other times she wanted to wring his neck, and this was one of those times when throttling seemed permissible. The past few days had been the worst. He'd hardly uttered more than a dozen words to her, and his tone dripped with boredom when he did speak.

She picked up her logbook and flipped to the last entry page. Inch by inch the drill bit burrowed into the hard ground, but the formations weren't as promising as she'd hoped. Her soil tests remained constant, revealing the possibility of oil farther down but nothing definite. Yesterday she'd done a drill stem test, which had depressed her even further. If she'd still been working for PATCO, she knew that the geologists would have ordered the well capped and abandoned, but she was a wildcatter now and her common sense had taken a backseat to mindless hope.

Houston rapped his knuckles against the outside of her trailer, signaling that she was in the water business again, and Faith dropped the logbook and sprang from the divan.

"Thanks, partner!" she called, knowing he could hear her through the thin walls.

She peeled off the kimono and her underwear and stepped into the bathroom again to wash off the itchy soap film. She hurried, sensing that Houston was probably keeping an eye on how much water she used and congratulated herself when she spent only two minutes under the spray. Twenty minutes later she emerged from her trailer and joined Houston at the rig.

"How's Black Fury biting today?" she asked, staring down at Houston's straw hat. He was crouched beside the hole, watching the up-and-down progression of the bit and pipe.

"Okay, I guess. This bit is still green, so I don't imagine we'll have to change it." He glanced up at her. "Shut her down. I've got to add more pipe."

She followed his instructions and watched as he added another length of pipe. The man knew his stuff, she thought with a smile. He was worth ten of PATCO's roughnecks. There wasn't anything on this rig he couldn't fix, and he'd proved himself invaluable to their shoestring operation. He paused to strip off his shirt before finishing the task and asking her to start up the rig again. Confident that everything was satisfactory, Houston gave a curt nod. He wadded his shirt in one hand and ran it across his chest and arms, and Faith felt her femininity respond to the blatant masculinity before her. She looked away, feeling lightheaded and weak willed.

"I'm going to take a shower and a nap," he announced, already moving toward his trailer. "If you need me, just holler."

"I will." Noticing his sagging shoulders, Faith realized that he was dead on his feet. He probably spent the night in the hammock, she surmised. Houston hated to leave the rig unattended, even though his trailer was only a few yards from it and he would be able to hear any rumble or rattle. Faith knew that he spent most nights under the stars, baby-sitting Black Fury. It made her feel guilty, but she preferred her own soft bed to sleeping in a hammock beside the noisy rig.

She sat at the card table she'd erected near the rig under a makeshift tent and adjusted her microscope. Staring at the three bound books of test results, she shook her head. Logs, logs, logs. What would she do without her logs? A geologist without log books was like a witch without a broomstick. Stranded.

Glancing around at the bleak countryside, she fell back in the metal folding chair as a sense of futility overwhelmed her. Was there oil under her feet, or was she standing in financial quicksand? Sharp particles of dust blew into her eyes, and she put on her sunglasses to shield them. Looking up at the Lone Star flag, she was surprised to find that it was standing straight out from the pole. Miracles of miracles, she thought with a wry twist of her lips. Was that a bonafide breeze? She bent over the microscope and studied the soil sample, enjoying the wind's cool breath against the back of her neck.

An hour later a sheaf of papers fluttered off the table, and Faith scrambled after them. The wind had picked up, blowing everything that wasn't tied down and blasting dirt against her exposed skin.

"Ouch!" Faith covered her stinging face with her hands for a moment, then captured the rest of her papers and stuck

them in her briefcase. She closed the case and locked it before glancing around at the swirling dust and dirt. The atmosphere was so choked with it that she could barely see
more than a few feet ahead of her.

"Welcome to west Texas," she murmured as she stowed
away her microscope and carried it to her trailer where it
would be safe from the clouds of dirt. She made several trips
back and forth, each time toting logs, books and surveyor
maps and dumping them in her trailer out of harm's way.

When the wind came sweeping down the plains in this arid
region, it could only mean one thing—a dust storm—and
Faith didn't want to spend any more time in it than was
necessary. After making sure that everything was tied down,
she escaped the wicked wind by ducking inside Houston's
trailer. She closed the door and leaned weakly against it for
a minute while her vision adjusted to the dim lighting.
Whipping off the sunglasses, she rubbed her stinging eyes
and felt grit on her face and hands.

"Houston?" she whispered, glancing around the empty
living and dining rooms. Would he want to shut down the
rig until the dust storm had blown itself out?

Tiptoeing across the carpet toward the higher end of the
trailer that housed Houston's bedroom, she paused at the
bottom of the three steps leading up to it and listened. He
was snoring. She smiled and crept up the three steps until she
could see him sprawled in the queen-sized bed.

"Houston?" she whispered again, hating to wake him,
but he didn't stir. His guttural snores escaped through his
parted lips, and his chest rose and fell with the rhythm of
deep sleep.

Faith's gaze fell on the bundle of clothing near the bed,
and after a quick inventory, she realized he was naked. Her
gaze returned to his sleeping form with the feverish interest
of an amateur voyeur. She sniffed the air, catching the faint

fragrance of soap and water before she noticed that his hair was still damp from the shower.

She loved his hair. She loved the light blond color of it and the way it fell in layers of flaxen silk. He brushed it straight back, but as the day wore on, it usually separated naturally in a place that was somewhere between a side and center part. More than once, she had wrestled with the urge to run her fingers through that mane. Did he ever want to glide his fingers through her golden hair and feel the weight of it where it settled across her shoulders?

The wind whistled around the trailer, and Houston stirred. His noisy snores ceased abruptly, and Faith held her breath until he appeared to drop back into unconsciousness. She took three tentative steps closer to the bed and indulged in a few minutes of visual delight that made her pulses flutter. His chest was wide and lightly dusted with curls of crisp, reddish-gold hair. His arms were corded with muscle, long arms that were tanned a golden brown.

Looking at his face again, she noticed that his brow was furrowed and that fret lines framed his wide mouth. What demonic dream gripped him? she wondered. What vile vision made his legs jerk convulsively under the top sheet? His full lips moved, but no sound escaped; then he moaned deep in his throat and his eyes popped open. He sat bolt upright and stared at her. Faith backed up, alarmed at his wild-eyed glare.

"Houston, are you okay?" she asked, wondering if he were awake or still caught in his nightmare. "It's me—Faith."

He ran a hand over his face. "I haven't dreamed about that in years," he murmured. "Why now?"

"Dreamed about what?"

"The car acci—" His umber gaze sharpened. "Nothing. What are you doing here?"

"There's a dust storm blowing up out there, and I was wondering if we should shut down until it's over."

"Dust storm?" He cocked his head to one side and listened to the howling wind. "No, it'll cost too much money to shut down. Just keep an eye on the rig—through the windows," he added, catching her slight grimace. "What time is it?"

"A little after ten." She crossed her arms, feeling uncomfortable now that he was awake and aware of her. "Want some coffee?"

"There's some already made. Help yourself."

"Thanks, I will." She turned and escaped to the kitchen, wondering what sort of dream could make him break out in a sweat. Must be a humdinger, she thought. It would have to be to scare Houston Traynor. Had it been fright or anguish she had glimpsed on his face before he had awakened? Maybe a combination of both, she decided as she poured herself a cup of coffee and lightened it with milk.

Houston entered, pulling a T-shirt over his head as he did so and tugging it down over his chest. He peered out the window at the dust that nearly obliterated the sun.

"It's really blowing up out there," he said, then nodded when she held up her cup. "Don't mind if I do. How do the samples look?"

"The same as before." She set the other cup on the table and Houston sat in front of it. "I'm trying to remain optimistic."

"Having your doubts?" he asked, his coppery gaze pinning her across the table.

"I just thought we'd start seeing different formations by now."

"We're only at three thousand feet," he reminded her. "I don't think we'll hit until thirty-four hundred."

"Thirty-six," she corrected. "Maybe as far down as thirty-eight."

"So why are you singing the blues?"

"I'm not." She shrugged off the momentary pessimism. "I'm just tired of waiting."

"That's the name of the game, lady." He sipped the hot coffee and looked out the window when the wind shook the trailer. "Hot dog! It's really blowing and going out there. Hope it doesn't damage the rig." He sprang to his feet, grabbed his hat and tied a red bandanna across his nose and mouth.

"What are you doing?"

"I'm going to check on the rig," he said through the kerchief as he pulled his hat down low on his forehead. "Be back in a few minutes."

Not to be outdone by him, Faith grabbed a tea towel and tied it around her nose and mouth. She put on her hard hat and followed in his tracks, straining against the buffeting winds. Dust particles stabbed her eyes and shot past the fluttering cloth into her mouth and nose. She coughed and plowed through the wind current until she finally reached the rig. Houston was shutting it down and hauling the casing and bit out of the hole. She grabbed hold of it and helped him push it aside and secure it. He covered the hole, then pointed to the trailer, signaling for her to go back inside, but she stood her ground and waited for him. His hat blew off and slammed into her chest. Faith held on to it, stumbling backward when a solid sheet of air and dust pressed into her.

Houston turned her around, wrapped his arms around her and guided her back to his trailer. He pushed her up the steps and inside, then shut the door against the force of the storm. Coughing deeply, he ripped the kerchief from his face and tossed it aside.

"Drilling in this storm is about as useless as a hog with a sidesaddle," he choked out, running his hands through his tousled hair. "Hot *damn*, it's wicked out there!" He inched the tea towel down her face and grinned. "Who is this masked woman?"

She handed over his crushed hat and examined his joyful grin. The wind storm had swept away his moodiness, leaving him exhilarated, while she felt as if she'd been beaten. She laughed softly, thinking that she'd never understand the ways of men.

Houston removed her hard hat and surprised her by running his fingers through her tangled hair. His touch was gentle, and his smile matched it. She was acutely aware of how she must look—wind-whipped and bedraggled. Why was he being tender toward her now when she looked such a sight?

"Can I use your bathroom to freshen up? I probably look like a scarecrow."

"Not to my eyes," he murmured as if to himself while his gaze wandered lazily across her face and hair. "I don't think you could look unattractive even if you tried."

I could say the same thing about you. The words burned her tongue but went unspoken. She didn't know what to say to him when he was in this mood, but she was painfully aware of how susceptible she was to his charms. When he touched her or just *looked* at her with any degree of sensuality, she was powerless, defenseless and alarmingly passive.

"Can I use your bathroom, or are you going to send me back out in that?" she asked, desperately trying to break the spell, to overcome the sexual chemistry that drew her to him.

"What?" He blinked his eyes, and his hands fell away from her hair. "Sure, you can use my bathroom."

"Thanks," she replied, expelling her pent-up breath. "I won't be a minute. Got a brush in there?"

"Top drawer of the vanity."

She went into the bathroom and closed the door. Finding the brush, she ran it briskly through her hair until it crackled with static electricity; then she splashed water over her face, hands and arms. She felt halfway decent by the time she returned to the main part of the trailer. Houston turned from the kitchen sink and toweled off his wet face.

"Lots of dirt out there," he said, tossing aside the towel and pulling a comb from his back pocket which he used to tame his hair. "I don't think it'll last long."

Faith nodded as she looked out the kitchen window. "It's already died down a lot."

"We'll start up the rig again pretty soon. How about a sandwich while we wait?"

"Okay." She dropped into one of the kitchen chairs and cradled her chin in her hands. "What have you got?"

"Peanut butter, grape jelly, ham and some sausage and biscuits left over from breakfast."

"Sausage and biscuits for me."

"You've got it." He set them in front of her. "Want some mustard, too?"

"Yes." Faith cut open the two biscuits and placed sausage patties between them. "What are you going to have?"

"Ham will do me." He set the mustard on the table, then sat down. "How are we doing on money?"

"Not bad." She bit into one of the biscuits and tasted the spicy sausage and mustard. "We're keeping to our budget so far. Did you want to look at the financial books?"

"No, I'll leave that to you."

"Trust me?" she asked, grinning.

"Let's say that I have faith in you, Faith."

She swallowed the morsel of sausage and biscuit with a gulp. "Want a glass of milk?"

"Yes. I knew something was missing." He hooked an arm around her waist when she stood beside him to pour milk into the glasses. "Do you trust me?"

"Yes, of course." She laughed nervously as she set the milk carton on the table and started to wiggle from his embrace. "Houston!" She lost her balance when he pulled her against him, and she found herself sitting in his lap, her arms draped around his neck.

"Perfect landing," he said, grinning. "I want to apologize for being such a bear the past few days."

"Oh, that's okay. I haven't been Susie Sunshine myself." Part of her ached to be free of him, but another part longed to stay in his sheltering embrace forever.

One tanned hand moved down her waist and along her jeaned thigh. His fingers traced the inseam, down and up until she shifted away from his brazen caress.

"I'm not sure this is a risk we should take," she whispered, mesmerized by the way he was gazing at her lips as she spoke.

"I like the prospects," he whispered back, making her tremble.

"The samples have been pretty good, but it might be a false alarm," she said, enjoying the double entendres.

"I think we should catch some more samples and see what develops."

His lips brushed across hers, light and easy, but releasing a surge of passion in Faith. She flattened her hands at the back of his head and brought his lips to hers. If her strong reaction startled him, he showed no sign of it. His arms tightened around her waist, and his mouth slid down the side of her neck, the tip of his tongue leaving a trail of moisture. Faith tipped back her head, and her exhaled breath trembled with desire as she pushed her fingers through his hair and kissed the crown of his head.

She had always been aware of a wilder side lurking within her—had always been a little afraid of it, but was always able to control it. Not this time. Houston unleashed it, and Faith could do nothing but glory in the complete abandon it offered.

"Houston...Houston," she murmured between kisses she dropped hungrily upon his parted lips. She arched her body closer to his searching hands, filling them with her breasts. When his thumbs slipped across the hard nipples beneath her blouse, Faith thought she would die from the exquisite pleasure of it all.

The blaring of a horn outside tore through the intensity of the moment, and Faith was on her feet, eyes wide and unseeing, before she even realized she had reacted. Trembling uncontrollably, she stared at Houston and wondered what kind of magic he possessed that could transform her from a conservative, pragmatic woman into a wild creature of passion.

He tore his gaze from her when the horn blared again. "Now who's that?" he asked, looking at the windows.

Faith bent down to peer out the window and spotted a faded red pickup. A man and a woman slid off the tailgate, and the pickup drove away.

"That's Will Cheatum's truck," Houston said, getting to his feet, "but I don't know who in the hell...Holy Moses!"

His strange, strangled tone spun her back around to face him. His eyes were alight with...She felt her own eyes widen. Was he crying?

Houston moved with lightning speed to the door and flung it open, letting in a cloud of dust. From the joyous smile on his face, Faith knew who the woman was before he even spoke her name.

"Odessa!"

"Houston?" A husky voice rode on the wind, and then the woman was inside the trailer, Houston's arms were wrapped tightly around her waist and she was lifted off her feet in a mighty hug. "Houston! Houston, it's you! You're a sight for sore eyes!"

Houston buried his face in his sister's blond hair—hair that was piled high on her head and so stiff with hairspray that the wind had barely mussed it. Houston set her on her feet, and Odessa leaned back in the circle of his arms. She framed Houston's face between her hands to let her gaze move lovingly over his features.

She was older than Houston, and her heavy makeup couldn't disguise the ravages of hard times and hard knocks. Faith guessed that a few years ago Odessa had been attractive—the evidence was in her full-lipped mouth and high cheekbones—but the years had not been kind ot her. She probably wasn't older than thirty-five, but she looked forty.

"Oh, my! Aren't you handsome?" Odessa crooned in a voice that was smoky from too many cigarettes. "Do you realize that the last time I saw you, you were no more than a boy? You're a full-grown man!"

"Odessa," Houston said in a way that made Faith's heart constrict with emotion. "I've prayed that you'd come back. I wanted to see you again. I've missed you."

"Oh, you sweet thing!" Odessa delivered a smacking kiss to his lips, and her red lipstick left its mark. She ran her thumb across Houston's lips, smearing the color. "Speaking of full-grown men...I want you to meet someone." She turned and crooked her forefinger. "Come on in, honey. Houston, this here is Jimmy Ray Workman. He's my intended. Jimmy Ray, this long, tall Texan is my little brother!"

Faith didn't like Jimmy Ray on sight. He swaggered even when he stood still, and his smile was sly and cold. He pumped Houston's hand, then ran his palm down the leg of his jeans as if to erase Houston's imprint. His hair was black and slicked to his small head in a style reminiscent of the 1950s. His body was lean and corded with muscle. He was at least ten years younger than Odessa.

"Howdy, slick," Jimmy Ray said in a tone that was full of cocky contempt. "Hope you're receiving visitors." His icy blue eyes took in Faith. "I see you've already received one."

Faith cringed inwardly, not liking the innuendo in his observation. She couldn't bring herself to speak or smile.

"Oh, this is Faith Hutton. She's my partner in the oil business. We're drilling on this land. Faith, this is Odessa Traynor, my sister."

"Gibson," Odessa corrected with a shaky smile. "It's Odessa Gibson, hon. I got married a while back, but I'm divorced now."

"It's nice to meet you," Faith said, shaking Odessa's hand. "Houston's told me about you."

"Has he?" Odessa poked an elbow in Houston's ribs. "Don't that beat all? I thought you'd forgotten all about me."

"You should know better than that. I'd never forget you." Houston's gaze followed Odessa's to the food on the table. "Have you eaten? We were just sitting down to lunch."

"Sure looks good!" Odessa wasted no time in sitting at the table and tearing open the package of ham. "Me and Jimmy Ray didn't take time to eat before we hitched our way out here from Mentone. Sit down, Jimmy Ray, and help yourself." Odessa laughed and turned flirtatious eyes up to her brother. "Houston don't mind, do you?"

"Not at all."

Feeling out of place, Faith edged toward the door. "Houston, I'll leave you alone with your sister and her...Jimmy Ray."

"You don't have to go," Houston objected.

"I know, but I want to look at those samples again. Let me know when you're ready to start up the rig again."

"Okay." He opened the door for her. "What do you think about this? It must be my lucky day."

"Yes, it must be." She forced a smile to her lips and turned to leave. Before Houston closed the door behind her, she heard Jimmy Ray's slyly phrased question.

"So you're drilling for oil? Looks like me and Odessa arrived at just the right time, don't it?"

Faith hurried to her own trailer. She was glad that Houston was happy, but she couldn't share in it. For some reason she felt as if trouble had accompanied Odessa and Jimmy Ray, and that it wouldn't leave until they did.

"Where are your guests?" Faith asked as she sauntered up to stand beside Houston at the rig.

"They're catching some shut-eye." He took off his hard hat and mopped his brow with a handkerchief. "I guess I'll let them have my bed and I'll sleep on the couch."

"How long are they staying?" Faith tucked her hands into the back pockets of her jeans and tried to appear only mildly interested in his answer, although she was fervently hoping he would say that Odessa and her "intended" would be on their way tomorrow.

"I don't know. Until they get on their feet, I guess."

"On their feet?" she echoed, not liking the sound of it. "What does that mean?"

"Until they find jobs and a place to live." He shot her a questioning glance. "Something bothering you?"

"No." She shrugged and shifted her gaze to the rumbling rig. "What kind of work are they looking for?"

"I didn't ask for their résumés," he said with biting sarcasm. "She's my sister, and she can stay here as long as she wants."

His voice was flinty, and Faith backed off the subject, feeling small and petty for wanting to get rid of his long-lost sister and her greasy boyfriend. She knew how much it meant to Houston to have his sister back in his life, but she couldn't deny the aura of trouble that seemed to hang around Odessa and Jimmy Ray.

"Where has Odessa been all this time?"

"Here and there," he answered with a telling economy of words. "She's had a string of bad luck lately." He oiled one of Black Fury's crusted joints, then wiped his hands on the handkerchief. "She needs a car. You can't look for work on foot out here."

"That's true. Are you going to loan her your pickup?"

"No, I need that for myself." His eyes met hers, then returned to the soiled handkerchief. "I loaned her some money to buy a car and some clothes."

Cold fury settled between Faith's temples, but she managed to keep her voice level. "Your money or our money?"

Houston stuck the kerchief in his back pocket but kept his gaze averted from hers. "My money is our money, I guess."

"You *guess*?" Faith shot back.

He glared at her. "She's my sister. What did you expect me to do?" he asked, his voice rising with his temper.

"I expected you to ask me before you doled out our money!" She stepped closer to him, ready to do battle. "Do you have a short memory or what? Didn't you agree to discuss things with me? Aren't we supposed to be equal partners? I'm really getting tired of your throwing our money around. You're just like my father. You run through it like it's water!"

"Well, if that's the case, then I spend it a hell of a lot better than you do. Get out of my way." He shoved her unceremoniously aside and strode to his trailer. As the door banged shut behind him, Faith saw the draperies in the bedroom settle back into place. Someone—either Odessa or Jimmy Ray or both—had observed the altercation, and Faith placed her money on Jimmy Ray. The creep!

Faith spun around, presenting her back to the trailer and its occupants. Her anger spent itself, leaving her to wallow in self-pity and hurt feelings. He had shoved her! Tears burned her eyes, and she swallowed hard to keep from sobbing. She didn't blame him for giving Odessa money, but he could have asked her first. He *should* have asked her first.

She turned around and saw a gap in the draperies. Smiling sweetly, she lifted her hand, pressed her thumb to her nose and wiggled her fingers. The draperies fell back into place, and Faith laughed. Take that, Jimmy Ray Workman! Workman, hah! She kicked at the dirt and fell into the hammock, sending it rocking crazily from side to side. She doubted if that man had ever worked a day in his life!

Chapter Seven

So my little brother is an oilman!" Odessa propped her pink boots on the coffee table and settled back against the couch cushions. She waved her hands in the air to dry the gold polish she had applied to her fingernails, then paused to blow on them. "Don't that beat all? Before long I might be related to a millionaire!"

Houston sat in the leather recliner across from her. "Don't count the chickens until they've hatched."

"You hit something this morning," Odessa said. "That proves something's down there."

"It was just a pocket of gas, and that's no proof." He shrugged, and a grin lifted one corner of his mouth. "But I do think something's down there, or I wouldn't have invested every penny I have in that well."

"This is so exciting!" Odessa tested one of her nails. "Good. They're dry. Jimmy Ray should be back pretty soon."

"Did he go into Mentone looking for work?"

"No, he went in to pick up a few things for us. I imagine we'll have to look for work in Pecos, don't you?"

"Yes. Mentone doesn't have much to offer. What kind of work does Jimmy Ray do?"

"He's a jack-of-all-trades. He's worked on rigs before." Odessa stood up and went into the kitchen. "Want some more coffee?"

"No, thanks." Houston drummed his fingers on the chair arms, feeling restless and depressed. When they'd hit that gas pocket this morning, he'd thought it might have been the real thing. Now that it was over, he felt as if a lead weight had settled on his shoulders.

Odessa hummed merrily as she poured herself a cup of coffee and opened a package of cookies. Harsh sunlight fell across her face, callously revealing each wrinkle and the toughness of her skin.

Houston would have recognized her anywhere, but he'd been surprised to see how much she'd aged. He remembered a young strawberry blonde whose blue eyes had sparkled with a lust for life, but the years had extinguished the sparkle. She'd bleached her hair until it was a lifeless pale color, and she styled it in an upswept swirl of stiff curls that was in vogue among country-western starlets but looked ridiculous in the real world.

"How long have you been divorced?" he asked when she returned to the living room.

"It's been..." She paused and counted on her gold-tipped fingers. "Twelve years, I guess."

"Did I know him?"

"No. I met him at a carnival in Oklahoma. I was working in one of those shooting gallery booths and he was running the ring-toss game." She smiled wistfully and examined her polished nails. "Kiefer Gibson. What a man!"

"What happened?"

"Oh, the usual. After a couple of years he started chasing skirts. I was sick and tired of the carny life, so I got me a quick divorce and lit out for New Mexico."

"How long have you known Jimmy Ray?" Houston asked, feeling a little sick. Had her life been a series of men? Rounders, rogues, hard-drinkers and roustabouts? Just like their father.

"I ran into him in Dallas. The guy I'd been with had split and left me owing a three-weeks' motel bill. Jimmy Ray was working in the motel office, and he said he'd pay the bill if I'd go dancing with him." She giggled like a schoolgirl and blushed. "What a night! We've been together ever since."

"Since when?" Houston asked.

"Since two or three months ago." She waved a dismissive hand. "Enough about my love life. What's the story on you and your shapely partner?"

The weight settled more heavily between his shoulders. Had Odessa been kicking around like a tumbleweed all her life with nothing but lines and wrinkles to show for it? He shouldn't blame her, but—*damn it*—he did! She was living the life they had wanted to escape as children—knockabouts, ne'er-do-wells, poor relations. Whatever the name, they all meant the same: a shiftless, hollow-eyed existence.

"Aren't you going to tell me?" Odessa pressed. "Are you two sharing a mattress or what?"

Houston winced slightly at her ill-bred question. "No offense, but I don't see how that's any of your business."

Odessa's red-rimmed eyes widened in surprise. "Excuse me! I was just curious. With you two living out here all alone, I just figured that nature would have taken its course."

"Nature has nothing to do with it. Faith and I are business partners."

Odessa's eyes smiled at him over the rim of the coffee cup she held to her lips. "A little business, a little pleasure. A little yin, a little yang. Happens all the time." Her gaze shifted to the windows when a car door banged shut. "Speaking of pleasure, here's Jimmy Ray." Her lips tilted up at the corners when Jimmy Ray entered the trailer. "Hi, hon. What did you get us?"

Jimmy Ray shifted a grocery sack from the one hand to the other. "Just a little something to help the time go down better." He strode to the kitchen and opened the refrigerator.

"Did you remember my cigarettes?"

"Sure did." He lifted two six-packs of beer from the sack. "I remembered these, too."

"Goody!" Odessa sprang from the couch and grabbed the sack from Jimmy. She withdrew a carton of cigarettes from it and dropped the sack to the floor.

"That's what you went into town for?" Houston asked, not bothering to hide his disgust.

"I was fresh out of cigarettes," Odessa said, tearing into the carton and removing a pack. "And you didn't have any beer."

"That's because I don't drink. I lived with a drunk long enough to know that I could live without it." He lifted his brows when Odessa flashed him a pointed glare.

"Hell, beer isn't hard liquor," Jimmy Ray said as he popped the top on one of the cans.

"Tell that to Alcoholics Anonymous." Houston stood up, restless with irritation. "When I loaned you money, I thought you were going to use it for clothes and a car."

"We are, sugar," Odessa said, drawing deeply on the cigarette she'd lit. "I know what's bothering you. You're feeling down after that false alarm this morning. Don't you worry, sweetie. You'll hit something sooner or later."

"Sure you will, slick!" Jimmy Ray beamed, then guzzled the beer.

Houston gritted his teeth to keep from telling Jimmy Ray just what he thought of him. He hated being called "slick," and he hated the way Jimmy Ray said it.

"I got an idea," Odessa said, placing a hand on Houston's arm. "Why don't you and your little gal go dancing tonight? Jimmy Ray and me will watch the rig for you. You need to get away and kick up your heels."

"No, that's okay."

"Listen to me." Her fingers dug deeper into his arm. "Sister knows best. You've been stuck out here for weeks. A night out with that pretty blonde will do wonders for your frame of mind." She pursed her lips into a pout. "You've been so good to me, sugar. Let me do something for you."

"Ought to listen to her, slick." Jimmy Ray winked at Odessa. "I took her up on her generosity, and I've never been sorry for it."

"Oh, you!" Odessa giggled, then coughed spasmodically. Her voice was huskier when she spoke again. "Go on, Houston! If you won't do it for yourself, do it for your *all-business* partner out there." She nodded in the direction of the rig and grinned.

"What will you do while I'm gone?" Houston asked, his mind's eye projecting a drunken scene.

"Nothing. We'll just sit around and listen to the radio and keep an eye on your rig. You can trust me, little brother."

He stared into her pale blue eyes and decided that her heart was in the right place. She was trying to thank him for his hospitality, and he'd be a heel not to accept her offer. "Okay. I guess I could use a few hours away from here."

"Now you're talking!" Odessa laughed and stubbed out her cigarette in a saucer on the kitchen table.

"There's an ashtray on that end table," Houston said, pointing to it.

"Oh, thanks." Odessa sat on the couch and reached for another cigarette.

Houston left her and Jimmy Ray to their beer and cigarettes and went into his bedroom for a few minutes of blessed solitude. He stared at his unmade bed for a moment or two as anger gnawed at his insides. The least she could have done was to make the bed this morning, he thought, automatically straightening the sheets and tucking them in at the corners. He smoothed the bedspread into place, then looked out the window at the rig.

Faith was in her usual place at the card table. She was bent over her microscope and logbooks, her golden hair gathered into a ponytail. If that woman was awake, she was working. Faith Hutton didn't have a lazy bone in her body, he thought, mentally comparing her energy to his sister's lethargy.

Sitting on the bed, he continued to watch her through the windows as she jotted notations in one of the logbooks. He could see the look of concentration on her face; then it disappeared as she glanced up and spotted something that made her frown. Houston leaned sideways until he could see Jimmy Ray through the window. Not caring that he was eavesdropping, Houston cranked the slatted windows open so that he could hear what Jimmy Ray was saying.

"Nice day!"

Faith bent to her microscope again, ignoring him with cool determination.

"I got a surprise for you," Jimmy Ray said, raising his voice to be heard over the rig. When Faith continued to ignore him, he stepped closer. "Did you hear me?"

"Yes. Your voice carries."

Houston grinned, hearing the icy quality of her voice. If Jimmy Ray was smart—which he wasn't—he'd leave her alone with her microscope.

"I'm giving you time off for good behavior," Jimmy Ray persisted. "I'm going to watch the rig while you go into town for a manhunt. Of course, you don't have to go into town to find one. I'd be glad to quench your thirst."

Houston sprang to his feet and strode through the trailer. That filthy-minded little pipsqueak!

"Where you going, sugar?" Odessa asked as he flung open the front door.

"Outside!" Houston slammed the door behind him and made fast tracks to the rig. Faith was on her feet, her face flushed an angry red.

"Think you're too good for me?" Jimmy Ray asked in an angry tone.

"No. I *know* I'm too good for you," Faith answered, then shifted her gaze to Houston. "What's all this about your sister and Jimmy Ray watching the rig?"

"It's not definite. I wanted to talk to you about it." Houston eyed Jimmy Ray. "Alone."

"Hey, I don't have to be told twice!" Jimmy Ray chuckled and threw his cigarette to the ground. "She's all yours, slick."

"My name isn't 'slick,' " Houston said through clenched teeth. "If you don't like calling me Houston, then you can call me Mr. Traynor."

Jimmy Ray squared his narrow shoulders. "I was just trying to be friendly."

"Don't try so hard," Houston shot back. "Now if you'll excuse us, I'd appreciate it."

The look Jimmy Ray gave him triggered a warning in Houston's mind. Jimmy Ray was a hothead and not the kind of man to turn your back on. He wouldn't fight fair; he'd fight dirty. Houston waited until Jimmy Ray had disappeared into the trailer before he breathed a sigh of relief.

"Now what's all this about leaving the rig?" Faith asked, propping her fists at her hips.

"Odessa said she'd look after the rig if we wanted to go into town for dinner or something tonight."

"Or something?" she asked, lifting one winged brow.

"Don't start on me." Houston curled his upper lip in a snarl and dropped into the other folding chair. "I'm trying to be nice, and so is Odessa. We've been anchored to Black Fury for weeks, and I just thought you might like a change of scenery while we've got someone here to baby-sit the rig for us."

Faith sat in her chair and covered the microscope with a drop cloth. "What if something happens while we're gone? Odessa couldn't—"

"Jimmy Ray has worked on rigs. He'd know what to do."

"Jimmy Ray has *worked?* You'll pardon me if I find that a trifle hard to believe."

Houston felt one side of his mouth twitch as laughter bubbled up inside him. "Well, let's say that he's been around rigs and observed what happens when a well strikes." He matched her smile and covered her hand with his on the table. "What do you say? It would be nice to spend an evening away from this noisy piece of junk. After that false alarm this morning, I could use a diversion."

"And I'm a diversion?" she asked, watching as his thumb skimmed across the top of her hand.

"The best kind," Houston agreed. "Come on, partner. Mentone isn't Dallas, but it has its own kind of charm. We could have dinner and then do a little two-stepping. We'll nice to each other instead of at each other's throats."

Faith gave a contrite smile. "That would be an interesting change of pace. Are you sure we can leave the rig with Odessa and Jimmy Ray?"

"It'll be fine. Nothing's showing, right?" He glanced at the open logbook.

"No such luck." She closed the book with a sigh. "I think we'll have to go down another hundred feet or so before we hit anything worthwhile."

"So you'll go out on the town with me?"

She smiled and gave a swift shrug. "Why not? I'd rather do that than eat dirt with a rusty spoon."

He scowled playfully. "Thanks a truckload, partner."

"You're welcome. What time will you call for me?"

"I'll give you a couple of hours to gussy up, and then we'll hit the road."

She stood up and stretched her arms above her head, giving Houston a provocative glimpse of jutting breasts. "See you in a couple of hours, partner. Should I wear a dress, or will slacks do?"

"Slacks. Mentone has a casual dress code." He turned to watch the sway of her hips as she made her way to the tiny trailer.

She was a good-looking woman, he thought with a satisfied smile. In fact, she was about the prettiest woman he'd ever come across. It wasn't so much her looks—although they were picture perfect—but it was the way she conducted herself. So proud and spirited. She was smart and independent, and he liked that. In fact, he liked everything about her except for her sharp tongue and wicked temper. Suddenly he grinned. Oh, hell! He even liked those things!

Anticipation coiled in his stomach and he was glad she'd agreed to a night out. The monotony had been getting to him lately, making him feel like a machine. He wanted to feel like a man again, and Faith was just the ticket.

In the circle of Houston's arms, Faith felt tranquil and protected. Following his lead, she moved ever so slightly to the beat of a slow dance. The limited dance area was crowded with couples, leaving no room for anything fancy. Booted feet shuffled. Hands traced shoulder blades and narrow waists. Eyes spoke lavishly. Lips touched and parted.

Faith roused herself from a self-induced trance and smiled at Houston when the song ended.

"Want to sit the next one out?" he asked.

"Yes. Do you mind?"

"Not a bit." He led her to a table and ordered two soft drinks. "This place will close down in another hour, and then I guess we'd better head back to the ranch."

"Guess so." She fell back in the chair. "This has been nice. I haven't been so relaxed in weeks."

"I know what you mean." His gaze wandered over her face, her loose white shirt and her navy-blue front-pleated trousers. Her attire was casual, but she stood out from the other women. She possessed a touch of class no matter what she wore. He'd seen her in shapeless overalls and she still looked like a million bucks.

"What are you thinking about?" she asked, noticing his thoughtful smile.

"I was just thinking about how pretty you look." His gaze moved slowly over her golden hair. "I guess lots of men have told you that."

"A few, but it's nice to hear." She pushed up the sleeves of her shirt and sipped the iced cola.

"Can I get you folks anything else?" the waitress asked.

"No, this will do us," Houston said.

"I'm surprised to see you in here, Houston," the waitress said as she ran a moist cloth over the table next to them.

"Why's that, Alma?" Houston turned sideways in the chair to look back at her.

"You keep to yourself. I never figured you to be the kind who liked to socialize."

"I keep busy, that's all. Don't have much time to show my face at these places."

"Come on, now," Alma scoffed. "Everybody knows you're a loner."

Houston shrugged and faced Faith again. "What's the use? People think what they want to think."

When Alma had moved out of earshot, Faith crossed her arms on the table and held Houston's gaze.

"Why do people have the wrong idea about you? Everyone told me that you were cold and aloof, that you lived by yourself and liked it that way."

"You don't think I'm like that?"

"No!" She shook her head in a vehement denial. "You like being around people, and you're certainly not cold or unfriendly. All anyone has to do is take a good look at you and they'd see how warmhearted and kind you are."

"Maybe you're the only one who's taken the time to look," he said in a near whisper. "I'm glad you did."

She felt her color heighten, and she averted her gaze from the intimacy of his. "How did you get your unfounded reputation?"

"It's not completely unfounded."

"Oh?" Her gaze swept back to his. "How's that?"

"I sort of started out with two strikes against me, and I added the third one myself." He hooked one elbow over the back of the chair and stared moodily at the glass of cola. "I told you about my dad, and how everybody around here thought I'd be like him."

"I don't follow you," Faith said, uneasy with the dull, painful expression in his eyes.

"Well, when I was seventeen I had a crush on a pretty gal named Tracie Lou Holden. I never had more than a dollar or two in my pocket and Tracie Lou was from a well-to-do family, but she liked me. She was sweet sixteen. Red hair, green eyes, perky nose. A real cutie." A wistful smile touched the corners of his mouth, then was gone. "You know how boys are when they're seventeen or eighteen. I had a yearning to be a man, and I was impatient with it all. Single-minded. I wanted to impress her, so I sort of borrowed one of Mac's cars."

"Borrowed? You mean you didn't tell Mac you were taking it?"

"Right." He exhaled his breath in a sharp burst of frustration. "It was a dumb thing to do, but I was pretty stupid in those days. We lived in a shack on Mac's land, and Mac had always been good to me. I shouldn't have taken advantage of his friendship like that, but I did."

"What happened? Were you caught?"

"Worse." He glanced at her, then resumed his gloomy examination of the cola glass. "We were cruising along a country road. I wasn't going more than twenty, although everybody swore I must have been doing sixty or seventy, but I wasn't in any hurry. I just wanted to take Tracie Lou for a drive and then park somewhere for a little smooch." He laughed softly under his breath, but there was no humor in it. "I took my eyes off the road for a second to give Tracie Lou a little kiss, and when I looked back, there was a bull in the middle of the road. I hadn't driven a car more than a couple of times before then, and I panicked. I swerved the car off the road and hit the ditch. The car sailed end over end."

"Oh, no!" Faith reached across the table and covered one of his hands with hers. "Were you hurt?"

"That's where I got this," he said, touching the scar on his chin.

"Sounds like you were lucky to come away with nothing but that cut."

"Lucky?" He removed his hand from hers as if her touch made him uncomfortable. "Luck has never been my companion. Tracie Lou was killed in the car wreck."

"Oh, Houston..." Faith shook her head, unable to think of the right words to comfort him.

"When the dust settled and I had my senses back, I looked at her and I knew she was dead." His voice broke, and he swallowed hard. "And I knew that everybody would be ready to pack me off to the penitentiary. I was right."

"You went to prison?"

"No, but I came close to it." He looked off to the side where the club patrons were filing toward the door. "Mac spoke up for me during the arraignment. He said that stealing his car was my first offense and that I shouldn't be sent to jail for it. He asked the judge to let me work off the price of the car I swiped, and the judge agreed to it since he was friends with Mac."

"So you worked for Mac?"

"I worked on his place for a couple of years, long after I'd paid for his car. I didn't have anywhere else to go."

"What made you finally leave?" Faith asked, struggling to get the words past her constricted throat.

Houston looked around the empty dance floor and sighed. "Hatred. The folks around here never forgot Tracie Lou—neither did I. They were just waiting for me to mess up again so that they could say, 'I told you so. He's just like his old man. No good.'" He paused to finish his soft drink and drop a couple of bills on the table. "Let's go."

Faith stood up, feeling as if she were wrapped in a clinging sheet of sadness. Alma looked up from the cash register as they passed by and gave an automatic smile.

"Y'all come back real soon. Nice to see you, Houston."

"Good night, Alma." Houston grabbed his Stetson off the tree near the door and put it on. "Be careful going home. Need a lift?"

"No, thanks. My hubby's picking me up."

"Okay." Houston opened the door and let Faith precede him into the warm night. "She's married to the guy who runs the filling station."

"You know everybody around here, don't you?"

"Just about." He opened the pickup door and waited for her to slide across the seat before he sat behind the wheel and snapped his safety belt together. "Better buckle up." He glanced at her to make sure she was obeying his request. "I shouldn't have gone on and on about my past. It spoiled the evening."

"No, it didn't," Faith objected, twisting against the confining belt to look at him. The green light from the dashboard illuminated his frowning countenance. She remembered the times he had cautioned her to drive safely, realizing that it had been more than just a parting remark. He'd meant it. "So you finally left Loving County and joined the Marines."

"Yes, and the rest is history." He smiled to take the edge off his words. "Let's talk about you for a change. Did you love your father?"

She was taken aback for a moment by his swift conversation shift. "Yes, I loved him." She slid one arm along the back of the seat and stared into the tunnel of light ahead. "There were things about him that were hard to live with, but nobody's perfect."

"What things were hard to live with?"

"He had an infuriating habit of spending money as if it grew on trees. My mother used to say that if Dad had a buck in his pocket, he'd spend it in a flash. He loved *things*: boats, yachts, houses, antiques, art, jewels, you name it. He'd buy things and tire of them quickly, then practically give them away. He should have been a wealthy man, but he wasn't. He died penniless and a failure."

"You're being too hard on him. There's more to being a good man than knowing how to manage money. He might have been penniless, but that doesn't mean he was a failure. Now if he'd drunk himself to death and had never done any good for anybody, then he'd have been a failure."

Faith stared at him for a long moment before averting her eyes. She felt ashamed as she realized how unfair she'd been to her father's memory. Houston was right. Her father *had* been a good man. More than a hundred people had attended his funeral, and it seemed as if each one had related a story about him to her, each a heartfelt testimony to his sense of humor, his wit, his generosity and his love for his family. Just because he had lived with the idea that money was meant to be spent, not saved, didn't give her the right to call him a failure.

Lost in her thoughts and her memories of her father, Faith was surprised to see the oasis of light ahead. She sat up straighter and ran her hands across her eyes, realizing that time had slipped by unmeasured and that they were home.

"How about a glass of iced tea?" she asked when Houston had parked the pickup.

He glanced at his own trailer, then nodded. "Don't mind if I do. Looks like Odessa and Jimmy Ray have turned in for the night. I'll check the rig while you brew the tea."

"Okay." Faith stepped out of the truck and went to her trailer. She turned on the lights inside and picked up a few magazines she had tossed onto the divan. Living space was tight, and even a small amount of clutter made her trailer appear disheveled. She stacked the magazines on the coffee table, then put on the tea to brew.

She was pouring it when Houston stepped inside and tossed his hat onto the coffee table.

"Everything shipshape?" she asked.

"Everything's fine, but we're not millionaires yet." He levered himself into one side of the kitchen booth. "How do you like your trailer?"

"I'd like it a little larger." She grinned as she sat opposite him. "Is that music to your ears?"

He drank some of the tea before he answered, "I made the same mistake. The first trailer I bought was about this size, and I thought it was perfect until I lived in it for a few weeks. I guess we all have to live and learn."

"Thanks for not saying 'I told you so.'" She settled back in the booth with a sigh. "Another few hundred feet and we're going to strike something."

"Is that a promise?"

"No, it's a prediction."

"I don't know." He ran his fingers down the glass. "Sometimes I think I'm jinxed."

"Oh, don't be ridiculous," Faith admonished. "Luck has little to do with success. The soil samples look good. Something's trapped down there, and we're going to find it."

"Do you think it's possible that bad luck might be hereditary?"

"Stop it, Houston." She slid her hands across the table and gripped his wrists. "That's superstition and you know it. Besides, what you think of yourself is more important than what others think of you."

"What do *you* think of me?" he asked, his eyes taking on an engaging shimmer.

Faith started to remove her hands, but he captured them in a light grasp. She stared at her hands being held by his and felt her senses blossom. Was she falling in love with him? she wondered as her heartbeat accelerated. Had her initial attraction deepened over the weeks until she was on the verge of commitment? Lifting her gaze, she found the answer to her questions in his eyes. He was looking at her with open adoration, and she didn't care if her own eyes reflected the love she felt for him. She'd never felt so close to a man before or so passionately aware of every expression on his face, every move he made, every breath he took. If this wasn't love, it was a kissing cousin to it.

"No comment?" he asked, reminding her of the question he'd posed.

Faith wet her dry lips with the tip of her tongue, surprised at how difficult it was to answer him. Was she afraid of exposing too much to his eager eyes, or was she afraid he didn't want to hear the truth?

"I think you're the sweetest and kindest man I've ever known," she said, barely able to speak above a whisper. "What do you think of me?" When he didn't answer immediately, she met his level gaze and her breath caught in her throat. She'd never been looked at with such raw sexuality before, and it set her heart to racing. He brought her hands to his lips and kissed each finger in turn.

"I think you're the best thing that ever happened to me." He tugged at her hands, and she stood up and slipped into the booth next to him. He kissed her forehead and her eyelids as his hands moved slowly down her back, then back up to her shoulders. "I mean that. I'm not just feeding you a line."

"I know." She smiled and touched her lips to his. "And you're right. I am the best thing that ever happened to you."

He grinned appreciatively and moved her hair away from her neck so that his lips could caress her skin. "When you want me to leave, tell me."

"And you'll go? Just like that?"

"Sure." He leaned back to look at her. "I don't stay where I'm not wanted."

She laughed and stood up. "You're either a gentleman or a fool."

"I guess it depends on you. If you tell me to go, then I'm a fool; but if you tell me to stay, I'm a gentleman."

Why had he placed the entire burden of this decision on her? Faith wondered as she took in his rapt, expectant expression. Did she want him to stay just because she was lonely and needed the company of a man who understood loneliness, or had she actually fallen in love with Houston Traynor? Gazing at him, she felt a tenderness that she hadn't experienced since her father had died, and she knew that the impossible had happened: she'd fallen in love with a wildcatter.

She laughed lightly at the self-directed joke, then reached out and ran her fingertips across Houston's frowning mouth.

"I'm not laughing at you," she explained. "I'm laughing at me."

"Why?" He captured her hand and pressed a tingling kiss to her palm.

"Because I can't believe this. How did this happen? When did you weave yourself into my life?"

His frown returned. "I'm not sure I understand...."

Faith laughed again. "Neither do I."

Scenes of the past few weeks flashed through her mind. Day after day she'd worked beside this man, conversed with him, laughed with him, argued with him. She'd spent more time with him than with anyone other than members of her immediate family. What had begun as a business association had slowly evolved into a personal relationship. They had moved from business partners to friends and now...to lovers?

A tingle raced up her spine, followed by a wave of intense longing. Her desire for him engulfed her, and she realized that it must be apparent on her face because Houston straightened and his eyes darkened to an earthy umber. Suddenly she felt shy. She'd never considered herself to be a timid person, but faced with the burden of starting a love affair, she was completely dumbstruck. For the life of her, she couldn't tell him she wanted him. She was aggressive, Faith thought, but not *that* aggressive.

"Faith...?" He rose slowly to his feet and rested his hands at her waist, gazing into her eyes. He must have seen the wavering doubt in her expression, because his hands tensed and he drew her to him. "To hell with being a noble gentleman," he said, his voice matching the urgency of his touch. "I'm not leaving here without making love to you."

"Thank you," she managed to whisper before his mouth met hers in a rough yet tender kiss.

His lips softened against hers, growing lazier with each lingering kiss. Dropping kisses on her eyelids, nose and cheeks, he primed her passion for what was to come.

"I've dreamed of this moment, but now that it's here I think I've forgotten how it's done," he said with a little laugh that seemed to break through her shyness. "Can you jar my memory?"

Smiling, she framed his face in her hands and brought his lips down to hers. "I remember the procedure. It starts something like this." She kissed him, enjoying the firm but gentle caress of his mouth on hers. Reaching behind her, she found the light switch and flipped it down, throwing the room into semidarkness. Her clock-radio provided a soft blue illumination, lighting the way to the divan.

Without a word, Houston shoved aside the coffee table and unfolded the divan to make a bed for two. Turning back to her, he began unbuttoning his shirt as a look of pleasure spread across his face.

Faith mirrored his actions, her fingers trembling slightly as she unbuttoned her blouse and shrugged out of it. Her slacks and shoes followed the blouse to the floor, but modesty kept her from shedding the rest of her clothing. Houston sat on the bed and removed his boots, socks and jeans, the held out his arms to her.

"Come to me, Faith." His voice was punctuated with underlying emotion.

Pausing a few moments to take in the lean, bronze shape of him, Faith sat on his lap and lost herself in the bend of his embrace. His hair-roughened thighs were taut with muscle beneath hers. His kisses were feathery light, but grew bolder with each touch. He pushed down the thin straps of her bra and buried his face between her breasts.

A maelstrom overtook her, laying waste to her modesty and uncertainty. She raked her fingers through his hair, and he fell back on the bed, taking her with him. She rained kisses across his face and shoulders while he removed the last of their clothing, then enfolded her in a shelter of warm skin and white-hot sensations.

Faith had never loved anyone before with such intense devotion. She yearned to please him, to give him something he would never forget. She wanted to become a part of him, wanted him to remember her no matter what happened after tonight. Houston had broken through her defenses and had conquered the sweet, feminine center of her, and she wanted desperately to claim a piece of his soul and a part of his heart.

The sentimental journey she took with him raised her consciousness of her own feminine prowess. Her slightest touch enticed him. The merest caress of her lips engaged him. A flick of her tongue enthralled him. His moans of pleasure increased her boldness, and she ran her hands down his chest and stomach until her eager fingers found the most sensitized part of him. He trembled and uttered broken words of encouragement as she stroked him and marveled at the softness of his skin and the power that coursed beneath it.

"Have you really dreamed of me?" she asked shyly.

He smiled and touched his lips to the tip of her nose. "Every time I closed my eyes."

He bent his head and his lips closed around the straining peak of one of her breasts. Faith shivered, gripped by an ecstasy that obliterated everything but the pleasure he could effortlessly release within her. The dim light illuminated him, letting her view the myriad expressions that raced across his face. The scar on his chin was white, reminding her of the pain he'd endured and the courage he possessed. When his body joined hers, she closed her eyes and let the tumultuous experience of being one with him consume her.

He was a gentle yet thorough lover. Moving with a liquid ease, he guided her to the plateau of fulfillment. She wrapped herself around him, holding on tightly as he surged through her like a hot Texas wind. Breathlessly she murmured his name as a feeling of satisfaction spread through her, bringing a peaceful smile to her lips.

Houston kissed her smile and returned it. "I feel as if I should thank you."

Faith laughed, shaking her head. "Don't. I took as much as I gave."

"You sure did." His lips rested on hers, briefly and reverently, then he rolled onto his back and pulled her to his side. "It just can't get much better than this. I don't know when I've been this happy."

Kissing his shoulder, Faith released a long sigh. He was such a remarkable man, she thought. He said things that most men kept to themselves for fear of exposing the tender side of their personalities.

"You're a living, breathing miracle, Houston Traynor," she murmured, then smiled when she realized that he had fallen asleep.

She awoke slowly, lazily. Opening her eyes, she found herself staring at Houston. He was dressed, his hair was combed and he was heading for the door.

"Hey!" Faith sat up in bed and smiled. "Where's the fire?"

"It's after eight," he said, looking everywhere but at her. "I've got to get out to the rig."

She let the sheet slip just enough to expose one of her breasts. "Come back to bed. Black Fury can wait another hour or so."

"No, I've got to get out there."

"Houston..." Wariness chased aside her playful mood, and she hitched up the sheet. "Didn't we make love last night?"

"Sure." He grabbed his hat and fitted it on his head. "I'll see you out there."

"Houston, wait just a minute." She folded her arms across her breasts and glared at him. "How about a good-morning kiss, or is that too much to ask?"

He shuffled his booted feet before moving to the bed and dropping a light kiss on her forehead. Faith wrapped her arms around his neck, preventing him from straightening.

"You call that a kiss?"

He tried again.

"Better, but not your best effort. What's wrong?"

He gently disengaged himself from her and put some distance between himself and the bed. "I'm an honest man, Faith."

She didn't like his tone and lifted an invisible shield around her as she tipped up her chin in a direct challenge. "So?"

"I don't want to lead you astray."

Disappointment slammed into her. She'd heard this song before: same tune, different singers. Remaining stoically silent, she fed him more rope and mentally prepared for a lynching.

Houston tucked his fingers into the front pockets of his jeans and rocked back and forth on the balls of his feet. "You see, until I can stand on my own feet—financially speaking—I don't want to share a double yoke." His glance was fleeting and guilt-ridden.

Faith swallowed the bitterness that rose in her throat. "Since we're using unattractive metaphors, would it be correct to say that I'm so sweet honeybees keep buzzing around my head and you're afraid of getting stung?"

He delivered a narrow-eyed glare. "I'm trying to be serious."

"So am I, but it's difficult." She squared her shoulders and presented an outward calm. "You don't have to worry, Houston. I have no intention of getting *hitched* to anyone. You're safe with me." Flinging out her hands, she smiled. "My parents are dead, so there's no chance of a shotgun wedding. Feel better now?" With an economy of movement, she tucked the sheet around her and got out of bed. Standing before him, she felt less vulnerable and more in command of the situation.

"I'm sorry, Faith. I didn't mean that the way it sounded. You took it all wrong. What I meant was—"

"I got your message loud and clear," Faith cut in. "You're a maverick, and I won't rope you in and brand you."

"Will you stop with the...the..."

"Metaphors?" She shrugged, heaving a weary sigh. "I thought you enjoyed them."

A look of frustration clouded his face, and his mouth stretched into a tight line. The scar on his chin was white against his tan and more noticeable than usual. "I'm trying to level with you and make you understand how—"

"I understand," she said brightly. "And I want *you* to understand that I'm not living for the day I'll march down the aisle and say those sacred vows. I've got better things to do with my life."

"If you'd shut up for a minute and let me explain—"

"No need." She wrapped the sheet tighter around her and opened the door for him. "We eased our loneliness last night. It was a natural reaction."

"It was more than a reaction. It was—" He chopped off the sentence and glared at her when she gave him a little push toward the door. "Quit shoving!"

"I thought you were in a hurry to get to the rig. Move along, little doggie."

Giving her a murderous glare, he opened his mouth, but no words spilled out. Finally he heaved a sigh. "Well, hell!"

Faith shut the door, blocking him out before he could see the tears of anger and disappointment fill her eyes. She choked back the bitter emotions and released a trembling sigh.

Leaning back against the door, she stared at the bed that had held heaven last night. She ripped the sheet from her body and flung it aside as a cold fury blasted through her.

"Well, hell," she whispered as a single tear trickled down her cheek.

Chapter Eight

It was a little past noon when Houston rapped his knuckles on Faith's trailer door.

"Your shift!"

Faith sprang from the divan and stared at the door. "What?"

"Your shift! I'm going into Mentone for supplies," he called through the door.

"Okay. Be right there." She grabbed her hard hat and pushed her feet into canvas slings, then stepped outside into the hot Texas afternoon. Heat made the rig undulate, and Faith could feel the warmth of the earth through the soles of her shoes as she moved lethargically to the card table and chair.

Houston's truck roared past in a cloud of dust, and Faith sensed his anger by the way he steered the truck in an uncharacteristic show of speed and carelessness. Her first impression was that he was still angry with her, but she rejected it. Something else was on his mind. She shifted uneasily in the hard chair, waiting for the other shoe to drop. Looking toward the trailer, she wondered if Houston's burst of anger had anything to do with Odessa and Jimmy Ray.

Since he had left her this morning, she had showered and puttered around her confined surroundings while her mind had gone over and over the heated words she and Houston had exchanged. She had been sarcastic—too sarcastic—but he had been self-centered and cowardly. She had fully intended to offer an olive branch later on in the day, but now Houston was on his way to Mentone, leaving her to misery and self-recrimination. Did he need supplies, or did he need to get away? she wondered, glancing at his trailer again in time to see Odessa skip down the steps and start toward her.

Dressed in tight, *tight* jeans and a skimpy blue polka-dot blouse with short puffed sleeves, Odessa patted her stiff curls, and her ruby-red lips stretched into a smile that didn't reach her eyes.

"Morning!"

"Good afternoon," Faith replied, uncovering her microscope. "Thanks for looking after the rig last night."

"Oh, that was nothing." Odessa perched on the other folding chair and lit up a cigarette. "Houston gone?"

"Yes, he said he was going into Mentone for supplies." Faith pushed aside the microscope and studied Odessa carefully for any reaction.

"I don't know what you two did last night, but it must have been awful!" Odessa's heavily mascaraed eyes widened for effect.

"What makes you think that?"

"Didn't you hear the ruckus this morning?"

"No."

Odessa blew out a stream of smoke. "I didn't think anyone could sleep through that!"

"Through what? When did this ruckus happen?"

"About nine or so."

"I must have been in the shower." She propped her chin in one hand, anxious for the juicy details. "What went down?"

Odessa rolled her blue eyes. "We were in bed—me and Jimmy Ray—and Houston comes roaring into the bedroom slinging beer cans at us! Can you believe that?"

"Beer cans?" Faith replied, finding it difficult to picture such an outburst.

"Our empties," Odessa supplied between puffs on the cigarette. "He was hollering about turning his place into a pigsty, what with the empty cans and overflowing ashtrays." She paused and pushed her lower lip into a pout. "It wasn't that bad. We were going to pick things up this morning." She dropped the cigarette, ground it into the earth with the heel of her boot and lit up another one. "I think he was upset that we spent money on beer and cigarettes."

"I think you're right." Faith arched one brow when Odessa shot her a cutting glare. "He thought you'd spend it on clothes and food and looking for work."

"We did! Two six-packs and a carton of cigarettes! What's the big deal?" She sighed heavily and tapped her golden fingernails on the tabletop. "Anyway, he said some ugly things about Jimmy Ray being a lazy good-for-nothing." A smile tipped up one corner of her rouged lips. "Jimmy Ray has a temper, and he don't take nothing off nobody. He took a swing at Houston and the fight was on!" She tipped back her head and laughed until tears glistened in her eyes and ran in black trails down her cheeks.

"They fought?" Faith straightened, suddenly gripped by the story and her mental pictures. Had Houston really socked Jimmy Ray? How glorious!

"It was a barn burner!" Odessa swiped at the moisture on her face and smeared the mascara trails. "Busting up lamps and sending tables every which way! At first I thought Jimmy Ray was going to whip Houston good, but then Houston really got mad and—boy howdy!—that man is like a locomotive when he gets his dander up. Jimmy Ray kicked him while he was down…'' She paused to deliver a sheepish glance. "He kind of fights dirty, but he usually wins. Anyway, when Jimmy Ray did that, Houston got madder than a wet hen, and the feathers flew!'' She slapped her thigh and cackled. "Jimmy Ray didn't rightly know what hit him. Houston's left connected and Jimmy Ray went out like a light.''

"Houston decked him?'' Faith felt triumphant, as if she shared in Houston's victory.

"And how! Jimmy Ray came to a while ago and he's fit to be tied.'' The exuberance left her face and she looked old and frightened. "He holds a grudge. Things can't be the same no more.''

"He'll get over it and so will Houston.'' Faith offered a halfhearted shrug. "Men will be men. Women are wise enough to know that the first person who raises a fist is the loser.''

Odessa blinked her eyes in confusion, then shook her head. "That's over my head, honey. All's I know is that I'll take a tough, two-fisted man over a wimp any day.''

Realizing that she was facing a communication gap, Faith steered the conversation to something Odessa could understand. "Are you going to look for a job today?''

"Job, job, job!'' Odessa stubbed out the cigarette and sprang to her feet. "Is that all you and Houston have on your minds? *Work?* Honey, you need to smell the roses once in a while!''

"I know it's a boring subject, Odessa, but smelling flowers doesn't pay the rent or the grocery bills.''

"What rent?'' Odessa glanced at the two trailers.

"The rent on this rig. It's eating our lunch. For the past couple of months we've spent money, but we haven't made one red cent. I know that Houston wants to help you—he adores you—but he can't support you and Jimmy Ray."

"Well, who the hell asked him to?" Odessa planted her fists at her waist, and her words dripped venom. "Let me tell you something, Miss Holier Than Thou: I've worked all my life because I've *had* to—not because I wanted a *career* or to land me a corporate executive so's I could take tennis lessons and go to the opry. So don't you sit there and preach me a sermon about hard work!" She held out her hands, which were rough and red-knuckled. "These here hands have known many a long day of hot, sudsy water and steel-wood pads. They've picked cotton and oranges and you name it. They've slung hash and dug ditches. I know all about work. More than you'll ever know!"

Faith stared at her a moment, surprised by the outburst but not subdued by it. "And what about Jimmy Ray?"

"What about him?"

"Has he ever worked?"

Odessa's face hardened, and her lips pulled back to bare her teeth. "You don't fool me. You don't care about his work record. You're jealous because he pleasures me and not you!"

"Don't be ridiculous," Faith said, laughing a little at the absurdity.

"He's a young buck and he's used to women falling at his feet. He's told me about how you can't keep your hands and eyes off of him. You might have Houston fooled, but I know your kind."

Faith rose slowly to her feet, warning herself not to slap Odessa's face. Odessa was Houston's sister, and because of Faith's deep feelings for Houston, she held herself in check. "Odessa, you might think that Jimmy Ray is God's gift to the female population, but frankly, he turns my stomach. I suggest we end this discussion before it gets out of hand. I don't want to insult you."

"You've insulted me from the moment you laid eyes on me." Odessa tipped up her chin and delivered a cold glare that brimmed with hatred. "You think I'm trash, but I don't mind. At least I know what I am and I'm not pretending anything different. You're trying to turn Houston against me, but you won't. He's my flesh and blood, and you're just passing through. Six months from now he won't even remember your name."

"Houston isn't the issue. Half of the money—"

"Money!" Odessa scoffed, and jerked down her blouse's hemline. "You can't stand the competition, that's all. I've got Jimmy Ray and Houston, and you've got..." Her gaze dropped to the logbooks. "Your numbers and samples."

"I'm not drilling for men; I'm drilling for oil. Men aren't that hard to get. I could go into Pecos and find a willing one in ten minutes, but I want more out of life than a series of one-nighters." She bit her tongue, knowing she'd gone too far when Odessa's lower lip trembled.

"I'll take my one-nighter and leave your precious oil operation! See how Houston likes that once he knows that you're the one who threw me off his land!"

"I'm not throwing you off his land!" Faith reached out, but Odessa turned away and started for the trailer. "Odessa! Odessa, don't be stupid!" Faith sighed and dropped back into the chair as Odessa slammed the door behind her. "What a mess," she murmured, feeling the nudge of depression. She turned and looked down the road, hoping that Houston would show up before his sister hit the trail.

An hour later Odessa and Jimmy Ray sauntered out to the rig again to interrupt Faith's study of yesterday's soil samples. The sample was different from any she had seen on this site, and she was so engrossed by the possibility of pressure faults in the soil that she let out a shriek when Odessa tapped her shoulder.

"What?" Faith asked, smoothing back her hair and feeling stupid for having screamed bloody murder. "I'm sorry. You scared me."

"I came out to apologize," Odessa said, glancing at Jimmy Ray. "We're both going to shape up."

"So you're not leaving?" Faith asked, barely able to keep the smile from her lips when she saw Jimmy Ray's battered face. His nose and lower lip were swollen, and one eye was so puffy that it was closed and the skin was reddish purple. He looked as if he'd been run over by the back wheels of a truck.

"No, we're not leaving," Jimmy Ray said, and his words were slurred because of his swollen lip. "Not yet, anyhow."

"That's good. I was afraid you might leave without telling Houston goodbye."

"We wouldn't do *that!*" Jimmy Ray's good eye twinkled and his mouth slanted into a careful grin. "Right, Odessa?"

"Right, hon," Odessa whispered, staring at the ground. "Well, we'll leave you so you can work. I'll be in the trailer if you need anything."

"Thanks." Faith smiled but couldn't shake off the niggling worry at the back of her mind. "I'm glad you've decided to stay and...well, mend your fences. Houston thinks the world of you, Odessa."

A look of pain shot through Odessa's pale blue eyes. Her lips parted, twisted, then she whirled and hurried to Houston's trailer. Perplexed, Faith glanced at Jimmy Ray. A wicked glint entered his eyes as he wet his lips with the tip of his tongue.

"You're looking real pretty today, old Faithful."

Faith stared holes through him. "And I've never seen you look better. Purple is definitely your color, kid."

His hands balled into tight fists of rage, and for a few clammy moments Faith thought he was going to tear into her, but he turned on his heel and marched across the dry ground to Houston's trailer. Faith released her pent-up breath and counted her lucky stars. Jimmy Ray was a dangerous animal, she warned herself, and she was foolish to provoke him. Houston might have been able to get the best of him, but Jimmy Ray could make mincemeat out of her.

Looking down the road again, Faith wished Houston would return. She didn't like being alone with Jimmy Ray and Odessa. Her sixth sense told her that something was afoot. She flung a worried frown at the fifth-wheel trailer, then forced her attention back to her work.

The sun was making its way to the horizon when Houston drove the chugging pickup along the potholed road that led to his land.

The old buggy needed a tune-up, he thought. He rounded his shoulders and rested his arms along the curve of the steering wheel, narrowing his eyes against the blinding orange light of the afternoon sun. The bruised skin stretching across his left cheekbone throbbed, and he glanced in the rearview mirror at the damage. The bruise had deepened from pink to blue. By night it would be close to purple, he imagined. The tip of his tongue darted out to assess the cut at the corner of his mouth, then he frowned.

He hadn't slugged it out with anyone since he was a kid. What had gotten into him this morning?

Faith.

His frown became more pronounced. Heaven help him, he was falling in love with her, and as usual, his timing was rotten. If there were just the two of them, he might be able to handle it. But there were Odessa, Jimmy Ray and Black Fury. Everything he had was tied up in the rig. If the well was dry, he'd have nothing to offer Faith except poverty and a hole in the ground. She deserved so much more than he'd ever have to offer.

A wicked grin spread across his face, stinging the cut, as he recalled his rampage. He'd never have had the gumption to order Odessa and Jimmy Ray to clean up the trailer and then get out and find work if it hadn't been for Faith. He had left her trailer feeling like a kicked dog, and the sight of the empty beer cans and smelly ashtrays in his own trailer had been more than he could handle in that frame of mind. Maybe he'd taken things too far, but it had felt good when his fist had connected with Jimmy Ray's jaw. That lazy, good-for-nothing...

Houston sighed heavily, wondering how many Jimmy Rays there had been in Odessa's life and how many more would be added to the list. Why didn't she get a permanent job and settle down? She was too old to be knocking around the West with a series of two-bit Romeos.

Odessa had been pleased when Houston had knocked Jimmy Ray into next week. What had she said? He flashed back to the scene, seeing her shining eyes and bubbly grin.

"It's about time someone gave him a taste of his own medicine! Maybe he won't be so quick to slap me around now that he knows how it feels."

Houston winced and swallowed the bile that rose in this throat. Did Jimmy Ray beat her? Why did women stay around men like that? Did violence breed violence?

The Traynor home had been a battleground. Houston's childhood memories were marred by hazy recollections of his father hitting his mother. The drunken brawls, screaming fights, and mental and physical abuse had hardened Houston against liquor and uncontrolled temper tantrums, but had Odessa embraced them as acceptable behavior? *Normal* behavior, even? Was she one of those poor, wretched women who thought that being loved by a man meant he had the right to punish her as if she were an unruly dog?

Shaking off the sickening thoughts, he squinted against the piercing sunlight and spotted Faith. She was in the hammock, and it looked as if she'd fallen asleep. As he got out of the truck, he glanced around with a worried frown. Something was missing.... His brows shot up. Her car! Where was Faith's car? Had she loaned it to Odessa and Jimmy Ray? Good. They were probably in Pecos looking for work. Maybe they'd buy their own car and quit using everyone else's.

He placed his feet carefully and quietly so as not to awaken Faith. She was curled on her side, her lashes long and spiky where they dusted her cheeks. Lovely, he thought with an appreciative grin. He'd never held a woman who felt as good...as right as she did. Last night had changed him. No longer would he be able to live alone with nothing but time and his own company. Faith had made him realize how much he needed companionship. The tribal instinct was strong in him now, and he realized that he needed to create his own family because he wasn't the type of man who could live with loneliness. He needed a woman. A woman of faith and convictions.

"Faith?" He touched her shoulder and she stirred. Her eyelashes fluttered and lifted. "Sorry I was away for so long."

"Houston...Oh, that's okay." She sat up, letting him assist her to her feet. "What time is it?"

"About six. Where's Odessa and Jimmy Ray?"

"I don't know." She rubbed her eyes and yawned. "Odessa and I had a fight."

"What about?"

"You name it." She shrugged and then stretched lazily. "You, me, her, Jimmy Ray. The whole ball of wax and then some. But don't worry. After she cooled off, we buried the hatchet.'' She looked at him fully, then grinned. "Looks like you ran into somebody's fist.''

"You should see the other guy.'' He drew back when her fingertips touched the tender skin across his cheekbone.

"I did.'' Faith laughed and covered her mouth with her hand. "I shouldn't laugh about it. Jimmy Ray looked sort of pitiful with his black eye and swollen lip. I almost felt sorry for him until he opened his mouth.'' She stomped one foot and released a puff of breath. "Oh, I hate that guy! He's so crude! I don't understand how Odessa can tolerate him.''

He glanced over his shoulder to the place where her car was usually parked. "Did you loan them your car?''

"My car...'' Her eyes widened to their limits. "My car! Where is it?''

"I don't know.'' He turned to watch her pace off the empty space where it had been. "I thought that you'd loaned it to Odessa.''

"I didn't loan anything to Odessa! She...they took it while I was asleep!''

Houston held up his hands to halt her panic. "They'll bring it back. They probably did what I told them to do this morning—they went into Pecos to look for work.''

"But they swiped my car!'' She held her arms out to her sides to emphasize the emptiness around her.

"Maybe they'll buy one so this kind of thing won't happen again.''

"Houston, they could have asked me!''

"I know.'' He shrugged, understanding her indignation. "It was a lousy thing to do. They'll bring it back.''

"I don't know.'' She looked toward his trailer, and an expression of anxiety crossed her face. "Odessa was angry this afternoon and Jimmy Ray was spiteful....''

"You said that you and Odessa made peace.''

"Yes, but I got the feeling that her heart wasn't completely in it."

"I know what you're thinking, but you're wrong. Odessa wouldn't leave without telling me goodbye." His head snapped back when she confronted him with eyes that held pity and regret. "She wouldn't, Faith. She loves me."

"Yes, well..." She looked down at the cracked earth and tucked her fingers into the back pockets of her jeans. "You're probably right."

He could tell that she didn't share in his belief, but he didn't want to argue the point. He'd argued enough with her already. "Are you still sore at me?"

Her blue eyes swept over him. "No. I think we both overreacted this morning. Maybe I expected too much of you."

"What do you mean?" he asked, moving closer until he was standing directly in front of her.

"I was hoping that you'd wake me up with kisses. I didn't expect to wake up and find you taking a powder."

"I wasn't taking a powder!" He took a deep breath and reined in his temper. "I was going to let you sleep in."

"Living with you is like living with Janus."

"Who's she?"

She laughed softly under her breath. "*He* is the Roman god of beginnings and endings. He represents the extremities of human nature. Like Dr. Jekyll and Mr. Hyde. Do those names ring a bell?"

"You're calling me a monster, is that it?" He crossed his arms against his chest and glared at her, reminding himself that he had meant to repair the damage instead of adding to it.

"I'm not calling you anything, Houston. Forget it." She started past him, but he gripped her forearm. "I don't want to fight with you. Let go."

"I don't want to fight, either." He pulled her into his arms and kissed her motionless lips. His mouth was tender, and her firm, unrelenting lips didn't lessen his discomfort. "It's better when you help." He grinned, trying to lighten her moodiness, then kissed her again, but she didn't respond. "What's wrong?"

"Nothing except that this hasn't been one of my best days. It started with a fight, moved rapidly to another fight, then to a halfhearted apology, and now my car has been ripped off. Sorry, but I can't stomach a kiss-and-make-up scene right now."

"I know that you don't like Odessa, but—"

"It's not that!" She jerked free of his hold. "It's not a matter of liking or not liking your sister. I just don't like the way she uses you, and I don't like the way you *let* her use you."

"She's not using me. She's family."

"So what?" she demanded, her voice rising.

"So...it's none of your damned business!" He clenched his teeth, furious with himself and with her for goading him into another angry confrontation.

"Houston..." She rested her hands lightly on his forearms and looked up at him in a way that made his insides melt. "You're so kind and generous, but I'm afraid you're going to get hurt."

"I can handle it."

"I know you can, but I wish you'd try to avoid it. You've spent years dreaming of this family reunion, and I think it's wonderful that Odessa has come back, but she isn't the sister of your dreams. I get the feeling that you love her a lot more than she loves you."

"Don't you think I know that?" He rested his hands at her waist and bent closer until his forehead touched hers. "I don't want to talk about Odessa. I want to talk about us."

"What about us?"

"We became lovers last night, and that changes things. I know I'll never be able to look at another woman again without thinking of you."

"Oh, Houston..." She closed her eyes, and her body sagged wearily against his. "Why didn't you say that this morning when I desperately needed to hear it?"

"Doesn't it count for anything that I'm saying it now?"

"It counts." Her lips searched for his, brushing across his chin until they found his mouth. "It counts for a lot."

Her lips parted beneath his and her tongue entered his mouth, moving sensuously against his. Fingers of heat ran up his thighs, and the earth trembled under his feet. The blood roared in his ears, surprising him with its intensity. He found it difficult to keep his balance, the earth was shuddering so violently.

"Houston!" She broke free of his embrace, and her blue eyes were deep pools of excitement. "We've done it!"

"I know, it's wonderful." He reached for her, wanting to mold her body to his.

"No, no!" She slapped at his hands and raced toward the rig. "Come on! Hurry!"

He stared after her for a few mindless seconds until reality jarred him back to his senses. Holy Moses! He looked at the trembling rig. They'd hit something!

Faith was at the blowout preventer, and her laughter winged across the flat land. Houston's mind switched to automatic and he began barking orders to her as the ground beneath Black Fury grumbled and quaked.

"Open it up!" he yelled.

"No!" She shook her head, turning the wheel of the preventer.

"Let's see what we've got!" He pushed her aside and opened up the valve, then grabbed her hand and ran with her to a safe distance from Black Fury. The grumbling earth began to groan, crying for release. "Come on, honey,"

Houston whispered. "Come on. We're almost there. Let it go...let me have it." He felt Faith's wondering stare, but he was too full of the moment to share it. His heart was hammering against his rib cage, and he thought he might explode before the well did.

The rig shuddered, the earth belched and a black fountain arched into the sky.

"Hot damn!" Houston tore his hat off his head and tossed it into the air. "It's oil, sweetheart! Oil!" He wound his arms about Faith's narrow waist and swung her around in a dizzy circle of euphoria. Her laughter fell around him as droplets of oily water splattered his skin. The air grew heavy with it, and the strong stench of crude filled his nasal passages. Faith's mouth clung to his and her laughter mingled with his own.

"Houston...Houston! I love you!"

Her declaration rang through him like the pealing of church bells on a Sunday morning. He kissed her hard, feeling fiercely possessive as the earth spewed forth a rainbow of dreams-come-true and a pot of black gold.

Houston grabbed the empty champagne bottle and flung it across the flat land.

"So much for riches untold," he said with a snarl.

Faith sighed and sat cross-legged on the wet, sticky ground. "It's dropped off to nothing," she said, more for her benefit than for his. "Another false alarm, but for a while there, I was sure it was going to flow a hundred barrels a day." She rolled her shoulders, trying to loosen the tight muscles there, and glanced at her watch. "It's seven. No wonder I'm tired. We've been up all night."

"I'm shutting it down," Houston said, already throwing levers and silencing Black Fury. "It was just top pressure— a little pocket of nothing." He kicked at the rig, and his booted foot clunked harmlessly against the metal. "Damn you, Black Fury!"

Faith averted her gaze from his crestfallen expression. She couldn't bear to witness his disappointment. She had her own to deal with. The strong smell of oil still lingered on her clothes as a painful reminder of what might have been. "Well, we'll just have to make more hole. It's down there. I know it is."

"What's the use?" Houston flung himself into the hammock and covered his eyes with his oily forearm.

Faith turned her head to look at him, hating him for acting like a broken man. "Stop it, Houston. We're both disappointed, but his isn't helping anything. You aren't the only one who's hurting. I feel awful, too, but it's not the end of the world."

"Isn't it? Sure feels like it to me."

Gritting her teeth to keep from screaming at him, Faith looked around her at the oily patches of ground. For a while, champagne had flowed along with the oil, but the oil had run out before the champagne, and the celebration had come to an abrupt halt. Their giddiness had become doubt and then despair. Now what? she wondered. Nothing left to do but pick up the pieces, dust off Black Fury and start all over again.

The approach of a truck roused her from her self-pity, and she looked over her shoulder. A towtruck bounced along the road, and behind it was a blue car. Faith stood up, shading her eyes with one hand.

"Houston! That's my car!" She ran forward, waving at whomever was behind the steering wheel. The truck stopped in a cloud of billowing dust, and Peewee Porter stepped out of it. "Peewee! Where did you find my car?"

"Just outside Pecos. I recognized it, so I thought I'd bring it to you. I thought you must have run out of gas and left it."

"No..." She looked back at Houston. "Someone borrowed it."

Houston rolled out of the hammock and held out his hand as he approached Peewee. "Howdy. Thanks for bringing it."

"Oh, it was nothing. I filled it up." Peewee shook Houston's hand, studied the residue of oil Houston had left on his palm and wiped it off on his bib overalls. "It took ten dollars," he murmured, turning back to Faith.

"I'll pay you for your trouble," Faith said, already moving toward her trailer. She stepped inside it and removed some money from her billfold, then returned to Peewee and Houston. The two men were walking around the rig, and Faith knew that Houston was telling Peewee of their false alarm. "Here you go, Peewee. There's a little extra for your trouble."

"Thanks." Peewee pocketed the money without counting it. "You're not packing it in, are you?"

"Packing it..." Faith glanced at Houston. "No, we're not. We're going to reenter. There's oil down there. My samples indicate that—"

"Your samples," Houston cut in with drawling sarcasm. "Your samples aren't worth a plugged nickel!" He stared at the ground for a few moments as if trying to control his temper. "Good to see you, Peewee. Thanks for bringing the car out to us." He gave a short nod, then went to his trailer, slamming the door behind him with unnecessary force.

Faith glanced at Peewee, embarrassed by Houston's ill-tempered outburst. "He's tired. We've been at it since yesterday afternoon."

"Guess you're pretty tuckered out yourself," Peewee said, then sent a stream of brown juice to the ground. "This oil business can wear you to a frazzle."

Faith shrugged and walked over to her car. "Was there anyone with the car?"

"Nope."

She frowned, wondering where Jimmy Ray and Odessa could be. They'd be back for their belongings, but when? How could they do this to Houston after all he'd done for them?

"Still think there's oil down there, do you?"

Faith nodded absently. "Of course. Another few hundred feet and we'll hit the pay zone."

"I heard-tell that Houston's sister was here."

"She was...she is." Faith leaned against the side of the car, suddenly too tired to stand on her own strength. "She and her friend showed up a few days ago. Do you know her?"

"Odessa Lynn?" Peewee grinned. "Hell, yes. I used to go with her. She was a pretty thing back then." He chuckled and ran a hand across his mouth. "Course, so was I. That was twenty or so years ago, mind you."

Faith smiled, taking in his round body and the loose skin that wiggled under his chin when he talked.

"You've had a patch of bad luck," he said, shooting a glance at the rig. "I'd say that Odessa Lynn has hit the road, wouldn't you?"

"I don't think so. She'll be back for her things."

"Wouldn't count on it." Peewee ambled toward his truck and opened the door, which let out a nerve-racking creak. "Don't give up on Black Fury. She'd got a nose for oil."

"We're not giving up," Faith said, straightening up from the car.

Peewee looked at the fifth-wheel before struggling into the truck and squeezing his big body behind the steering wheel. "He is," he shouted over the roar of the engine.

Faith stepped away from the choking dust as a cloud of apprehension billowed around her. Houston wasn't giving up, was he? She went to his trailer and knocked on the door.

"Houston? Can I come in?"

"It's open." His voice was weary and lifeless.

Opening the door, she stepped inside the dark trailer and blinked until her eyes adjusted. Houston was sprawled on the couch. He stared at the ceiling, not moving a muscle.

"Wasn't it nice of Peewee to bring my car out to me?" She waited for his reply, but he remained silent. "I wonder where Odessa and Jimmy Ray are?" Still no answer. Faith moved closer to him. "Houston? Are you still with me?" She ran her fingertips lightly through the silky hair that fell across his forehead. "How about some coffee? I bet some eggs and bacon would hit the spot."

"Leave me alone."

"No." Anger nipped at her, and she dropped to her knees beside the couch. "We're in this together. I know what you're feeling, but we're not doing any good by sitting around licking our wounds. We'll rest today and then start up again tomorrow."

His eyes slid sideways to look at her. "It's over."

"No, it isn't. It's not over until the fat lady sings or we hit oil." She tried to smile, but it didn't feel right. "Come on, Houston," she urged, pressing her fingers into his shoulders. "This isn't like you. Tomorrow we'll start all over and—"

"No!" His voice rang out as he jerked up to a sitting position and glared at her. "Read my lips. It's over! We'll cut our losses and pack it in. Let PATCO have the damned lease if they want it."

"Over my dead body!" Faith gripped his knees and leaned into him until her face was inches from his. "Will you snap out of it? So we hit a pocket. Big deal. That's part of the risk. Next time we'll—"

"There won't be a next time for us. We're nearly broke—busted. Now that you've got your car, you can pack up and clear out. I'll tie up the loose ends."

She stared at his dirt-streaked face and wanted to slap it. "What do you mean we're nearly broke? We've still got—"

"Nothing. We've got nothing except a hole in the ground." He ran an oily hand through his hair, pushing it off his forehead. "Odessa and Jimmy Ray aren't coming back. They've cleaned me out."

"Cleaned you..." Faith sprang to her feet and went to the kitchen cupboard where she knew Houston kept their nest egg in a coffee can. Pulling it off the shelf, she pried off the plastic lid and stared into the dark emptiness. "The money..." She swallowed hard and felt her heart sink. "It's gone." Flinging the can aside, she whirled to look across the dim room at Houston. "How could they have stolen your money—*our* money? We were good to them. We tried to help them."

Houston shrugged off the questions and cradled his head in his hands as he propped his elbows on his bent knees. "I shouldn't have lost my temper. I should have known that Jimmy Ray wouldn't take a beating without striking back."

"He deserved that thrashing. The lazy, slimy..." She clamped her lips together and crossed the room to sit beside Houston. "Well, that's that. There's nothing we can do about it."

"Now you're making sense."

"We'll pick ourselves up and—"

"Will you stop it?" He glared at her, his eyes stormy and swimming with defeat. "Your optimism is turning my stomach."

"Houston..." She slipped an arm across his wide shoulders and gave him a swift, confident hug. "You're feeling betrayed. I understand that, but life goes on. We still have the rig, and—"

He shot up from the couch and grabbed his jean jacket. "I'm out of here."

"Where are you going?"

"Anywhere but here." He stuck his arms into the sleeves and swept his truck keys off the coffee table. "Start packing your things, Faith. There's nothing here for you anymore."

"Houston, don't go. Let's talk about this."

"Nothing to talk about." He opened the door and looked over his shoulder at her. "Goodbye, Faith, and good luck."

"Houston..." She held out her hands to him, beseeching him to stay and let her comfort him, but he shook his head and closed the door behind him. Moments later, Faith heard the roar of the pickup as it raced away from the Double H.

"The Double H," she repeated aloud, wondering if that were true any longer. He'd told her to clear out of his life as if they had nothing between them except the oil venture. Didn't he know that she loved him? Didn't he love her?

Faith fell back on the couch and closed her eyes. It couldn't be over, she thought with a sob. She wouldn't allow it. She'd be here when he returned, and she'd tell him that she had no intention of leaving him. She had too much invested...and she had too much to lose.

Stepping outside Houston's trailer, Faith shook the throw rug vigorously as her gaze went automatically to the empty road.

"Where the hell is he?" she wondered aloud as she draped the rug over her arm. She'd spent four days cleaning his trailer, cleaning hers, washing her car, looking for Houston's truck on the lonely road. Nights had been the worst as she'd managed to doze fitfully, alert to every sound and every shadow.

She placed the rug on the tiled area just inside the door, then walked aimlessly toward the hulking silent rig. Every day that it sat there doing nothing was costing hundreds of dollars. What was Houston thinking of, letting this rig sit silently when he knew there wasn't enough money to pay for its rental? How could he leave her for so long?

Faith ran a light hand down the length of pipe, then squatted near the hole in the ground and checked the drill bit. It was still green and ready to chew up earth. Should she start it up? She looked down the road again and sighed. If she did, she'd be stuck here. She wouldn't be able to leave the rig unattended.

Before she started it up again, there was something she had to do. During the past four days she had seesawed indecisively, but suddenly she had made up her mind.

Rising to her feet, she went to her trailer for a quick shower. She dressed carefully, realizing that it was the first time in months that she'd worn a skirt, blouse and blazer. The low-heeled pumps felt strange after wearing tennis shoes and boots, and putting on makeup wasn't an automatic process as it once had been. Staring at herself in the bathroom mirror, it occurred to her that she had changed. Her skin was smooth and deeply tanned. Her hair was lighter, having been bleached by the sun. But it wasn't just a physical metamorphosis, she told herself. It was mainly an internal transformation from a self-centered businesswoman to a team player. She and Houston were a team, whether he liked it or not. Their lives were tightly interwoven, and their future hung in the balance.

A few months ago she had believed that PATCO was still, and always would be, part of her life. Although she had resigned, she had held on to a piece of it out of sheer stubbornness. Now she realized that she had lost any claim to PATCO the day her father had taken his own life. She had hung on out of misdirected loyalty, but PATCO didn't deserve her loyalty, her father did. He had been a desperate man, trying to keep his head above financial waters, and the company officials had turned against him. Instead of reaching out a helping hand, they had pushed him under and watched him struggle helplessly.

She had been angry with her father instead of with the PATCO board of directors.

"Forgive me, Dad?" she whispered, fighting back tears. "Please forgive me. I loved you, you know. You were my whole life." Turning away from the mirror, she ran trembling fingers beneath her eyes. "Oh, Houston! Where are you when I need you?"

Houston was her life now, and without him she felt frail and afraid, just as she had when she'd lost her father. A smile quivered on her lips as she picked up her purse and a thick portfolio and went outside to her car. Sitting behind the wheel, she reflected on her weakness for men who were generous to a fault. Oh, well, she had her own faults. No one was perfect. She started the car and headed towards Pecos. Samson Applegate would be surprised to see her, but delighted with her offer. He'd finally be rid of the Patton/Hutton clans. Jack Campbell would probably throw a party to announce the end of Cain Patton's heirs to the throne.

"It's been real and it's been fun," she said, thinking of her years with PATCO. "But it hasn't been real fun." She laughed, hoping that she'd spot Houston in Pecos or Mentone. He must be in one of those places. Should she search for him?

She discarded the notion. When he was ready to come home to her, he would.

The sun glared through the windshield, and Faith slowed the car while she flipped open the glove compartment to locate her sunglasses. A piece of note paper fluttered to the carpet and Faith glanced at it, then stopped the car when she saw that it was a note to Houston from Odessa. Pulling to the side of the road, she stopped the car and picked up the note, reading it aloud slowly as she struggled with the numerous misspellings and the childish scrawl.

Deer Houston, I bet you hate me and I don't blaim you. I won't bother you agin. It sure was good to see you one more time. Me and Jimmy Ray are heading for parts unnown. We like the gipsy life. I know you don't unnerstand that, but its jist the way we are. You want a home and famly and respict and me...well I want to have fun and kick up my heals. I tryed the family life and it wasn't for me.

Sure hope you strick oil. Maybe when we get ahead a little I'll pay you back the money we took. This old car has run out of gas so we're going to hitch and buy a pickup in the next town we come to. I know I dissapointed you, sugar, but it's just the way I am. Guess I've got a lot of the old man in me. You took after Mama. She was a good person who didn't diserve the mizery Daddy saddled her with—and you don't diserve getting dumped on by me so jist be glad I'm gone.

You'll always be my little brother, honey. Your sis, Odessa Lynn.

Faith folded the note and put it in her purse. She'd give it to Houston when he came home. How would he take it? Would it break his heart or ease his mind? Leaning her forehead on the steering wheel, she wished she could put her arms around Houston and kiss away his troubles. Her thoughts moved back to the night they'd made love, and a warmth spread through her as she remembered with startling clarity the way he felt, the way he moved within her, the way his mouth had worshiped her.

He was one in a million, she thought as she straightened and steered the car onto the road again. Once she told him that they were financially stable again, he'd catch the wildcatter fever and start up Black Fury.

She pulled her lower lip between her teeth and chewed on it, fighting off the wave of pessimism that washed over her. Was she whistling in the dark by thinking that Houston would come back to her with open arms?

Chapter Nine

Mac puffed noisily on his pipe, his youthful blue eyes sparkling with a humor he never seemed to be without. Faith smiled at him and knew her smile lacked conviction. She looked awkwardly around the comfortable den in the lengthening silence.

"Want some more coffee?" Mac asked finally, leaning forward to pour it.

"No, thanks." Faith covered the cup with her hand. "Am I keeping you from anything?"

"Nope." Mac grinned and settled back in his chair.

"So Bonita Kaye's in Mentone today?"

"That's right. Some kind of church social."

"Oh." Faith nodded absently. "But it's Wednesday, isn't it?"

"Church is open all the time."

"Yes, of course." She laughed softly at herself. "Why didn't you go?"

"I'll go tonight. They're getting things ready for it to-day. Decorating the hall and cooking the food—stuff like that. The social isn't until this evening. Want to come with us?"

"No, thanks." She clutched her purse and decided to leave. "I've got to go."

"But you haven't got what you came for, have you?"

Her gaze collided with his, and she dissolved into nervous laughter. "Mac, you're downright scary sometimes. What do you think I came for?"

"Advice, I imagine. Or maybe a sympathetic ear." His mustache twitched from side to side. "I've got both."

"I need both." She relaxed, crossing her legs and smoothing her skirt.

"Has he got you worried?"

She nodded. They both knew who "he" was. "He's driving me crazy with worry. I haven't seen him in almost a week."

"He's in Mentone."

Her gaze swept to his. "You've seen him?"

"Bonita Kaye saw him. He's hanging out at the pool hall mostly, although I heard that he'd worked a couple of days at the grocery store. The owner's wife took sick, and Houston filled in until she was back on her feet. He gave Houston some clothes and food for his help." Mac paused to light his pipe, then spoke around it. "Houston's just biding his time."

"Until what?"

"Until he can face you again, I reckon." He squinted through a cloud of smoke at her. "I hear you hit a pocket that fizzled out."

"Yes, and Odessa and Jimmy Ray split." She stopped short of telling Mac about the theft, feeling as if that were a private matter. "He said that he doesn't want to continue with the drilling, but I don't believe him.'' She took a deep breath, then exhaled it. "I sold my shares in PATCO, Mac."

His bushy white brows lifted. "That so? Why did you sell them?"

"I needed the money."

"Gone through your investment money already?" His brows lowered, forming a bridge over his eyes. "Wouldn't think you would have run out of your money this soon."

"Well...let's just say that we had some unexpected costs to deal with. I want to find Houston to tell him that we're financially stable again and that we can start drilling."

"Going to throw that money down the well, too?" Mac puffed on his pipe for a few moments, studying her decisive nod and grave expression. "Are you interested in the business or the personal investment?"

She felt heat wash across her face and kept her gaze glued to the clenched hands in her lap. "Both, I guess."

"Let's walk over to the garages. I had one of the Mercedes painted last week. You can tell me if you like the color."

"Okay." She stood up, linked her arm in Mac's and walked beside him outside to the long garages. "Cars must be one of your weaknesses, Mac."

"I confess," he said, patting her hand in the crook of his arm. "I think they're the best inventions since sliced bread. They fascinate me." He nodded at one of the ranch hands. "Brought this pretty lady out here to see my new paint job, Fernando."

Fernando pulled back one of the garage doors to let sunlight spill across the hood of a Mercedes. Faith squeezed Mac's arm and laughed as she blinked against the blinding gold.

"It's an eye-opener," Faith said, not quite sure what to say about the gaudy car. She let go of Mac and moved inside the garage to peer through the car windows. "Black velvet interior. Plush."

"Know why I did this?" Mac asked, running a finger along the side of the car.

"Did it have anything to do with a full moon?"

"No," he said with a chuckle. "Because Nita's daughter loves this color." His gaze swept slyly to hers and one corner of his mustache tipped up. "Nita's been working for us for more than twenty-five years, and her youngest daughter is getting married Saturday afternoon. They're having the ceremony in our living room." He turned and leaned back against the gold Mercedes. "Not one of our kids got married in our living room. They all married in places that were a long ways from here, and we found out about it thanks to long distance." He crossed his ankles and stared at the tips of his black boots as a dark expression flitted across his face, then was gone like a cloud sailing across the sun. "But Nita's girl wanted to get married here, and we're going to throw her some shindig!"

Faith examined the car again. "You're not going to give this car to her, are you?" she asked, thinking that such a wedding gift was a bit extravagant.

"No. They wouldn't take it. They're proud people." He looked over his shoulder at the blazing bonnet and grinned. "I'm letting them borrow it. They're driving to Los Angeles and San Francisco for their honeymoon, and they're going there in style." He laughed lightly, his shining eyes reaching across the dim interior of the garage to Faith. "I can always have the car repainted, but for now it's a golden chariot for Nita's baby girl." He rounded his shoulders in a stiff shrug. "Don't know if Nita's girl will appreciate the gesture or not."

"Oh, she will." Faith fingered the hood ornament. "Anyone would love it."

"Can't tell about folks. I've done good deeds before and got nothing but the back of someone's hand for my trouble. Didn't keep me from trying to help folks when I could, but it was upsetting nonetheless."

Faith stepped back from the gleaming car and examined the cagey man with the infectious grin. Mac never did anything just for the heck of it. He'd showed her this car for a specific reason, and she was beginning to get his subtle message.

"You know about Odessa and Jimmy Ray, don't you?" she asked in a near whisper that reflected the awe she held for Asa MacQuay.

He crossed his arms and grinned shyly. "I've put two and two together, if that's what you mean."

"Amazing."

"Not really." His mustache lifted at the corners, and he laughed. "I knew Odessa way back when she was a wild young filly. I didn't think that age would tame her much."

"It didn't. Just slowed her down a little," Faith said with a helpless shrug. "She still bucks and kicks up her heels."

Mac chuckled and stroked his mustache thoughtfully. "She always took up with the wrong kind of man. Guess that hasn't changed either."

"No. Jimmy Ray Workman is a sleaze." Faith ran her hands down her arms and shivered. "It's been spooky out at the Double H at night without Houston. I'm afraid Jimmy Ray and Odessa will come back, and I don't want to be alone with them out there."

Mac's eyes lost their sparkle. "You should've come and stayed here. You know you're welcome here."

"I know." She shrugged helplessly, knowing that her next words would be revealing. "I wanted to be there in case Houston came home."

"Yep." He grinned and straightened from his lounging position against the gold car. Approaching her, he placed an arm around her shoulders and moved with her into the sunlight.

"Nita's daughter will love that car, Mac."

"No way of telling how she'll react." Mac's gnarled hand squeezed her shoulder. "But I've enjoyed getting it ready for her and her husband-to-be, and I'll enjoy loaning it to them. Sometimes you've gotta do things because they feel good and not because they'll make somebody else feel good." He stopped and looked at his oil-derricked land, where pumps moved up and down with a lazy rhythm as they drew wealth up from the core of the earth. "And sometimes people take advantage of your good intentions. There's always people who take more than you offered, but that isn't a poor reflection on you. It puts *them* in a bad light, that's all."

"It can harden your heart," Faith murmured.

"If you let it," Mac agreed. "But that's up to you, isn't it?"

Faith leaned her head against Mac's shoulder and sighed. "I love him, Mac. I don't know when it happened or how, but I love him. It hurt me when Odessa and Jimmy Ray hurt him. I could see it coming, but I couldn't stop it. I knew the moment they showed up that they'd trample on his feelings."

"He'll get over it. He's like a cat: always lands on his feet." Mac laughed and moved with Faith back to the house. "After all he's been through, it's a wonder his heart hasn't turned to stone."

"He told me about that car accident and how you stood up for him. That was good of you."

"I saw the good in him."

"So do I."

Mac opened the front door and let Faith enter before him. "Ever had a strawberry-banana sling?"

"Can't say that I have. What is it?"

His brows moved up and down comically. "Cool and refreshing. Come on into the kitchen and I'll stir us up a couple while we try to piece together Houston Huey Traynor."

"Huey?" She tipped back her head and laughed. "How awful!"

"That was his father's name. Huey Traynor. His mother was Rose. She was a sweet soul, but weak of spirit." He entered the kitchen and went to the refrigerator for ice, strawberries and bananas, which he placed near a blender on the counter. "I remember the first time I saw Houston. He was a little tow-headed tyke, quiet and thoughtful. Huey blustered and blew, spouting one lie after another, and I got the feeling that Houston knew his daddy was lying and that it bothered him. That's when I thought there was hope for the boy."

Faith paid attention as ice cubes, a pint of strawberries and three bananas went into the blender. Mac switched on the noisy machine and let it whir for a couple of minutes before he turned it off. He poured the pink concoction into two tall glasses and handed one to Faith as he sat at the kitchen table with her.

"Looks scrumptious," Faith said, then took a long sip of the frosty drink. It was tangy, tart and so cold that it made her temples throb. "Hmm. Just the thing on a hot Texas day."

"That's what Bonita Kaye says." Mac flicked drops of frothy pink from his mustache. "The strawberries make it pretty and sweet, and the bananas make it stick to your ribs." His eyes twinkled merrily, signaling something more to come. "And the ice gives you a headache so don't drink it too fast. Me and the missus are teetotalers, and this is as near to a cocktail as we get."

"Houston's a teetotaler, too." She rolled her eyes, realizing that she had steered the conversation back to Houston again. "I'm sorry. He's on my mind, and it's stuck there like a broken record."

"No need to apologize." Mac sat back in his chair and ran his fingers down the sides of the frosty glass. "What did he tell you about the accident?"

"Just the facts, and that people around here kind of turned against him—except for you and Bonita Kaye."

"The folks in this county are close-knit. More than you'd think." He took another sip of his drink and ran his hand across his mustache. "This is a big county with less than a hundred people in it, and that means everybody knows of everybody else. Can't do anything without somebody knowing about it and spreading the news. But these people admit when they're wrong, too, and they were wrong about Houston. When he came back a few years ago, people tried to make amends, but Houston had been burned and he didn't trust their overtures."

"They seem to like him," Faith interjected. "When I've been out with him people go out of their way to say hello and chat. The only thing is they think he's a loner—a hermit. He isn't."

"Depends on where you're standing." He grinned when she shook her head in confusion. "If you're standing here at six o'clock, you'd say the sun was setting, but if you're standing on the other side of the world, you'd say it was rising." He chuckled, amused by her wondering expression. "If you lived in Mentone and you saw Houston coming into town for supplies, then hightailing it back to his lonely piece of land, you'd say that he was a man who thrived on solitude. But if you lived out here and you saw how delighted he was when he received visitors, you'd say that he was a friendly guy who happened to live alone."

"Oh, I see. It depends on your perspective." She nodded, catching his drift. "Has he dated much since he's been back?"

"Not much in the way of available women in Loving County. Most of them are married with kids."

"Just the way I like it," Faith said, smiling. "Competition brings out the worse in me. LaQuita made a play for him one evening and I nearly lost my cool." She sighed, recalling the evening and the way Houston had accepted her challenge. Wetting her lips, she warmed to the thought of his kisses. Oh, she missed him! She looked at Mac and knew that he was reading her mind, so she switched tracks. "I guess that accident he had when he was a teenager changed his life."

"In a way." Mac nodded and took another sip of the sling. His tongue gathered up the stray droplets. "He was guilt-ridden. He *should* have felt guilty about stealing my car, but it was more than that. He kept thinking of Tracie Lou and..." He stared at the frosted glass and an uncharacteristic sadness doused the light in his eyes. "For a while there I thought he might do something crazy. He moped around here, not saying much and not looking anyone in the eye. He was like a horse that'd had its spirit broken."

"But he snapped out of it?" Faith asked.

"Yes, but it took a while. He finally took off, and I didn't think I'd see him again." He looked at her beneath scruffy brows. "He came back for Odessa. Family ties are important to Houston; I guess because he's never had any to speak of. Sometimes I catch him looking at me and Bonita Kaye— a kind of wishful look on his face—and it makes me thank heaven above that I've got my Bonita Kaye." Mac cleared his throat and blinked away the moisture in his eyes. "Odessa let him down; now you've got to pick him up."

"I'd be happy to, if I could find him."

"Go into Mentone. He's there. I imagine he'll be shooting pool around sundown."

"Do you think he'll come back to the rig with me?"

Mac grinned, his eyes twinkling with mischief. "I imagine you can be mighty persuasive when you want to be. If womanly wiles don't do the trick, then give him a swift kick. Works every time with me. Bonita Kaye's left her footprint on my seat many a time."

Faith laughed and held up her glass. "To pushy women."

Chuckling, Mac touched his glass to hers. "Bless them, one and all."

Wednesday night in Mentone was as exciting as watching grass grow.

Faith drove past the Mentone church. Its small parking lot was full of vehicles, and light spilled from the multicolored windows. The church social, she thought, spotting one of Mac's Mercedes parked near the side entrance. Except for the activity at the church, the tiny town was dark and lifeless. Faith drove on to the next block of buildings, where a square of yellow light fell on the street. Three pickups were parked outside the pool hall, and one of them was faded blue with several scrapes and dents. Houston's truck, Faith thought, feeling her spirits lift. Mac had been as right as rain.

A red-haired woman with a saucy smile and pendulum hips emerged from the pool hall as Faith approached it. The flame-haired woman clung to the lanky man beside her and laughed. Faith turned her head as the strong stench of alcohol enveloped her. She stepped inside and looked across the planked floor to the two green-topped tables at the back of the room. Houston was setting up a shot. The tiffany lamp suspended over the table sent shards of bright light across his face. Faith smiled, noticing that he still wore the imprint of Jimmy Ray's fist on his cheekbone. The bruised skin was healing, and Faith hoped that Houston's hurt feelings and failing spirits were on the mend, too. His red shirt was unbuttoned, and the tails hung in loose wrinkles.

Faith swallowed nervously as her femininity responded to the sight of his bronze, hair-roughened chest. He looked disheveled and preoccupied, and a weakness stole through her. When it came to Houston Traynor, she was a sucker, Faith thought with a quick frown.

Her low heels clicked confidently against the floor as she approached, and the two men with Houston looked up. One of them grinned, revealing empty spaces between this tobacco-stained teeth. The other stranger backed away and seemed uncomfortable now that there was a woman in the room.

"Evening, honey. Looking for some action?" he asked, nudging the other man, who blushed and kept his eyes averted from Faith.

"I've found what I'm looking for," she said politely but coldly as she stared at Houston. "The game's over, Houston. It's time to face your responsibilities."

He didn't flinch but continued to set up his shot. The pool stick darted forward, but he missed the shot. He frowned and straightened. "Your shot, Claude."

"Looks like you've got a visitor, Houston," Claude said, still grinning.

"I'm playing pool, not greeting visitors. Take your shot." He refused to look at her, preferring to stare at the table.

Faith set her mouth in a firm line and glared at him. "I want to talk to you—now."

"I thought you would have cleared off my land by now," he said, still staring at the table. "I'm going to start charging you rent."

"Go ahead. I can afford it." She confronted the other men, offering a cool smile. "Would you gentlemen excuse us, please? I have some business to discuss with Mr. Traynor."

One glance at her stern expression sent the men to the rack, where they placed their sticks. Houston scowled at them with disgust, then glowered at Faith from beneath lowered brows. A shiver of apprehension stole through her when she witnessed his state of fury.

"What gives you the right to barge in here and interrupt my game? I don't want you here!"

"Tough." She nodded at each man as they filed out of the room. "Thank you, gentlemen. This won't take long."

"Come back here, guys!" Houston motioned for them with a sweeping arm. "You don't have to take orders from her."

"That's okay," Claude said. "She's got something on her mind, and it don't concern us. We'll be out here tossing back a few brews." Claude touched his forehead in a salute. "Ma'am, you take all the time you need."

"Thank you, Claude." She bestowed a sweet smile on him before letting it go when she faced Houston again. "I've been waiting for you back at the Double H. How could you leave me out there all alone?"

"I told you to pack up and leave."

"I don't take orders from you. You'd be sorry if something bad had happened to me while you were in town spending money you don't have."

"What could have happened to you?"

"I could have...Jimmy Ray might have shown up or some other scoundrel. I was defenseless out there by myself."

"You're never defenseless, Faith." He sat on the edge of the table and laughed softly. "You'd have run over any scoundrel like a Mack truck."

"I'm flattered...I think." She met his gaze and held it. "I want you to come back, Houston."

"No." He shook his head slowly. "Not while you're there."

"Why? We've got work to do. Black Fury is sitting out there costing us money."

"I'll tell Peewee to come and get her."

"No!" She drew a deep breath and strove for a calm tone. "We're not finished. There's oil down there."

"The hell you say," he bit out as he placed his feet on the floor and stood up. "The deal's off. We're out of money and—"

"No, we're not." She reached into her purse and withdrew a stack of green bills. Waving them at him, she smiled. "I sold my shares in PATCO. We're in the black again."

"You did *what*?" His mouth dropped open, then he closed it with a distinct click of his teeth as his jawline became as hard as granite. He came around the table, moving rigidly, as if he were trying to hold himself in check. "Are you crazy? Nobody asked you to do that!"

"Nobody had to. I wanted to sell them. This oil venture is important to me—to us." She stiffened against the anger that seemed to radiate from him. His face grew pale, making his dark eyes more noticeable as they fairly smoldered.

"I won't take another dime from you," he said, grounding out each word as he lifted a finger and shook it in her face. "Do you hear me? Not another dime!"

Faith tipped up her chin and looked down her nose at him. "You have no choice. A deal's a deal. We shook on it, remember?"

His eyes narrowed to fierce slits, then he swung around and swept the balls off the table with a vicious swipe of his arm. "Get out of here. I mean it. I don't want you around me."

"You don't know what you're saying." She stood beside him, her gaze taking in his broad shoulders, his tousled hair.

He turned around, his expression dark and gloomy. "You represent failure to me, Faith, and I don't need the reminder."

"You don't mean that."

"Yes, I do," he said, softly and emphatically.

Faith shook her head, refusing to believe him. "We mean something to each other. I know we do, and it's more than just a hole in the ground or the possibility of oil. We're partners in every sense of the word."

"Partners," he said, delivering the word with a snarl. "You're a stubborn woman, Faith. You should learn how to surrender gracefully. We're whipped, can't you see that?"

"No, I can't. It isn't over until both of us concede. I'm still on my feet and I'm not ready to cry uncle."

He pushed his hair back on his forehead with both hands and sighed heavily. "Find another partner."

"No, Houston." She rested her hands on his shoulders, but he brought his up and broke the contact. Blinking in startled confusion, she backed away from him and tried to read past his angry expression. "Don't make me go home alone."

"We have no home," he said slowly, as if to make sure she understood each painful word. "I have some land with a trailer on it. You're a squatter on my land, but it's not your home."

She picked up the money and her purse from the pool table and stuffed the wad of bills back inside her purse. "I'll be waiting for you."

He cursed under his breath and strode past her. Turning, she watched him push past the screen door and climb into his pickup.

"Houston?" Faith turned her back on the curious stares of the men in the other room. She took a few seconds to compose herself, then strode from the pool hall with her head held high.

She'd be the talk of the town tomorrow, she thought. Everyone would be gossiping about the blond woman who'd begged Houston Traynor to come back to her and how he'd walked out on her without a backward glance. By tomorrow, however, she'd be too busy to care that she was the

source of gossip in Mentone. By morning she and Black
Fury would be back in business. Let Houston wallow in his
self-pity! She had better things to do, she thought as she
fought back tears of humiliation and despair.

"Faith?"

Her hand dropped from the handle on her car door, and
she turned and looked at a pool of shadows. Mac stepped
from it and smiled.

"Mac! What are you doing here?"

"My curiosity got the best of me."

"Is the church social over?" she asked, running her fingers under her eyes to check for telltale tears.

"It is for me." He moved closer to her and held out his
hand. "Bonita Kaye has to hang around and help clean up
after everyone. How about if you give me a ride to my
place?"

"Sure. No problem. Hop in." She started to turn away
from him, but his hand cupped her elbow.

"You could spend the night with us, if you like. We'd be
pleased if you did."

She felt her lips tremble as she dropped her car keys in his
hand. "You drive." Impulsively, she threw her arms around
his neck and gave him a fierce hug. "Thanks, Mac," she
whispered close to his ear. "Thanks for being my friend."

He smiled and helped her into the car. "You'll stay at our
place tonight?"

"Yes." She swallowed past the emotion that tightened her
throat. "I don't want to be alone tonight."

Mac closed the door, then went around to the other side
and got in. He slipped the key into the ignition and glanced
at her for a moment. Then, with an uncharacteristic frown,
he started the car and pulled out of the parking space.

"I thought Houston was smart, but he's acting like an
idiot," he grumbled. "What are you going to do now?"

"I'm going to drill for oil." Faith looked at him with a perky grin. "He might be a quitter, but I'm not."

"There you go," Mac said, chuckling. "If you need an over-the-hill roughneck, I'm available, and I work cheap."

"I'll keep that in mind." She turned her head and stared at her reflection in the glass. Her face was superimposed over the full moon, and she smiled sadly. Was waiting for Houston to come back to her like reaching for the moon? she wondered. Suddenly her sadness gave way to aggravation. How could Houston wash his hands of her and their partnership? She'd done everything but get down on her knees in front of him—and she wouldn't do that for *any* man. If he wanted to shuffle off into the darkness and sulk, let him! She wasn't about to cave in now that they were so close to hitting pay dirt!

"To hell with him!"

"Say what?" Mac asked.

She faced front again and puffed out an angry sigh. "To hell with Houston Traynor. He'll come back quick enough when I strike oil. When he does, I'll remind him that he dissolved the partnership and that the oil belongs to me!"

"It's on his land," Mac reminded her.

"But he abandoned the operation!" she countered.

"Well, I guess you can iron that out when the time comes." Mac threw her an amused glance. "Glad to see the sunshine back in your eyes. Gloomy gray isn't your color."

Peering into her microscope, she heard the approaching pickup but didn't look up. By the chugging of the engine and the rattle of loose parts, she knew it was Houston's truck. So he'd finally come to his senses, she thought. It had been two days since he'd stormed out of the pool hall in Mentone.

The truck skidded to a stop and the door slammed shut. His boots scraped across the dry ground, sending pebbles rolling. From the corner of her eye she saw his belt buckle as he stopped beside her.

"Faith?"

She lifted her eyes from the microscope and looked at him with what she hoped was complete contempt. "You're early."

"Early for what?" He glanced around, wondering what the hell she was talking about.

"I haven't struck oil yet. I didn't expect to see you until I had a gusher on my hands."

He rolled his eyes and placed his hands lightly at his waist. "Sarcasm is your strong suit all right.... I've changed my mind. I can't go back on my word, so I'm here to see this thing to the finish."

"What...thing?" she asked, leaning back and folding her arms against her waist.

"The oil deal." He examined her cool expression, knowing he deserved it but not liking it one bit. "What did you think I was talking about?"

"Beats me." She shrugged and eased from the chair. "Most of the time you don't make sense. One minute you're calling me 'partner,' and the next you're telling me to clear out."

"Okay, okay." He held up his hands in surrender. He deserved this, but that didn't make it any easier. "I know I acted like a fool, but I was disappointed and—"

"And I wasn't?" she charged, eyes glinting with blue fire. "If you're going to go off half-cocked every time we hit a snag, you'd better pack it in right now. I've had it with your childish tantrums!"

"Wait just a darned minute!" he fumed. "I had a right to be mad. My sister took off with—"

"You didn't have a right to be mad at me," she cut in with glaring righteousness. "Now you come back with your tail between your legs and expect me to jump for joy." She planted her feet firmly on the cracked ground. "Sorry to disappoint you—again."

He glared at her, feeling like a damned fool to expect her to fling her arms around him and mend his broken promise with her kiss. He should have known better than to predict a reaction from her. She never did what he expected her to do. Never!

"Did you run out of money? Is that why you've come back?"

He forced back his anger with effort. "No, I came back to make good on my promise."

"Which promise?"

"You're not making this easy for me."

"I have no intention of making it easy for you!" she said, her voice rising with each syllable. "I went into Mentone the other night and put my pride on the line, and you stepped all over it!"

"I didn't mean to—"

"Yes, you did!" She pressed her fingertips against his shoulders and pushed against them, wishing she had the strength to knock him flat on his rump. "You humiliated me in front of everyone!"

"Everyone?" he repeated. "I don't recall a crowd." He waved a hand, dismissing the argument. "Let's bury the hatchet and get back to work."

"No, damn you! I want my pound of flesh." A sob broke the last word in two, and she struck out, slamming her fist into his shoulder. He blinked, more from surprise than anything else. "If I were a man, I'd—"

"Well, you're not, so quit trying to act like one." He reached out and pinned her arms to her sides, bringing her up close to him. "I know you're furious with me and you've got every right to want to knock my block off, but you can't. Not that way. If you want to hurt me, then tell me that you hate me. Tell me that you don't want me anymore, and you'll bring me to my knees." He lowered his head until his mouth was close to hers. "Go ahead, Faith. Take your pound of flesh."

"You're disgusting," she said, staring deeply into his eyes, unable to land the final blow.

"I'm an emotional mess without you," he admitted.

"You're stubborn," she said, wishing he would kiss her.

"I'm a sucker for cool blondes with hot tempers."

"You're a quitter," she whispered, her voice becoming soft and yearning.

"I'm a winner when I'm with you."

His mouth clung to hers for a dizzying moment. "You make me so mad," she murmured. "I've never chased a man in my life! I feel like a damned fool."

"You are a fool if you think you're the one who's done all the chasing," he said with a devilish grin. "I'm all tuckered out from running after you, honey."

"You? You haven't—"

His mouth stopped her denial. "I think we've both been running in circles after each other. We need to stop and hold on to what we've got. I've caught you, and you've caught me."

"Have I really caught you?" she asked, still unsure of her effect on him.

"You caught me a long time ago, sweetheart." His eyes darkened and his face set in hard lines of determination. "I've never wanted a woman so much…."

His mouth fastened on hers, and he lifted her into his arms. Her arms stole around his neck as he mounted the steps outside the trailer and opened the door. He tore his mouth from hers to get his bearings, then let her slip from his arms when he saw the subtle touches that had made his home hers—theirs. A colorful afghan was draped across the back of the couch. Silk flowers spilled from a vase on top of the television. Fashion and petroleum magazines were scattered across the coffee table. The smell of pot roast and steamed vegetables wafted from the kitchen.

"I...I've been living here," she stammered, her huge blue eyes searching his face. "I hope you don't mind. I felt safer in here."

He crossed the room and touched a blue ginger-jar lamp. The bulb glowed at his touch, and he looked back at Faith. "This is new." He touched it again and the bulb died.

"You broke the other one during that fight with Jimmy Ray. If you don't like it, I can—"

"No, I like it." He stroked the afghan. "Did you make this?"

"No, my grandmother made it."

"It's pretty." A feeling of security warmed him, and he liked the sensation. He looked around the room again. Home. Home, at last.

"You're upset because I've moved things around and added my own stuff. I'll take them back to my place later," she promised.

"No, don't do that." He smiled, giving her a sign of what he was feeling inside. "They look good in here."

"You really don't mind?"

"Not a bit." He held out his hand and clutched hers as he moved toward the bedroom. "Have you added anything in here?"

"No, except for clean sheets and cold cream soap." She laughed and shook her head. "And my toothbrush and nightgowns. Personal things."

"I like the sound of that," he said, letting go of her hand and drawing back the bedspread to expose the white sheets that were strewn with pink and blue print flowers. "My mother had some sheets like this when I was a boy." He turned to face her, saw the trembling uncertainty in her eyes and pulled her to him. He kissed the top of her head, easing her doubts. "We belong together. Don't move out now that I'm here."

"Are you going to charge me rent?" she asked, smiling as her fingers stretched his shirt until the snaps gave way.

"Nothing you can't afford."

She pressed her mouth against his skin, and her tongue moistened the patch of hair on his chest. His hands moved down her back to cradle her hips, drawing her intimately against him. She had intended to browbeat him and make him plead for her forgiveness. Silly, she thought as she rained kisses across his breastbone. Revenge was silly, especially when she wanted nothing more than to be loved by him.

"So we're partners again?" she asked, pushing down on his shoulders until he sat on the bed, his hands spanning her waist.

"Partners," he murmured, then shrugged out of his shirt while she unbuttoned her blouse. "You're beautiful."

"I've been lonely without you." She flung aside her blouse, smiling when his hands cupped her breasts and his mouth fastened on one taut nipple. "Are you sure we should leave Black Fury alone out there?"

"She'll be fine for an hour or two...or three...or four." He pressed hot kisses across her breasts. Her skin was as smooth and fragrant as he remembered.

The memory of her had kept him up nights. He'd paced the small motel room he'd stayed in while visions of her soulful blue eyes and shimmering golden hair had filled his mind. When he could stand it no longer, he had swallowed the bitter medicine of his pride and had decided to come back to her. He didn't want to live without her. This woman—this beautifully delicate woman—had reduced him to a mass of miserable longing.

He unsnapped her jeans and helped her wriggle out of them. His hands moved down her supple thighs, then back up to remove the last lacy scrap of clothing.

"A work of art," he whispered, and she laughed. "I love to hear you laugh." His gaze lifted to hers. "It's lusty. Comes right from the center of you." He leaned forward and kissed her smooth stomach. A series of quick kisses brought his mouth up to the warm skin between her breasts. He turned his head to let his lips skim across the soft, pillowy curves before his tongue flicked across the nipple that was beginning to harden with desire.

"Oh, Houston." She spoke with the yearning sigh of a spring breeze. "You've turned me inside out...."

He smiled, then took the taut nipple into his mouth and let it quiver against his flicking tongue. Her fingers drove through his hair, her fingernails making his scalp tingle. Switching to the other breast, he feasted for a few moments before she backed away from him.

Faith moved from his embrace and walked around to the other side of the bed to slip beneath the crisp sheet. Houston stood up, quickly discarded his clothes and joined her in the cool bed. Her hands moved appreciatively, almost reverently, across his shoulders and down his back. He was truly a work of art, she thought. Long muscles flexed down his sides as he laughed softly when her teeth nipped his shoulder. She breathed in the scent of him, and no man had ever smelled so good to her. He smelled of earth, wind and blooming things. A man of nature, she thought. A man for all seasons.

For a few moments she mentally chastised herself for giving in to him so quickly, but the following minutes were too full of pleasure for her to dwell on her weaknesses. She had never needed anyone as much as she needed him. Her fierce independence was a paper lion when it came to Houston Traynor.

She wrapped her arms around him tightly, holding him with trembling possessiveness. He seemed to enjoy it. His kisses became more drugging, his hands grew gentler. She brought her legs up to embrace him, and her calves stroked up and down his lower back. He responded instantly, shifting slightly until his lower body corresponded perfectly with hers. One arm moved between them until his searching fingers found and entered her. She moaned, surprised by her own readiness. Houston's breath warmed the side of her face, and his leathery cheek rubbed against hers.

"So nice," he whispered. "You make me feel wanted, and I love the feeling."

When his piercing masculinity replaced his fingers and he moved within her, it felt as if the sun had broken through a bank of clouds to spill golden light in every corner of her being. Faith shut her eyes tightly and surrendered to mindless passion, letting her body respond to each silky stroke of him. She flung her arms around his neck and fell in with his measured rhythm, which increased slightly with each plunge. She quivered around him, filled with the exquisite agony of unleashed desire.

Houston buried his face in her hair, receiving its silky caress and distinct bouquet. No one smelled like her, he thought with a wondrous smile. No one felt like her or made love like her. She was both aggressive and passive, moving from one to the other with ease. One minute she was silently directing him, and the next minute she was soft and clinging and waiting for him to take the initiative.

Houston knew that he could live a hundred years with her and still find mystery in the way she responded to him. Every night would be the first. Every kiss would be a revelation.

Passion began to build until his thighs trembled. A raging storm of emotion whipped through him, and he cried out her name in mindless ecstasy as her arms and legs tightened around him. He kissed her parted lips and murmured her name over and over, and the sound of his voice mingled with her soft, mewling sounds. His love flowed into her, hot and binding. He felt joined to her, body and soul, and he blinked back tears of wonder. She was like a flower opening up to him, and he longed to climb into her and let her petals enfold him. Safe, safe, he thought with a smile. He was safely at home with her.

He relaxed as the tension flowed from him in quivering spasms, leaving him as limp as a rag doll. The events of the past few days flitted through his mind, and he realized how close he'd come to throwing away all this happiness. She had saved his life, he thought as he raised himself up on his elbows and smoothed her golden hair back from her face. Her lids lifted to reveal eyes that glittered with unshed tears of pleasure. He kissed her parted lips, soft and yielding beneath his. The tip of this tongue peeked out to outline her lips and leave a moist path down her chin, across her shoulder and back up to the curve of her neck.

"You're my anchor, Faith." He smiled at her look of surprise. "That shouldn't come as a shock."

"Is being your anchor good or bad?" she asked, her voice weak and whispery.

"Good. Great!" He ran his thumbs across her high cheekbones and took a few moments to appreciate her beauty. "All my life I've wanted someone to hold on to. Thanks for letting me hold on to you. You could have let me drown in self-pity, but you reached out a hand and saved me."

Tears burned the backs of her eyes, and she brought his lips to hers. Oh, he said the most wonderful things! Just when she needed to believe that she had a claim on him—however temporary—he came through with shining colors.

He lifted his head and looked out the window. "How did the samples look?"

"Typically male," she said, smiling to take the edge off her words. "Now that you're satisfied, it's back to business."

"I didn't mean for it to sound that way." He rolled onto his side and drew his fingertips down her arm. His fingers laced between hers, and the simple gesture made him feel secure. "And I'm not satisfied...yet."

"Oh, no!" She sprang from the bed, evading his questing fingers. "I've worked double shifts since you've been gone." She crooked a finger and fixed a stern expression on her face. "Out of that bed, buddy. There's work to be done."

"Come back here," he protested, holding out a hand to her.

"No. It's your shift, so get a move on."

"You're pushy and bossy," he accused with a grin.

"I thought I was a work of art!"

"Only when you're horizontal." He laughed when the pillow slammed into his face.

"You know, I was thinking that we might be drilling in the wrong place," Houston said as he chewed thoughtfully on a dried blade of grass. He tipped back his hard hat and shifted to his side to look at Faith. She was bent over the microscope, and he wasn't sure she was listening to him. She had an uncanny way of tuning him out when she was studying soil samples. He sighed and lay back on the rig platform, enjoying the warmth of the sun. "I was walking off the land the other day. The far northwest corner of my land looks promising. There's kind of a waffle effect."

"Surface geology," Faith said with a drawling sarcasm.

"That's right." He grinned. At least she was listening to him. "I know you don't think I can see oil formations, but I swear there's something under that northwest corner. We ought to take a spin out there later and have another look."

"You can have another look. I can't tell beans by the way the land lays. We're in the right place, anyway. There's something right under our feet."

"I thought so, but now I'm not so sure. How far down are we?"

"Thirty-seven hundred feet."

"That's deeper than I thought we'd have to go."

"What if we have to go down four thousand? If it's there, then we keep going down."

"Mac's wells are all between three and four thousand feet," Houston said, feeling the beginnings of doubt. "We should have struck something big by now. What does the soil sample look like?"

"I'm getting to it."

"What have you been looking at all this time?" he asked, craning his neck around to see her.

"The sample I took right after we hit that little pocket."

"That's history," he said, frowning. "What does the latest sample tell you?"

"Keep your pants on." She sighed and straightened from the microscope. "While I was in Pecos the other day I met with a PATCO geologist and went over my logbooks with him."

"And?"

"And he confirmed my own beliefs. Something is trapped down there. The formation structure is showing holes in the rock, and there are signs of friction."

"I think you're more interested in that dirt than you are in me." He flashed her a grin, then pushed his lower lip into a pout. "It makes me feel left out sometimes."

"Poor Houston." She pressed her hands to the small of her back and swayed from side to side as if to stretch out cramped muscles. "Soil is very interesting. It tells me stories of dinosaurs and hidden treasure."

"I can tell you stories."

"Yes, but if I plant corn in you, will it grow?"

He laughed. "No, I don't think so. Your standards are tough."

"You just don't have enough to offer," she teased.

"Well, if corn turns you on, then I'm all ears." He smothered his laughter when she groaned.

"That was awful," she said, still moaning. "Spare me any more kernels of wit."

"Ouch!" He sat up and enjoyed her smile. "Look who's talking." Sharing her smile and her tender gaze made him want to pinch himself to make sure he wasn't dreaming. "I'm so glad we're together again."

A blush tinted her skin, and she adjusted her microscope. "So am I," she whispered before bending over the instrument again.

Houston sighed, disappointed to have lost her attention again. He watched the red flag tied around the drill stem go up and down, and the monotony of it all seemed to surround him. How many more days would they sit beside this rig and listen to its rattling voice as it chewed up earth? He wanted to take Faith away from this dry land and live it up a little, but for now they were anchored to this spot in Texas.

Suddenly the rig belched, and muddy water slapped Houston in the face. Faith cried out, and Houston was on his feet before he had time to assess the situation. A hose flapped wildly, missing Faith by inches.

"Damn!" He pushed her off the platform, then made a grab for the broken hose as it sprayed everything with muddy water.

"Shut her down!" Faith screamed above the chaos.

He dodged the severed hose, but it smacked his shoulder and sent him stumbling. His hands closed over a lever, and he yanked it hard. Black Fury groaned to a halt, and the ripped hose dropped lifelessly to the platform.

"Damn it! Just what we need." Houston wiped muddy water from his eyes and bent to examine the hose.

"It's a wonder the rig didn't shake to pieces," Faith said, squatting next to him. "This hose is ripped to shreds."

"Sure is." He flung the hose aside and looked at Faith. A grin spread across his face. "You're filthy."

"So are you!" She ran a finger down the side of his face and showed him the caked mud. "Do we have an extra hose?"

"No. I'll have to go into Pecos for one." He sighed and stood up, then helped Faith to her feet. "I'll get cleaned up and go. You stay here with the rig, okay?"

"That's what I do best."

"I guess you're in heaven, aren't you?" He smiled when she shook her head in confusion. "Well, you love dirt and you've got it all over you."

She cuffed him playfully. "Go take a shower. I'm going to clean off my logbooks and equipment. Everything got splattered."

"Right." He started off but stopped when she called to him. "Yes?"

"You'll be back soon, won't you?"

His heart constricted painfully at the doubt in her voice. "Of course I will. I'll be back in time to tuck you into bed."

Chapter Ten

Shading her eyes with her hand, Faith smiled when she recognized the burgundy Mercedes. "Mac," she said, then waved as the car stopped a few feet from her.

"Hello, Mac." She hugged him, then looked at the short man who emerged from the passenger side of the Mercedes. "It's good to see you." She held out her hand to the newcomer. "Cliff Richards, what brings you out here?" She shook his hand, glancing over his tan slacks and pale yellow shirt. What was PATCO up to now? she wondered. Why send out a landman when the company knew that this was a wildcat venture?

"Hello, Faith." Cliff's gaze focused on the hard hat she wore, and he smiled. "What does OM stand for?"

"Oil Millionaire," she said, looking at Mac. "It's a present from Mr. MacQuay."

"That's funny." He laughed loudly, making Faith back away from him apprehensively.

It's not *that* funny, Faith thought with a slight frown. She didn't like Cliff's cocky attitude or the way he looked at the silent rig with a smug grin.

"Got a problem with your rig?" Cliff asked, stuffing his hands into his pants pockets and arching one thin eyebrow.

"Broken hose." Faith shrugged off the trouble. "It happens. Houston went into Pecos for another one."

"LaQuita saw him in Pecos earlier," Mac said. "He was trying to run down the hose, but he was having trouble with his pickup. He sent a message with LaQuita to tell you that he might be later than expected."

"Oh, okay." She swept off the hard hat and ran a hand across her brow. She'd hoped Houston would be back before dark, but the chances of that were slim. She bundled up her hair and put the hat back on. "What's up Cliff? This isn't a social visit, is it?"

"Oh, no." He chuckled and wandered closer to the rig. "I'm on company time. I dropped by the MacQuays, and Mac offered to give me a lift out here."

"That's nice." She held Mac's sparkling gaze for a few moments and knew that something was afoot. "What's on your mind?"

"We thought you might be interested in a lease by now." He turned on his heel to look at her. "Haven't hit pay dirt, have you?"

"We've hit a few patches, but the pay zone is a little further down. As soon as Houston gets back we'll fix the rig and start down again."

"That's the right direction," Cliff said, chuckling at his inane joke. "The question is, is it worth it? You've sunk a lot of money into this hole, and there's a good chance you won't break even."

"That's a matter of opinion," she noted, propping her hands at her waist and growing impatient with Cliff's roundabout offer. He was talking to a former landman, she thought with a spurt of irritation. He didn't have to do this song and dance with her. She knew the routine by heart, and he was well aware of it. "So far you haven't told me anything that I don't already know. Why don't you make your offer so that I can refuse it and you can be on your way?"

Mac chuckled, and Cliff shot him a piercing glare. Mac covered his grin with one hand and moved to the rig for a close inspection.

"Don't be so hasty," Cliff warned, looking at Faith again. "You've always been a level-headed little lady."

"Level-headed, yes. Little, hardly. Lady? It depends on the day and the company I'm keeping." Tapping one booted foot impatiently, Faith stared at him until he looked away. She grasped the tiny triumph and walked to the rig, leaving Cliff to follow her. "PATCO must smell oil or they wouldn't have sent you out here to sweet-talk me."

"Well, the company has a soft spot for you. I guess that the top brass is kind of looking out for your best interests."

Angrily she whirled to face him. "Who are you trying to kid, Cliff? The top brass has never been concerned with my best interests unless they could take advantage of them."

"Faith, that's not true. You're *the* Patton heir. PATCO has always held your family in high esteem."

Faith reined in her anger with difficulty. "Cliff, I know you're just doing your job and repeating what the brass has told you, but it's drivel and insulting."

"Not true." Cliff delivered a cagey smile. "Yesterday Jack Campbell himself said that you were a fine young woman, and Samson Applegate agreed whole-heartedly."

"That's because I sold them my company stock. That's their way of looking after my best interests," she added with biting sarcasm. "I figured that they'd send someone out to kick me while I'm down, but as you can see, I'm not on my knees. I sold that stock because it no longer holds any interest for me. I don't want any part of PATCO."

"But your grandfather founded the company," Cliff objected.

"The company Cain Patton founded died with him, and it was buried with my father."

Cliff cleared his throat and pulled a lease agreement from his back pocket. He unfolded it and held it out to her. "I think that when you look at this generous lease agreement, you'll want to eat those words. PATCO is offering you double what they'd pay for any other site."

Faith shook her head, then grasped the paper when her gaze fell on the company logo. She stared at the new name and felt something shrivel and die inside her. "When did this happen?" she asked, pointing to the top of the page.

"What's that?" Cliff asked, glancing at the lease.

"CAMCO Petroleum, formerly PATCO," she read aloud. "By any chance does CAMCO stand for Campbell Company?"

"Oh, right." He shrugged and offered a sheepish grin. "It's so new that I haven't got used to the new name. I think the board voted on that a few weeks ago."

"So Jack Campbell has finally exorcised the ghost of Cain Patton," she said, handing the lease back to him. When he didn't take it, she grabbed his wrist and forced the paper into his resisting hand. "Good for him. I hope the board is as loyal to him as they were to my father."

"Well, I don't imagine Jack will get into the hot water old Terrence did. He's a clever man."

"He's a coldhearted, back stabbing opportunist and just the kind of man your employers need at the helm. He fits it perfectly. What about Samson Applegate? Is he vice-president now?"

"Yes." Cliff looked perplexed. "How did you know?"

"Elementary, my dear Cliff. Elementary." She laughed at his confusion. "Don't turn your back on them, Cliff, unless you don't mind wearing a knife between your shoulder blades.''

Cliff stared at his feet for a few uneasy moments. ''I can understand your bitterness, but it might be time to put that aside and deal with logic.''

''For the first time in years that's exactly what I'm doing,'' Faith said, feeling as if a burden had been lifted. ''I have had plenty of reasons to be bitter, but I've come to grips with the past and it can't hurt me anymore.'' She held out her arms to encompass the land around her. ''This is my new lease on life. If I don't strike anything but salt water, I'll walk away from here a wealthy woman.'' She regarded Cliff's puzzled expression for a few moments, wondering if she should tell him the details of how Jack Campbell had betrayed her father, then decided against it. Cliff wouldn't be sympathetic, and he'd run back to Jack and tell him everything she'd said. She didn't like Cliff Richards and she wasn't going to give him any information that he could turn into ''brownie points''.

''You should look at this lease, Faith,'' Cliff said, smoothing the crumpled pages. ''It's extremely generous.''

''I don't want the company's generosity. *If* we lease this land to someone, it won't be PA—CAMCO.'' She pulled work gloves from her pocket and slipped them on. ''You'll have to excuse me. I've got work to do, Cliff.''

''I hate to see Traynor milk you dry.''

Faith's head snapped up and her temper flared. ''Get out of here, Cliff, and don't come back.''

''I'll drive you back to my place,'' Mac said, moving from the silent rig to his Mercedes.

''Right.'' Cliff squared his shoulders and stuffed the lease in his back pocket. ''You'll keep us in mind should you actually strike something, won't you?''

''No.'' Faith looked away from Cliff. ''Out of sight, out of mind.''

"Better be going," Mac said as he folded his wiry frame behind the steering wheel.

"Have you got a crew hired to complete the well if you strike?" Cliff asked, looking at Faith over the hood of the car.

"Yes." She flashed him a frown of irritation. "We've put Anderson Oil on alert."

"Anderson?" Cliff laughed derisively. "They're small potatoes."

"Goodbye, Cliff." Faith smiled at Mac. "See you around, Mac."

Mac gave her a sly wink as Cliff slid onto the car seat. "Those Anderson folks are right nice. You made a wise choice. Listen, if Houston isn't back by sundown, you come on over and spend the night at our place."

"Thanks." She backed away from the Mercedes and waved as it pulled away and headed for Mac's oil-rich land. A deep feeling of affection seized her, and she blinked away sentimental tears.

Mac and Bonita Kaye had become important people in her life since she'd embarked on her career as a wildcatter. How long had it been? she wondered, and counted backward. Only a little more than two months, yet it seemed ages ago. Moving to the rig, she thought of how her life had changed completely over such a short span of time.

Before Houston Traynor had swept into her life like a Texas tornado, she had been a self-confident woman who knew who she was and where she was going—or so she'd thought. Laughing at herself, she sat cross-legged on the drilling platform and leaned against Black Fury. Tipping back her head, she watched a flock of crows fly across the cloudless sky. They formed a black arrowhead that pointed south, and their raucous song drifted down to Faith. She pulled the hard hat from her head, letting her hair spill to her shoulders, then clasped her hands behind her head as her thoughts moved in lazy circles that matched her mood. When she pictured the woman she used to be and compared her with the woman she had become, Faith decided she was happy with the latter. She was still self-confident, but not self-centered as she used to be. And she still knew what she wanted, but her goals had changed.

Everything she'd wanted before had been centered on herself, but now they included another person, a very important person, a very special man. Her lips curved into a giddy grin; she couldn't remember ever having been as happy as she was now, sitting beneath a canopy of blue, leaning against a rusty rig and waiting for her man to come home to her.

An old memory floated to her, and she lived it again, feeling the strength of her love for her father as she had on the occasion of her sixteenth birthday. He had thrown a party for two—just her and him. He'd sung "Happy Birthday to You" and urged her to blow out the candles on her cake and make a wish, then he'd given her keys to a canary-yellow Stingray with a dark blue suede interior.

"I wanted to give you the sun and the moon, but I couldn't manage it," he'd told her, kissing her forehead. "So I bought you a car that's as bright as the sun on the outside and as soft as moonbeams on the inside."

He was always buying her things that symbolized his love for her, and he had spoiled her rotten. But he'd spoiled everyone he had cared for. He'd spoiled her mother, his in-laws, his friends and associates. Every Thanksgiving and Christmas he had thrown company parties and had given each employee a ham or turkey. Santa Claus had always made an appearance at the Christmas party and distributed presents to all the children. Faith had been nine years old when she'd finally recognized her father behind that cottony white beard and mustache. Instead of being disappointed, she'd been thrilled. It had seemed logical that her generous father had turned out to be Father Christmas.

She might not have recognized him if he hadn't let the cat out of the bag. Sitting on Santa's lap, she'd been confused when he'd said, "Give Daddy a kiss." She remembered staring into his green eyes, then kissing him soundly when she'd realized that she was the daughter of Santa Claus!

Memories of his unconditional love washed over her, bringing tears to her eyes. Her mother had loved her, too, but not as blindly as her father had. When he'd looked at her, he had seen perfection. Oh, she would never be loved like that again! Why hadn't she fully appreciated it when she'd had it?

She stared up at the sky and saw her father's face. He was smiling the way he did when she walked into a room or opened a present or kissed him good night. He'd always smiled at her in a way that had made her feel precious.

"I love you, Daddy," she whispered brokenly. She wiped away her tears and drew a shaky breath. Sometimes you have to look really hard to see the sterling qualities in a person, she thought. She'd dwelled on her father's faults instead of seeing past them to his tender heart and his need to be loved and respected.

She'd almost made the same mistake with Houston, believing at first all the gossip she'd heard about him. Thank heavens she'd backed off and taken a good, hard look at him to discover his quiet strength, his kind heart and his struggle to shake off a tragic past.

Shifting to a more comfortable position, she closed her eyes and daydreamed about what might happen in the future. An oil strike, a marriage, another oil strike? They were all interesting possibilities, and she embroidered upon them until her daydreams rocked her to sleep.

Awakening slowly, she frowned and wondered why the bed was so hard and scratchy. She reached out for the bedside lamp, and her hand fell limply against wood planks. Faith sat up and rubbed her eyes in a sleepy daze. What time was it? She peered at her watch, forcing her eyes to focus on the illuminated numbers. Eight-thirty! Struggling to her feet, she realized that she had slept for hours on the rig platform. She'd had no idea she was so exhausted, although the past few nights had been uneasy ones without Houston, so it was only natural that her body would eventually rebel against the sleepless nights.

She stretched, and her cramped muscles complained. The sky was no longer blue, but dark and star-studded. A quarter moon perched above her, giving off cold, milky beams. Faith shivered, suddenly feeling small and vulnerable. A jackrabbit raced from the edge of the rig to a concealing scrub brush a few yards away, and Faith knew exactly how defenseless he felt. She moved quickly to Houston's trailer, needing her own veil of concealment from the enveloping darkness.

Drawing herself a hot bath, she stripped off her clothes and submerged her tired body in the rose-scented water, silently thanking Odessa for leaving the vial of perfumed bath oil. Odessa!

Her eyes popped open as she remembered the note Odessa had left for Houston. It was still in her purse, and she made a mental note to give it to Houston as soon as he returned home. What was keeping him. Was he stuck on some lonely road with a broken-down pickup? If he wasn't back by morning, she'd go over to Mac's and use his telephone to call the supply houses in Pecos for any news of Houston. If need be, she'd form a search party. A good man is hard to find, she thought, and she wasn't letting this one get away.

Relaxing in the lapping water, she fantasized about how she and Houston would scout the country for another oil venture. Wildcatting was fun, she decided. It had never been something she'd aspired to, but that was another crucial change in her life. It had opened her eyes to the very roots of the petroleum industry. The oil companies had lost contact with those roots; leases, engineering, logbooks and conferences where decisions were made to continue an operation or abandon it had sucked the blood out of what discovering oil was all about. Instinct, courage, guesswork, despair and the excitement of the unknown were the heart and soul of the oil business. Cain Patton had been a roughneck before he'd struck it rich on a patch of land he'd leased in Oklahoma. He'd built a company by hiring former wildcatters and making them respectable businessmen.

Terrence Hutton had excelled as a petroleum engineering student and had won the heart of one of his classmates, who just happened to be the daughter of Cain Patton. If Terrence hadn't married Emily Patton, he would probably have joined the ranks of wildcatters, but Emily had encouraged him to fall in with PATCO. Looking back, Faith wondered if her father had regretted giving in to his wife. He had never seemed happy being groomed by Cain Patton, and Cain Patton had never been fully satisfied with his son-in-law.

She recalled a snatch of conversation she'd overheard one evening when her grandfather had joined her family for dinner. She'd stood outside the living room and listened to the heated discussion, although her young mind had not fully grasped its context.

"The oil business is a marvelous game of chance," her father had said with a laugh.

"This isn't a *game*, Terrence," her grandfather had bellowed, obviously angered by her father's ingenuous appraisal. "That's always been your problem. You've always thought of this as some kind of parlor game, but this is serious business."

"Calm down, Cain. I didn't mean anything—"

"Sometimes I shudder to think that this company will be placed in your hands when I'm gone."

"If that's the way you feel, leave it to someone else."

"I wouldn't do that to Emily," Cain had barked, then asked, "What did you say?"

"Nothing."

"I heard you mumble something under your breath," Cain had accused. "What was it?"

"I said that Emily would get over it."

"Why should she suffer just because her husband doesn't have the know-how to run a company effectively?"

"Why, indeed?" And then he had spotted Faith standing on the threshold. "There's my girl!" He had beamed and held out his arms to her. "Here's what living is all about, Cain. Say 'hello' to Granddad, Faith."

She had looked up into her grandfather's cool smile. "Hello, Granddad."

"Hello, dear."

Terrence had hugged her and kissed her cheek. "My little sunshine, that's what you are. The light of my life."

Faith sighed away the memory and sat up in the tub. The water had grown cold, and she stood up and toweled herself dry as the vestiges of the memory nagged at her.

There had been such antagonism between her father and grandfather, but she'd never known the extent of it until now. And what of her parents' relationship? Hadn't that suffered over the years? Her father had grieved when her mother had died, but Faith wondered if he had missed her companionship more than he had missed her waning love for him. She had tried to fill the void her mother had left by playing hostess during company gatherings and by supervising the household staff that had dwindled down to nothing over the years. By the time she'd left for college, her father had lived alone without any domestic help. There hadn't been enough money for such luxuries, especially with her college expenses.

She hadn't known how perilously close to bankruptcy her father had been until after his death when his will was read. She'd had to sell the family home to pay off the mortgage and second mortgage. Other than company stock and a trust fund her mother had set up for her, there was nothing left of the Patton/Hutton fortune.

"Poor little rich girl," Faith murmured with a smile of irony. She had finished college and accepted a position with PATCO, and that had been a big mistake. She had always been treated like a second-class citizen at PATCO or, more to the point, a poor relation.

Poor relation. Her brows shot up. That was something she had in common with Houston. He knew the humiliation of being thought of as a wart on an otherwise perfect face. He knew what it was to struggle against unfounded prejudice and preconceived notions of what people *thought* he was and what they *thought* he wanted. They were both fighters, in that sense, and both winners.

Slipping into a pink nightgown, she went to the living room windows and looked out at the night. No headlights broke through the darkness, and she turned away with a long sigh. What now? she wondered. Then, realizing she was hungry, she moved to the kitchen.

After a light dinner of tomato soup and a toasted cheese sandwich, she went back into the bedroom with a few magazines. Sitting in the center of the bed, she began flipping through them while she waited for the sound of Houston's pickup.

It was after midnight when she heard the approaching vehicle. Springing from the bed, she grabbed her dressing gown and put it on as she raced into the living room and threw open the door.

"Houston!" she cried, flinging her arms around his neck. "I was so worried!"

"Didn't you get my message? I saw LaQuita and told her—"

"Yes, Mac told me, but I was still worried that you might be stranded somewhere."

"I was for most of the night. The carburetor conked out and I had to wait for Peewee to fix it. You know how he is— slow as molasses."

"Yes, I know." She pulled him inside. "Are you hungry?"

"And how! No, no." He caught her hand as she started past him to the kitchen. "I'll just throw together a sandwich."

"How about tomato soup and a toasted cheese sandwich? That's what I had, and it will only take a minute to fix."

He shrugged out of his denim jacket and grinned. "I never refuse an offer from a beautiful woman, especially when I feel like a horse that's been rode too hard and put up wet."

"Go get cleaned up and I'll have your supper on the table by the time you're finished."

He nodded and moved slowly toward the back of the trailer. Faith watched him go, amazed at the sweet sensations that flowed through her like a gentle spring. If a mystic had told her three months ago that she would be head over heels in love with a wildcatter and would be fighting back tears of joy at every turn, she would have laughed long and loud. But here she was, puttering around the kitchen fixing her man a late, late dinner while he grabbed a quick shower. Here she was, facing a future of one test well after another and filled with excitement instead of dread. Here she was, purring like a kitten as she daydreamed of him. Love reduced the most staid woman to a giggling girl again, and she was no exception.

How did it affect him? she wondered as she warmed the soup over the burner and waited for the cheese sandwich to toast in the oven. Did he feel so damned good at times that he wanted to cry? No, not Houston, she thought with a shake of her head. But she'd seen the glimmer of something sentimental in his eyes when he'd made love to her, something that came straight from the heart.

She shivered thinking of how he looked when he looked at her, then she laughed softly to herself. Grow up, Faith, she ordered firmly. You're too old to go bananas over a guy! But the euphoria persisted, and she gave in to it. Her mouth curved into a smile and she laughed.

"What's so funny about tomato soup?" Houston asked, entering the kitchen and sniffing the air. "Smells like that cheese sandwich is well done and going on burned."

"Oh, my gosh!" She whipped open the oven door and grabbed a pot holder. "It's burned around the edges. I'll fix another one."

"No, it'll do me just fine." He sat at the kitchen table and threw her a quizzical look when she placed the sandwich in front of him and smiled lovingly. "What?" He glanced at his bare chest and jeans. "What's so amusing?"

"I'm happy." She sat next to him and pushed the bowl of soup closer to his elbow. "Are you?"

"Sure." He glanced at her, shook his head in confusion and reached for a paper napkin. "I'm always delirious when the carburetor in my pickup conks. It makes my day."

She watched him devour the sandwich and realized that he couldn't know she'd spent the last few hours evaluating her past, present and future and had decided that this was the best time of all. Her gaze moved hungrily over his damp hair, wide chest and muscled arms. Her thoughts retreated to the coffee shop in Pecos where Houston had offered her a partnership. She had been interested in pulling the rug out from under PATCO when she'd agreed to the proposition, but that seemed utterly insignifcant now.

"A PATCO landman came out today," she said when he sat back with a satisfied sigh.

"What did he want?"

"He offered to lease the land again. Wasn't that generous of PATCO?"

Houston smiled. "Were you tempted?"

"Not in the least. I ordered him off the land."

Houston's brows shot up. "Was that necessary?"

"I thought it was. It was Cliff Richards, and I despise that guy. I guess the PATCO brass thought I was desperate because I sold—" She stood up as a thought struck her. "I keep forgetting that I have something for you. I'll get it." She went into the living room for her purse and brought back Odessa's note, which she handed to him. "I found this in the glove compartment of my car."

His brows met in a frown when he saw the childish handwriting. "Odessa?"

"Yes. She didn't leave without saying goodbye after all." Faith gathered up the dishes and rinsed them, giving him a few minutes to himself as he read the letter.

"She was always the worst speller I'd ever seen," he said, folding the note carefully. "It reminds me of that joke about the old boy who was such a bad speller that he paid forty dollars to sleep in a warehouse overnight." He chuckled, but it had a false ring to it. "I guess this isn't very funny—especially to you."

Faith sat down again and rested her hands on his forearm. "It's okay. I was mad at first, but I'm over it."

"I wish you hadn't sold your shares in PATCO. I'll never be able to repay you."

"There is no PATCO." She stroked the hair on his arm, loving the feel of him. "They've changed the name to CAMCO."

"What does that stand for?"

"Jack Campbell, chief executive officer and major shareholder. He's a weasel and I want no part of a company that bears his name."

"I guess that was pretty hard to swallow," he said, his voice low with sincerity. "PATCO is part of your life."

"*Was* part of my life." Her fingers dug into his skin. "This is my life now and I have no regrets." She wanted to tell him that she loved him, but she was too afraid. He had made it abundantly clear that he didn't want a commitment until he was financially stable, and she had no reason to think he'd changed his mind about it. "Do you feel better now that you've read Odessa's letter?"

"No, not really." He propped his chin in his hand and stared moodily at the far wall. "I feel like a fool for trusting her."

"You shouldn't."

"You saw this coming. You knew that she and Jimmy Ray were only interested in ripping me off."

"No, that's not true. Jimmy Ray might have thought along those lines, but Odessa went along against her will."

"She's weak willed."

"Yes, but she loves you."

He laughed harshly. "If that's love, I don't want any of it."

"What else could you do, Houston? You had to trust her. If you hadn't tried to help her, you would have disappointed me."

His gaze swept to hers slowly, wonderingly. "How's that?"

"One of the things I admire about you is your kindness, the way you give everyone a chance no matter what their past behavior dictates. It's taught me a valuable lesson."

"What lesson?"

"To be more trusting by giving people the benefit of the doubt."

"You can get hurt that way," he said, looking at her fingers as they moved against his arm.

"Yes, but you can become insulated and uncaring if you don't reach out to people. I'd rather take my chances instead of hiding in a shell while my heart turns to stone."

He smiled and leaned forward to kiss the tip of her nose. "You're in a generous mood tonight."

"I've done some house cleaning," she admitted. "I threw away a lot of emotional garbage today, and I feel lighter than air."

"Tell me about it." He sat back, waiting for her to continue.

"Well, I made peace with my father."

"I didn't know that you were at war with him." His dark eyes searched her face for any hint of emotion.

"I was, in a way. I blamed him for things that were of no consequence. When you love someone, you have no right to try to change him. You have to love him for what he is and not dwell on what he isn't." She glanced at him from beneath the concealment of her lashes and saw that he was regarding her intently. "Dad had a generous nature. He loved people and he wanted them to love him, so he gave and gave and gave, thinking that they would appreciate the gestures, but not everyone did."

"What led up to his death?"

"Bad advice from the notorious Jack Campbell." She took a deep breath and expelled it slowly to calm herself. "After Dad died I was burning with curiosity. I knew that he'd never take his own life if he hadn't been backed into a corner or bitterly disappointed or both. I realized that he had died after a board meeting, and I obtained the minutes of that meeting and read between the lines. I can't prove anything, mind you, but I know in my heart what went down."

"Look, if this is too painful—"

"No, I want to tell you," she insisted, surprised that she *did* want to confide in him. She hadn't told anyone of her findings, but she wanted to tell Houston. She *had* to tell Houston, and then, she knew, she would close the lid on the memories and be done with them. "I knew that Dad intended to meet with banker friends and ask for another loan. My college expenses were taken care of, but there wasn't much money left. When my mother died, Dad spent money like a madman. I guess Mother was the only restraint in his life, and when she was gone he was like a little boy set free in a candy store. Money had never been important to him except for the things it could buy.... I need a drink of water," she said, standing up and moving to the sink.

"Was he from a wealthy family?"

"No, the money was on my mother's side." She drank a glass of water, then returned to her chair.

"It sounds as if your dad didn't believe in saving for rainy days."

"No, he didn't." She shrugged aside her momentary sense of despair. "I wanted to help him, but I didn't know how. He took such pleasure in buying things. It seemed to be the only thing that made him happy."

"So did he borrow the money from the bank?"

"No." She steeled herself against the hatred she felt building within her. "Jack Campbell talked him out of it. This is where my guesswork comes into play. I think that Jack told Dad to borrow the money from the company, assuring him that the board would turn the other cheek and give him time to pay it back. The transcript reveals that Jack reported to the board that there was money missing from the executive account—money unaccounted for—and he asked

Dad in front of everyone if he knew what had happened to the money.''

"In other words, Campbell is the snake in the woodpile."

"That's it on the nose." She fought back the bitterness and continued, "Dad was an honest man, and Jack knew that Dad wouldn't lie to the board or try to cover up."

"Why didn't your dad tell about Jack's bad advice?"

"Jack would have denied it," Faith said with a shrug. "And the board would believe him before they believed Dad. Jack knew he had Dad just where he wanted him. Dad admitted that he took the money for personal use." She swallowed past the lump in her throat and felt her eyes burn. "The board made him an offer: sell his shares in the company and resign, and they wouldn't press charges. He walked out of that board meeting a broken man, and he went straight home and shot himself."

"Oh, honey." Houston shook his head sadly and took her hands within his. "You were at college?"

"Yes. Jack Campbell phoned and delivered the news, leaving out his own deception. Hatred has never been something I'm comfortable with, but I hate that man."

"I don't blame you. I hate him, too, and I've never laid eyes on him." He brought her hands up to his lips and kissed them. "You resented your father for getting into such a mess?"

"Yes." She pulled her hands from his and brushed the tears from her eyes. "I saw only his weakness and forgot about how wonderful he was. He loved me like no one has ever loved me. He called me his sunshine, the light of his life. How could I have forgotten about that? How could I have been so heartless?" She covered her face with her hands and fought back a wave of tears.

"You're not heartless," Houston objected, and put his arm around her shoulders. "Sometimes it takes a while to see things clearly."

"I don't like what I see," she said brokenly. "My behavior was unforgivable."

"Hush, honey." He pulled her up from the chair and walked with her to the bedroom. "You'll feel better after you've rested. You've had quite a night, haven't you?" He turned back the top sheet and helped her into bed, then tucked the sheet around her and kissed her forehead. "You're exhausted."

"You're coming to bed, aren't you?" she asked, needing him beside her.

"Yes." He stripped off his clothes and slid into bed, wrapping his arms around her and letting her rest her damp cheek on his shoulder. "Go to sleep, honey."

Faith closed her eyes and breathed in the clean smell of him. "I hope Odessa dumps Jimmy Ray and uses that money to start a better life for herself."

"Wishful thinking, sweetheart."

"It could happen," Faith murmured drowsily.

"If she dumps Jimmy Ray, she'll find another man to take his place. She's the type of woman who feels incomplete without a man in her life."

Faith nodded sleepily and snuggled closer to the man who had made her life more meaningful, more magical, more everything.

Houston stroked her golden hair and looked down into her lovely face. Poor darling, he thought, then grinned at himself for using endearments so naturally. He'd never been one to spout them before, but they seemed so right with her.

He knew *exactly* what she'd gone through during the hours when he'd been stuck at Peewee's place. He'd gone through the same thing years ago when he'd bounced around the country looking for something to believe in, someplace to belong to, someone to ease his acute loneliness. He had carried his past with him as if it were precious cargo he couldn't do without until he'd finally come to grips with the fact that his cargo was keeping him from the very things he sought.

So he'd had a bad father; so what?

So he'd used poor judgment as a teenager and had fallen into a pot of trouble; so what?

So he had no family to speak of; so what?

None of these things should have kept him from getting what he wanted out of life, he'd realized. Everyone had problems to overcome, and he was no different except that he'd worn those problems around his neck like a chain of guilt. He'd finally ripped off the necklace and made peace with himself and his past. He'd come back to the place where it had all started and had begun to heal slowly until he'd felt whole again.

The only part of his past he had clung to was Odessa, harboring the hope that she'd come to Loving County and strengthen the ties that had been weakened years ago when she'd left home without even saying good-bye.

He thought of her note and the lack of guilt in it. She didn't feel bad about stealing his money. She hadn't changed. She'd been self-centered and thoughtless as an adolescent, and those qualities had become stronger instead of weaker over the years. She was a user and too weak willed to stand on her own feet.

With a heavy sigh he released his last shred of hope where Odessa was concerned. She would always be part of him, but he could no longer dream of a sweet reunion. His arms tightened around Faith, and his heart soared with the realization that he didn't need those foolish dreams anymore because he had someone, someone who deserved all the love he had to give.

Faith hugged the pillow and buried her face in it to escape the noises that pierced her semiconsciousness. Giving up, she lifted her head and stared bleary-eyed at the violet light that told her it was early morning. She moaned and rolled onto her side to see the alarm clock, then she moaned again.

"Houston?" she called in a hoarse morning voice. "It's six o'clock, for crying out loud! Quit making that awful noise and come back to bed, you fool!" She fell back and stared at the ceiling, waiting for him to answer. He didn't. "Houston?" She raised her head and listened. The racket seemed to be coming from outside.

Flopping onto her stomach, she pulled back the curtains and angled her body on the bed until she could see out the window. Houston was scurrying around Black Fury.

Good, Faith thought, letting the curtain fall back into place. He's fixed the rig. We're back in the oil business—rather, the *awl bidness*. She closed her eyes and decided to catch another forty winks, but then her mind caught up with her eyesight and she sprang from the bed and looked out the window again. What was he doing with the blowout preventer? she wondered, watching as Houston tugged at the wheel that would shut the valve off and prevent the well from gushing. Gushing?

"Gushing!" she screeched, grabbing her dressing robe and pulling it on over her nightgown. "Saints preserve us, we've hit something!"

She was out of the trailer in a flash, hopping on one foot and then the other as she pulled on flimsy house shoes.

"What's going on?" she yelled above the rattle and rumble.

Houston straightened from the wheel, his eyes wide with excitement. "Oil!" He was breathless, and his chest rose and fell. "I started her up at sunrise and all of a sudden—Get back! She's going to blow!"

"Blow?" Faith stared at the preventer and realized he'd open it instead of shutting it down. "Are you nuts? Close it off!"

"No." He ran to her, wrapped an arm around her waist and hauled her several feet from the platform. "I want to see it. I want to take a bath in it!"

"It'll be the most expensive bath oil in town, Houston. This is crazy. For heaven's sake, shut it down before—" She bit off the words, realizing that it was too late to do anything about it. The ground trembled as if a herd of dinosaurs were galloping around them, and then a trickle of black liquid spilled over onto the platform.

Faith held her breath, praying that it would be more than a trickle this time. No more false alarms, she thought fervently. No more teasing and tempting. This had to be it. She looked at Houston, and his face was a study in tense anticipation. His arm was still around her waist, solid and motionless like a steel band.

"It'll happen this time," he murmured between clenched teeth. "I feel it in my bones."

"So do I," Faith agreed, swinging her gaze to the bubbling oil, which even as she spoke began to inch higher into the air. "Oh, my gosh, Houston! It's a...a..."

"Gusher!" Houston finished as a plume of crude shot into the air, then knifed back down, sending a shower of oil over them.

Faith held out her hands, letting the oil pool in her palms like a spring rain. She looked up at the black gold and laughed as her feet began to slide on the slippery ground. She clung to Houston to keep upright, and his arms wrapped around her waist. He pulled her up until his mouth could fasten on hers.

"We're home free, honey," he said, laughing, then kissing her soundly again. "This isn't a drop in the bucket—this *is* the bucket!'' He swung her around, lost his balance and fell to the smelly earth with her.

Faith giggled as he sent her rolling in the slimy pool of oil. Her nightclothes clung to her body and her hair stuck to her head in oily clumps. She framed Houston's oil-streaked face between her hands and laughed at the sight of him. He looked like a little boy who had found a big mud puddle, except that this mud was worth thousands of dollars.

''Hello, oilman,'' she said before bringing his mouth down to hers. Oooo! He tasted rich! ''How does it feel to be an independent oil producer?''

He threw back his head and laughed, letting the black drops splatter across his face. ''Terrific! We did it, Faith,'' he said, suddenly sobering as if the reality of it had just slammed into him. ''We did it.''

''Never a doubt,'' she said, smoothing her fingertips across his cheeks as her thumbs moved over the scar on his chin.

''Liar,'' he charged with a grin.

''No, I'm telling the truth. I always had faith in you—in us.''

A wondrous expression bathed his face, and his lips touched hers lightly, lovingly. ''What did I ever do to deserve you?''

''Just lucky, I guess.''

''My luck changed with you.''

She moved her head from side to side in the damp earth. ''There's that silly superstition again. Don't you know by now that we make our own luck—good or bad?''

''All I know is that I never really believed in myself until you believed in me.''

''Oh, Houston.'' She swallowed past the lump in her throat and raised her head to kiss his full lips.

''What, honey?''

She bit her lower lip, unable to put her feelings into words. Glancing sideways at the oil that shot skyward, she laughed. "Will you shut that thing off now? We're wasting money!"

"Spoilsport," Houston said as he scrambled to his feet, then helped her up. "It's just raining pennies from heaven."

"I wouldn't mind if we had a bucket to catch them in." She pushed him toward the platform. "Take care of business, oilman."

Chapter Eleven

Houston pulled a resisting Faith into the shower stall and turned on the water.

"Houston, I'm still dressed!" Faith looked down at her filthy dressing gown and oil-soaked house shoes.

"So am I," he said, plucking at his once white T-shirt. His chest expanded as he took a deep breath. "Smell that!"

Faith obeyed, and the stench of petroleum stung her nose. "I always wondered what success smelled like, and now I know."

Houston peeled off his T-shirt and dropped it to the floor of the shower. "We're filthy—rich," he said with a delighted chuckle as he pushed his jeans down his legs and kicked off his work shoes.

Faith pressed herself against the tiled wall and enjoyed the erotic striptease. She laughed as he hopped on one foot, then the other, to remove his soaked socks, but her laughter dwindled to a long sigh when he stripped off his undershorts and stood naked before her. He turned to face the stinging spray, and Faith couldn't keep her hands from resting on his broad shoulders or from slipping down the curve of his spine.

"Beware of Greek gods bearing gifts," she whispered, then pressed her lips to the patch of skin between his jutting shoulder blades.

"Greek god?" He laughed, letting the water fill his mouth. "I'm just a good old Texas boy, hon."

"I like the way they grow them here in Texas." Her hands moved from his shoulders down his arms to his elbows. "I never thought I'd say that, but I've done more than one about-face since I've met you."

He turned around slowly to untie the sash at her waist. The knot was wet and resistant, but he managed to loosen it and part the soggy fabric to reveal her thin cotton nightgown. The material stuck to her skin, molding to her breasts and leaving nothing to the imagination. Her nipples were erect buds of desire, and the pebbly skin of her aureoles drew his fingers like magnets. His fingertips touched her straining nipples, then moved down to the golden delta below her belly. She trembled but remained plastered against the wall, her hands splayed against the wet tile.

Houston dropped to his knees, caught the hem of her gown and inched it up until it was bunched around her waist. His lips feathered across her stomach, and he pushed the gown up until her breasts were free of it. In a swift, impatient gesture, Faith yanked the gown over her head and flung it over the shower curtain. Her hands cradled his head and pulled his mouth to her breast.

He kissed each tight bud, then rose to his feet. Her mouth sought his, and her tongue dipped inside as Houston drove his fingers through her hair, feeling the residue of oil. Abruptly, he broke free of her storming passion and reached behind her for the shampoo on the shelf.

"Let me wash you from top to bottom," he said, smiling at the flash of impatience in her eyes. "Turn around." He poured a measure of the green liquid on top of her head, then began working it into a lather. She stood motionless, although he could sense her growing irritation, but he was in no hurry. He rinsed the soap from her hair and ran his fingers through the wet strands of gold.

"Let's get out of here and—"

"Wait a minute," he said, cutting off her suggestion as he seized the bar of soap and worked it into a lather between his hands. "What's the hurry?"

"We're wasting water."

He shook his head in amazement. "No matter what state of mind you happen to be in, you still manage to count pennies."

"Force of habit." Her fingers stole down his chest in a wanton appeal. "I like having money a lot better than not having it."

"We're in agreement on that." He ran his sudsy hands along her arms, her waist, her rounded hips, and his blood began to sing a sweet, soaring song in his ears. "We're rich. We don't have to conserve water."

"No use being foolhardy just because we struck a little pool of oil."

"Little pool?" he scoffed, letting the shower spray rinse the lather from her body. "Honey, that well will flow five hundred barrels a day, or my name isn't Houston Traynor."

"Houston Huey Traynor," she amended.

He drew away from her, catching her gaze. "Who told you my middle name?"

"Mac." She grinned and stood on tiptoe to kiss his frowning mouth. "I think it's cute. I think *you're* cute." Her hands moved around him to cup his tightly muscled hips.

"We're clean enough. Let's make love." She reached up one hand and turned off the shower.

"Striking it rich brings out the animal in you," he said, shoving back the shower curtain and grabbing a fluffy towel off the bar. "I like it." He toweled her off, then dried himself, silently laughing at her sighs of impatience and her groans when he insisted on dusting her back and shoulders with fragrant powder.

"Anderson's crew didn't waste any time," he said. "They'll have the well completed in another hour or so."

"We'll stay in bed and out of their way and let them work," Faith said, smoothing the dusting powder over her arms. "Houston, come on." She seized one of his hands and pulled him with her to the bedroom. Falling back on the bed, she propped herself on her elbows and crooked a finger at him. "I've never wanted anyone as much as I want you."

Her rose-tipped breasts beckoned him; her luminous eyes challenged him; her parted thighs welcomed him. Houston pressed a knee into the mattress, and Faith's fingers laced behind his neck. His lips parted to take hers, and his tongue skimmed past her teeth to the dark, moist cavern within. She sucked gently on his tongue, and a flash of white-hot desire bolted through him like summer lightning. Making love had never been so natural, so sensual, so sacred as it was with her, he thought, tearing his mouth from hers and fastening his lips on one hard nipple that seemed to throb against his flicking tongue.

The sheen of excitement glowed on her skin, making her seem golden. Still riding high from the day's activities, Houston couldn't keep from showering her with soft, moist kisses or from touching every tantalizing part of her. She wrapped her limbs around him, clinging to him as if he were an anchor in a tumultuous sea of pleasure. His love for her submerged him in a pool of rich longing, and he wanted nothing more than to transmit the devotion he felt to her.

Faith dug her fingers into his hips, guiding him in a dance of passion. He filled her with a tender toughness that brought tears to the corners of her eyes. For a few precious minutes he was part of her, a true partner in the most intimate way possible. Since he had come home last night she had yearned to let all her barriers crumble, to allow him entrance to the secret chamber of her heart where no others had been before him. As he moved within her with unleashed power, she closed her eyes tightly and let him lift her to touch the clouds and lasso the sun. Heat radiated from his hands, his mouth, his tongue. Spears of sunlight warmed her heart. Flames of desire coursed through her veins. She cried out his name as the world flared around her, then burst into a fountain of burning embers.

They had conquered each other, and love was the ruling power, the victorious monarch.

"See this?" Faith asked, holding up the square of glass that held the first drop of crude Cain Patton had discovered.

Houston turned from the shaving mirror to look at the object. "What's that?"

"A drop of oil from my grandfather's first strike. I think we should get a drop from Double H number one, don't you?"

"It would be a nice keepsake, but I doubt if we'll need anything to remind us of this strike. I've heard that you never forget the first one, and that the others can't compare to it."

"Like your first love," Faith said, smiling into the mirror at him.

"Yes, like your first love," he agreed, dipping his razor into the sink and rinsing it off.

"Tracie Lou?" Faith asked, wanting him to correct her.

"That was a crush, not the real McCoy."

"Oh, I see." She leaned against the door frame. "Let me see...who would be my first love? There have been so many...."

"Are you trying to make me jealous?"

"Is it working?"

"Nope." He dodged her playful punch. "Do you remember when you drove up and I was shaving outside?"

"Yes. I thought you were a rude, hardheaded lone wolf, and I was right."

His brows lifted. "I could take lessons in being rude and hardheaded from you."

"Hah!" she laughed harshly, and handed him a towel. "I was only trying to make you see the folly of your ways."

"You were mouthing company garbage and you know it." He splashed after-shave on the lower half of his face, filling the bathroom with a spicy aroma. "If I'd listened to you, I'd be getting a small percentage of the profits instead of a big slice of them."

"They're putting in the pump," she said, looking out the window at the crew. "I miss Black Fury. I never thought I'd say that!" She turned around and eyed him speculatively as he put on a clean blue shirt. "Are you getting gussied up just for me?"

"I'm getting gussied up because I've got to hit the trail."

"Where are we going?" she asked, backing out of the room as he moved toward the doorway.

"I've got to go into Midland to sign the purchase agreement with Anderson."

"What about me?"

He pulled a battered piece of luggage from the closet and swung it onto the bed. "I'll sign for both of us. You gave me the authorization, remember?"

"Yes, I remember. You've got this all planned, don't you?" She frowned as he began throwing folded shirts and socks into the open suitcase. "I thought we'd come to an understanding, Houston. We're supposed to discuss things before you make plans for us."

He shot her a chastising frown. "That's what we're doing now. We're discussing things."

"But you've already decided! You're packing your suitcase and leaving me with the well again, for crying out loud!"

"Calm down." He held up placating hands. "Damn, you have a quick temper. It goes off like a firecracker."

"Forgive me, but this is a trifle unsettling considering that yesterday you were making love to me and today you're packing your suitcase. Why do you get to go into Midland while I'm stuck here in Loving County? Come to think of it, there's a pattern developing. I've been anchored here a hell of a lot more than you have the past few weeks, and I don't like it!" She shook off his hands when he tried to pull her to him for a hug. "This also reminds me of that scene in my trailer after you made love to me the first time. You couldn't wait to get away from me then, either."

"Here we go again!" He ran a hand through his hair in a fit of frustration. "Will you ever let me off that particular hook? I apologized, and I thought you forgave me."

"I did, but you seem to be giving me a repeat performance."

"Do you think I want to leave you?"

She regarded him for a few moments, taking in his pleading eyes and gentle smile. "Yes."

His smile vanished. "I can't talk to you when you're like this. It's hopeless!" He turned back to the suitcase and began arranging the clothes in it. "If you don't want to stay out here at night, you can stay at Mac's."

"May I? Will you let me do that, boss man?" she asked, her voice dripping with venom. "How long will this business trip last?"

"Several days. Maybe longer."

"To go to Midland? How are you getting there? By way of Seattle?"

He flashed a smoldering glare.

"Why don't *you* stay? I can wheel and deal in Midland."

"Okay!" He slammed the case shut and glared at her. "Fine. You go. I don't give a damn."

She sighed and walked toward the living room. "No, you go."

"Will you make up your mind?" he yelled after her.

"I did," she yelled back, throwing the words over her shoulder like darts. "You're going and I'm staying, so pack your bags and hit the road!" She flung herself onto the couch, seething inwardly at the way he had relegated her to junior partner status. She tipped up her chin and glared at him when he entered the living room.

"Let's eat something before I head out."

She waved toward the kitchen. "Be my guest."

"Faith, honey..."

"Don't 'Faith, honey' me! I'm mad." She stiffened when he dropped to one knee before her. Good grief! Was he going to...?

"Forgive me? I should have discussed this with you before I started packing. It's just that I'm so excited. Aren't you?"

"I was," she murmured, feeling strangely dejected. How silly of her to think he would propose on bended knee at a time like this. All he had on his mind was that stupid well.

He took her hands within his and kissed them. "I'll miss you." He looked up into her eyes, saw the resistance and frowned. "I *will* miss you. Faith, don't send me away like this."

She relaxed inch by inch, suddenly feeling the fight ooze from her body under the onslaught of his charm. She made a comical face at him and pulled her hands from his. "You'll probably run off with some Midland debutante and I'll never see you again."

"Fat chance." He stood up and pulled her to her feet. "You know I'll be back."

"Right. Because the oil is here."

"Because *you're* here." He kissed her and laughed. "You're adorable when you're pouting." He smacked her backside lightly before moving to the refrigerator. "Chili dogs?"

"Chili? What are you trying to do, kill me so that you don't have to share the profits?"

"Okay, then, how about ham and eggs?"

"And biscuits and gravy?"

He winked at her above the refrigerator door. "You've got it, cutie."

As he prepared the meal and chattered on and on about the strike, it occurred to Faith that he hadn't been this talkative since she'd known him. He was a veritable magpie! Chirping about how many hundreds of gallons their well would cough up, what kind of money it would bring in, whom he would contact in Midland, how happy Mac and Bonita Kaye would be when they heard the news. Faith marveled at his running monologue, smiling when he collapsed in the chair across from her and stopped talking long enough to take a big drink of milk. Her smile waned when she realized that he hadn't mentioned her in his plans. Not once.

"Dig in," he said cheerfully as he handed her the platter of ham and eggs. "You know, after we sign the deal with Anderson, I think I'll scout out the prospects near the border."

"What prospects?"

"I've heard that there's still some oil under the ground down that way. The first thing I want is a new pickup. My old pile of nuts and bolts has about had it." He paused to shovel some food into his mouth. "And I need some new clothes. I haven't bought any clothes in two years. I want a new trailer, too."

"What's wrong with this one?"

"Nothing." He shrugged. "I just want a new one."

Faith scrutinized him carefully. Was that greed lighting his eyes? Had the oil strike created a monster?

"You haven't said one thing about where I fit into all of this," she noted dryly.

"Where you...?" He swallowed hard, then grabbed his glass of milk and drank most of it. "I'd like to buy you a brand-new car and a mink coat. How does that sound?"

"Like I'm your kept woman." She flung her napkin into her plate and stood up. "I don't want you to buy things for me! You sound just like my father. Every time I had a problem or needed advice, he bought me something, as if that made everything better. Well, it doesn't! Money can't buy everything or everyone, Houston." She stared at him, feeling hurt and disappointed. "It certainly can't buy me."

"Who said I was trying to buy you?" he asked, rising slowly to face her. "I thought I already had you."

"No. You have to *earn* me."

"You're talking crazy again, and I'm fed up with it!" He flung aside his napkin and stalked toward the bedroom. "It's a good thing I'm leaving. Maybe by the time I get back you'll be in a better mood."

"And maybe I won't be here at all!"

He whirled to face her, his eyes narrowed to slits of rage. "What do you want from me? Why are you forcing this showdown?"

"I don't know." She pushed her hair back from her face in a weary gesture. "I guess I'm feeling...insecure. I just don't like it when you talk about buying me things as if I'm a child who'll forgive you if you buy me a new doll.''

"I didn't mean it that way and you know it."

"I know." She shrugged and sat down in the recliner. "I'm on edge, that's all." Faith looked at him warily when he came back into the living room with his suitcase in hand. "I guess this is goodbye."

"Faith, stop it." He grabbed her hands and hauled her up and into his arms. His mouth moved against hers, creating a delicious friction. "Do you think it's easy for me to leave? I'd love to spend two weeks in bed with you, but the sooner we get the contract signed, the sooner we can wrap things up here."

"Right." She smiled, trying to appear brave and cheerful. "Hurry home."

"I'll be back before you know it." He let her go and opened the front door. "I'll stop by Mac's before I head for Midland. He's been awful good to us."

"Yes, he's a good friend."

"I'm going to offer him a two percent override for selling me this land below appraised value. He didn't have to do that, and he sure didn't have to give me the mineral rights to it."

"Two percent?" Faith touched Houston's forearm in a warning gesture. "Houston, don't go promising things before we've settled up everything here."

"Settled up? Don't tell me you disagree with offering Mac and Bonita Kaye a cut after all they've done?"

"I just don't want you to promise anything to anybody until we've had time to discuss it thoroughly, and while you're in Midland don't buy anything we don't need."

"You don't trust me, do you?" He backed down the steps, breaking contact with her.

"It's not a matter of trusting...."

"Yes, it is. You think I'll throw money all over town like a slaphappy fool. It's my money, too!"

"Fine, just don't spend my share of it!"

He shook his head slowly, and a sad expression came over his face. "You're a stingy woman, Faith."

"I'm not a spendthrift," she corrected.

"And I am?" He pulled the brim of his Stetson lower. "Maybe you should think about getting another partner while I'm away. Somebody you can trust."

"Houston, don't go—" She bit off the words as he swung himself into the pickup. "Don't go away mad," she whispered as the pickup rattled down the road. Could she help it if she worried about him? Most of the time she trusted him, but sometimes he scared her with his talk of giving away two percent overrides and buying this and that with money he didn't even have yet. Just like Daddy, she thought, then slammed the front door and wished she could kick herself from here to Midland and back.

A week later Houston hadn't returned, but the Anderson pump was in place. Other company officials had stopped by but had hurried away when Faith had told them that Anderson had been given a production contract. News of an oil strike crisscrossed the area, and most of their neighbors stopped by to view the pump and congratulate Faith. She felt as if she were part of the community and invited each visitor inside Houston's trailer for a glass of iced tea and friendly conversation. It had helped to ease her loneliness, but at night she had pined for Houston like a lovesick fool.

Standing outside, Faith watched the pump's pony head move up and down like a huge rocking horse. She wondered when Houston would return. She hadn't expected him to be gone a week.

"I'll be on my way now," Bill McCormick, one of the Anderson Oil employees, said as he moved from the pump toward Faith. He mopped his brow with a handkerchief, checked over some notes on his clipboard, then tucked his handkerchief back into his hip pocket. "She's going at a good clip. Lots of oil under that ground, Miss Hutton."

"Call me Faith," she said, emerging slowly from her reverie. "Bill, didn't you say that you saw Houston in Midland a few days ago?"

"Yes," he said slowly as if recalling the incident. "He said he was going to check out another business opportunity before he'd be back here. Getting worried about him?"

"Sort of. I expected him back before now. He said he was looking into another business opportunity?"

"Sure did." McCormick winked at her good-naturedly. "He said he didn't have to hurry back here since you were the decision-maker."

"He said that?" Faith pulled her lower lip between her teeth and bit down hard, but it didn't assuage her guilt. Staring at her folded hands, she grappled with her own shortcomings: acid tongue, thoughtless remarks and, most important, her inability to trust the man she loved with all her heart.

"That's right," McCormick assured her. "Traynor said to deal with you. He said that you held the purse strings."

Faith flinched, feeling the sting of Houston's verbal whip. "He's a modest man," she said softly. "Houston Traynor and I are equal partners. I can't make any business decisions without consulting him first."

McCormick got into his car and rolled down the window. "He'll be back soon. Congratualtions! That's a mighty feisty well you have there, Miss—Faith." He smiled and put his car in gear. "Faith—that's a pretty name."

"Thanks. 'Bye now." She smiled and waved to him as he drove away. She had to admit that she was sorry to see him go. Any company—even that of a stranger—was better than none at all.

Alone with her thoughts, she yearned for the hungry months when she and Houston had been on solid footing. They had needed each other. It had been so lovely and uncomplicated before they had tapped that vein of black gold, she thought as she wandered from room to room in the quiet trailer. Falling in love with Houston Traynor had been fun, but the fun was over.

Was Houston scouting east Texas for another drilling site? The thought diminished Faith's hopes of a continued partnership. If Houston was looking for another business venture without her, then that could only mean one thing— their partnership was dissolving. By the time he returned there'd be nothing left to do but shake hands and part company.

She had hoped he hadn't meant what he'd said about finding another partner, but with each passing day she realized that it hadn't been an idle threat.

What would she do without him? she wondered. Work for another oil company? Try her hand as a solitary wildcatter? Nothing appealed to her. She'd even grown to hate the sight of the well, because it reminded her of a golden time that was no more.

Finding herself in the bedroom, Faith looked out the window at the oil pump, and her heart skipped a beat when she saw a woman wobbling on high heels as she picked her way along the rough terrain.

"Odessa!" she whispered.

Odessa's long legs were poured into green satin slacks, and a yellow tube top hugged her small, pointy breasts. Her hair, as usual, was a mass of concrete curls on the top of her head. She carried a huge purse and a small overnight case. As she passed the well, she stopped for a moment to study the pump in thoughtful contemplation, and Faith could almost see the dollar signs swimming in Odessa's pale blue eyes.

"Trouble," Faith whispered to herself as she moved from the window. "Just what I need—more trouble."

Gathering her composure, Faith went to the front door and opened it before Odessa had a chance to knock. Odessa's upraised fist tapped the sultry air, and she grinned sheepishly at Faith.

"Surprise," Odessa said, lowering her hand to clutch her overnight case again.

Faith's composure slipped when she saw the dark, ugly bruise that spread along Odessa's jawline. Her lower lip was puffy and painful-looking.

"What happened to you?"

Odessa seemed confused for a moment, then she laughed. "Oh, you mean this fat lip of mine?" She shrugged helplessly. "Jimmy Ray and me got into it and split up."

"That's good news—that you split up, not that he hit you," Faith hurried to explain. She moved back, rocking her head to one side. "Come in out of the heat."

"Don't mind if I do." Odessa trudged up the steps and dropped her overnight case and purse to the floor. "Ah! I bummed a ride to the turnoff, but I had to walk the rest of the way." She flexed her fingers and examined the calluses around them.

"Where have you been?"

"Dallas, mainly." She fanned her face with one hand and went to the air conditioner. Bending at the waist, she let the air from the vents blow into her face. "That feels good," she said, kicking off her high heels. "That feels better than good."

"Houston isn't here," Faith announced, and Odessa straightened slowly and turned to face her. "He's in Midland on a business trip."

"That right?" Odessa tugged down the hem of her tube top. "When will he be back?"

"I'm not sure. Soon, I hope."

"I guess I can wait."

Faith turned quickly so that Odessa wouldn't see her wince of frustration. *Wait?* She was going to *wait* for Houston? Faith sighed, thinking gloomily of hours in Odessa's company. Solitude seemed like heaven now.

"Got something cold to drink?" Odessa asked.

"Iced tea, water or milk?"

"No beer?"

"No beer." Faith threw her a cutting glance. "And no cigarettes."

Odessa folded her arms across her breasts and measured Faith with narrowed eyes. "You don't like me much, do you?"

"Whatever gave you that idea?" Faith asked with mocking sarcasm. "Why wouldn't I like you? Just because you dumped on your own brother and stole my money and my car doesn't give me any reason not to like you."

"You got your car back. I saw it parked outside."

"That doesn't alter the fact that you stole it."

"Jimmy Ray stole it," Odessa corrected.

"And you just watched?" Faith countered, refusing to give Odessa an inch because she knew from experience that the woman would take it and more.

"What was I supposed to do?" Odessa asked, throwing out her hands in complete helplessness. "I loved the guy!"

"And what about your brother?"

Odessa's hands fluttered to her sides. "Him, too." Her eyes widened as if she'd been struck with a resounding thought. "See what a fix I was in? Damned if I did and damned if I didn't. It was a no-win situation, don't you see?"

"No, I don't see." Faith shook her head, baffled by the other woman and her view of life and love. "Are you hungry?"

"Does a dog have fleas?"

Odessa laughed as if she didn't have a care in the world, and for a split second Faith envied her. Oh, to be so shallow that you could cast off your woes with a flick of your painted nails, Faith thought as she opened the refrigerator and took out a container of leftover vegetable soup. She dumped the contents into a saucepan and put it on the stove.

"I made vegetable soup yesterday," she said, turning on the burner. "There's some cheese and crackers, too."

"Yummy," Odessa said, dropping into one of the kitchen chairs and propping her feet on another. "I'll have iced tea with it."

Faith glanced at her, feeling a mixture of irritation and admiration. She had to hand it to Odessa Lynn Gibson, Faith thought. The woman had no shame, but a lot of guts. She plunked down a glass of tea in front of Odessa, feeling like a handmaiden to a queen.

"Thanks, hon." Odessa drank some of the tea and sighed. "Hits the spot. I was as dry as the Sahara." She sniffed the air. "Soup smells good. Did you say Houston was on a business trip?"

"Yes." Faith drew herself up, waiting for the inevitable.

"I noticed that the well was plugged. You hit pay dirt!"

"Yes."

"Good for you!" Odessa swung her feet off the chair and twisted to face Faith. "I guess you two are rich now, huh?"

"Not yet. We have a lot of expenses. After we pay off everything we might not have much left."

"Oh, go on!" Odessa batted the air with one hand. "You don't have to sing the blues to me. I know you're bound to have money left when all's said and done."

"Is that why you're here?" Faith asked, deciding to drive right to the heart of the matter. "Do you need money?"

"Yes, but not from you." Odessa pushed her lower lip into a pout, then winced with pain. She touched her swollen lip gingerly, and her fingers trembled. "I'll ask Houston for it."

"Houston's money *is* my money, Odessa."

"Since when?" Odessa sat up, squaring her shoulders. "You two ain't married or nothing."

"We're in business together. We pooled all of our money, and you took a lot of it."

Odessa turned her back on Faith. "I'll talk to Houston about it. I don't need any lectures from you."

"I don't intend to deliver any," Faith said, pouring the bubbling soup into a bowl and placing it in front of Odessa. "I'm sure my words would fall on deaf ears."

"I ain't deaf and I ain't dumb." Odessa slanted a sly glance at Faith. "And I know that you and Houston make more than business together. Who do you think you're fooling? Not me!" She giggled and blew at a spoonful of soup. "I know when two people are sharing the covers."

Faith dropped into one of the chairs and lifted her hand to her forehead, where a dull ache had taken root. The woman was giving her a headache! Sparring with Odessa was like shadow boxing. Just when she thought she'd made contact, Odessa sidestepped her. A smile of irony tipped up one corner of her mouth, and she realized with dismay that she was more amused by the woman than angry at her.

"I've got to hand it to you, Odessa," Faith admitted grudgingly. "You've got backbone. I never thought for one second that you'd have the gall to come waltzing back here and plop yourself down as if nothing had happened, but here you are and here I am waiting on you like a first-class *schlemiel*."

"*Schlemiel?*" Odessa wrinkled her nose, then carefully slipped another spoonful of the savory soup between her bruised lips. "I guess you're used to going first-class, aren't you?"

Faith rolled her eyes. The woman only heard what she wanted to hear, she thought. Amazing!

"Me, I've never even flown in one of those big planes. I took a spin in one of those planes they use to spray crops once. It was great."

"Odessa, don't you feel the least bit ashamed for stealing from your own brother?"

She regarded Faith thoughtfully for a few moments, then lifted one shoulder in a shrug. "I guess Houston's pretty mad at me."

"He's hurt, not mad. He wanted to trust you."

"Isn't he something?" She tried to smile, but her lower lip couldn't manage it. "He took care of all of us when he was little."

"What do you mean?"

"Mama was sickly, and Houston waited on her hand and foot, and Daddy was a handful. Houston tried to keep him sober enough to work, and that was a full-time job, I'm here to tell you." She giggled, then finished off the soup. "And me? Well, I was as wild as a March hare. I'd slip out and meet some old boy, and Houston would try to cover for me when Daddy found out I was gone."

Faith hung on Odessa's words, imagining a young Houston with responsibilities far too immense for a sensitive boy.

"The night I left for good was a night I'll never forget. I'd been out with a guy and I came home real late. Daddy was waiting for me with his belt in his hand." She shivered and rubbed her hands up and down her thin arms. "He was drunk and mean. Mama was dead by that time, so there wasn't anybody to stop him from beating on us. I can remember him standing in the middle of the living room, his hand wrapped around the strap of his belt and the buckle tapping against the floor. I knew that he was going to beat the living daylights out of me, and I started screaming and crying."

Faith felt her eyes widen with horror, and she shuddered at the picture Odessa had painted in her mind.

"Houston was just a tyke, but he charged at Daddy, tackled him around the knees, and they both fell to the floor. Houston yelled at me to run, and I did! I've thought about that over the years. Houston was a brave kid; a lot braver than me. I shudder to think what Daddy did to him after I left."

"Oh, Odessa..." Faith shook her head, trying to dispel the terror from her mind. "What he must have gone through? I knew it was bad, but I never imagined..." She stood up and paced to the window. "How could you have betrayed him after all he's done for you?" When Odessa didn't answer, Faith turned to face her again. "*How*, Odessa? It makes me furious!"

Odessa looked away from Faith's accusing glare, and tears sprang into her listless eyes. "I'm not strong like you. I know that."

"Strength has nothing to do with it."

"Oh, yes it does!" She plucked a napkin from its holder and dabbed at the corners of her eyes. "You can walk through this world all alone, but I can't. I need a man in my life. I always have and I always will. I'm just that kind of woman."

"You can change," Faith said.

"No." Odessa sniffed and wadded up the napkin. "I don't want to change. I like having a man around."

"So do I, but not at the exclusion of everything else."

"Well, that's the difference between us. Life ain't worth living unless I got me a man. I don't expect you to understand." She laughed shortly. "We're from two different worlds. I don't feel like I'm worth a nickel unless I've got a man to love me."

"Houston loves you," Faith reminded her sternly.

"Sure he does, but it's a different kind of love. I want to be loved as a woman, not as a sister." She spread out her hands in an enveloping gesture. "You feel good 'cause of your career and success. I feel good in knowing that a man finds me irresistible."

Faith sighed wearily. "It seems like a sad existence to me. What's it gotten you besides bruises and pain?"

"Hey!" Odessa laughed, and her eyes cleared. "Wasn't that great when Houston punched out Jimmy Ray?"

"Violence in any form sickens me. That's *another* difference between us." The sound of a vehicle outside made Faith turn to look out the window. "It's Peewee Porter."

"Peewee!" Odessa sprang from the chair and patted her hair. "I haven't seen old Peewee in years and years!"

Faith sighed. "Here's your chance." She went to the door and opened it as Peewee got out of his pickup. "Hello, Peewee. What brings you out this way?"

"Got a message from Houston for you." He paused to reposition the tobacco in his mouth. "He called earlier and said he'd be home late this evening or tomorrow morning."

"It was good of you to come out here and tell me." Faith felt Odessa squeeze beside her, and she stepped to one side. "Won't you come in for some iced tea?"

"Well..." Peewee squinted, then his eyes widened. "Lo and behold! Is that Odessa Lynn, the belle of Loving County?"

"Sure is!" Odessa giggled and covered her swollen lip with her hand. "Peewee Porter, how in the world are you?"

"Can't complain." Peewee grinned and glanced at Faith. "I'd like that glass of tea, ma'am."

"Come in." Faith moved from the door into the kitchen to pour the tea while Odessa linked her arm in Peewee's and pulled him into the house.

"I didn't think you'd recognize me," Odessa said breathlessly. "It's been a month of Sundays since I saw you."

"I'd recognize you anywhere," Peewee said, sitting in one of the kitchen chairs. "What happened to your lip?"

"Oh, I got in the way of a fist. It's nothing."

Faith lifted her gaze to the ceiling in mute frustration. It's nothing, she thought. Happens all the time. Just one of life's little jolts. She placed the glass of tea at Peewee's elbow.

"Thanks, ma'am," Peewee said, barely able to tear his gaze away from Odessa long enough to glance at Faith.

"You're welcome."

"You going to be around for a while, Odessa?" Peewee asked, hope soaring in his voice.

"I might." Odessa fluttered her heavily mascaraed lashes at him. "I'm footloose and fancy free right now. I was thinking of going into Pecos, but I don't have a ride."

"I'll take you," Peewee offered before Faith could mention that she would have been more than happy to have taken Odessa into Pecos. "Be glad to give you a lift."

"Oh, that's so sweet of you," Odessa purred, placing a hand on his sleeve. "You always were a sweet old thing. Did I hear that you took yourself a wife?"

"No." Peewee blushed and stared at Odessa's caressing hand. "I never got hitched."

"Hitched," Faith murmured with distaste, but neither Odessa nor Peewee seemed to hear her. They were obviously caught up in their own world.

"You must be the playboy of Pecos," Odessa said with a lilting laugh. "I bet you've got the women lined up at your door."

Faith lifted a hand to hide her smile as her gaze swept over Peewee's roly-poly body clad in grimy overalls and a faded red T-shirt. The playboy of Pecos excused himself to spit tobacco juice out the door, then returned to Odessa's admiring gaze.

"Where was Houston calling from?" Faith asked, breaking into the seduction.

"Uh...uh..." Peewee seemed at a loss.

"Dallas? Midland? Mars? Pluto?" Faith prompted, trying to help him form one word.

"Muleshoe," Peewee said, snapping out of his trance for a few moments. "Muleshoe, that was it."

"*Muleshoe?* What in the world was he doing in Muleshoe?"

"Uh...I dunno," Peewee said, slipping under Odessa's spell again.

"We'll be settling up with you soon, Peewee," Faith said, glancing from him to Odessa.

"Uh...right."

"When Houston gets beck we'll go through our account books. We haven't forgotten that we promised you a one percent override." Faith smiled knowingly when Odessa's eyes lit up.

"One percent override?" Odessa echoed, and her fingers bit into Peewee's arm. "Why, Peewee! You're a wheeler-dealer!"

"Uh...I do okay, I reckon."

"I reckon so!" Odessa let her fingers trail down his arm and across the back of his beefy hand. "How did I let you off the hook? You know, I never got you off my mind."

"You didn't?"

"You didn't?" Faith asked in unison with Peewee.

"I always wondered what would have happened if I hadn't taken off with that Tommy. You remember Tommy Smith, don't you?"

"Uh...I think so."

"He was a roughneck." Odessa flicked a hand. "But he was no good. Left me high and dry in Laredo."

"Can't imagine anyone leaving you," Peewee muttered, blushing a beet red. "You ready? I gotta get back to my business."

"Sure, hon!" Odessa patted her platinum curls and smiled at Faith. "Thanks for the soup. I hate to eat and run, but..."

"Houston will be sorry he missed you," Faith said without conviction.

"I'll drop him a line." Odessa rose from the chair and gathered up her belongings, then handed them to Peewee. "Here you go, big boy."

Peewee nodded at Faith and lumbered out the door with Odessa's overnight case and huge purse. Odessa slipped on her high heels and followed him, her steps light and carefree, but she paused on the threshold and turned back to Faith.

"You're a nice lady, and I hope you and Houston stick together. He needs a good woman, and whether you know it or not, you need a good man." She sighed and looked out at Peewee. "Now that old boy out there isn't the best-looking guy in Texas, but he's good at heart, and I'm a lady in distress who needs a gentleman right about now."

"Not to mention a one percent override," Faith noted grimly.

"Oh, hell!" Odessa laughed, and the sunlight made the bruises on her face stand out against her pale skin. "He won't give me his money. He's slow, but he ain't stupid." She looked down at her stiletto heels for a moment. "Tell Houston...tell him..."

"I'll tell him," Faith said, letting her off the hook.

"Thanks, hon." Odessa tipped up her chin and delivered a radiant smile to Peewee. "Coming, sugar!" She pranced down the steps and let Peewee help her into the pickup.

Faith waved at her from the doorway and laughed to herself when Odessa slid across the seat to snuggle against Peewee as the truck moved down the road.

"What a character," Faith murmured, closing the door. Poor Peewee. Faith giggled, then laughed at the memory of Peewee's flustered state. Old Peewee was in for the ride of his life! He'd be completely besotted by the time he reached Pecos.

She went into the bedroom to change, remembering that she had promised to have dinner with Mac and Bonita Kaye. Her spirits lifted when she recalled Peewee's message. Houston would be home soon—for better or for worse.

Chapter Twelve

Faith sat on the front porch with Bonita Kaye and soaked in the sultry beauty of a west Texas night. Earth and sky appeared to meet and end, creating a fetching illusion as stars seemed to sit on the ground and the moon sailed only inches from the treetops. She smiled thoughtfully and remembered a time not so long ago when she would never have used complimentary words to describe this dry, flat land. It felt like home now, and she liked it.

The air was heavy and still, but every so often a surprisingly strong gust of wind blew up out of nowhere. It was late, she surmised. Probably past ten. Mac had gone to bed, but Bonita Kaye had persuaded her to sit on the porch for a while before she headed back to the Double H. Bonita Kaye had served savory enchiladas and refried beans for dinner, then topped it off with pecan pralines. Faith had eaten too much but hadn't been able to resist the homemade sweets. She'd eaten two and hadn't argued when Bonita Kaye had insisted that she wrap up a couple more to take home with her.

"I should leave soon," Faith said, turning her head in a lazy roll against the back of the metal chair to look at Bonita Kaye. "Houston might be back tonight."

"He'll probably show up in the morning," Bonita Kaye reassured her. "Probably stopped off somewhere tonight to get some shut-eye."

Faith nodded absently, feeling the crowding of dread in her mind. She wanted to see him again, of course, but she was afraid. What if he returned only to finish off their business together and hit the road again?

"It's sticky out tonight," Bonita Kaye said, fanning her face with a folded newspaper. "The sky is a funny color. Kind of greenish." She examined the far horizon for a few moments as the newspaper fan stirred her white bangs. "You seem troubled tonight, Faith. Want to talk about it? Did Odessa upset you today?"

"No, not really." Faith sighed away her confusion at the mention of Odessa. "I've given up trying to figure her out. I guess you've just got to accept her the way she is and and live with it."

"Have to do that with most people," Bonita Kaye said, glancing at Faith's frowning regard of the dark horizon. "Are you feeling kind of at a loss now that the well has come in?"

"Well, the bloom is off the rose."

"You talking about the well or Houston?"

Faith smiled, realizing that Bonita Kaye had headed her off at the pass. "You're just like Mac. I swear that you and Mac can read minds."

"We can read people. Most of them are open books if you look hard enough. I'd guess that you and Houston had a tiff before he left."

"Good guess." Faith laced her hands behind her head and decided to get everything off her chest. Bonita Kaye was a wise woman, and Faith trusted her advice. "I said some things that I meant, but not in the way Houston took them. I was upset because he was leaving without discussing it with me. He'd just decided to take off while I kept the home fires burning. It drives me crazy when he takes me for granted!"

"Men do that," Bonita Kaye noted with a shrug of her round shoulders.

"And I hate the way he decided things without discussing them with me. He said...well, what started it all was when he said he was going to buy this and that and—" She paused, suddenly hating herself for her next admission. "And offering you and Mac a two percent override because you've been so good to him." She sat up straight, her back leaving the chair as she twisted in the chair to turn appealing eyes on Bonita Kaye. "Not that I object to that, but it was the way he told me what he was going to do instead of asking my opinion first. Do you see what I mean?" She held her breath, hoping that the other woman wouldn't be offended.

Bonita Kaye nodded slowly, and moonlight skimmed across her white hair. "That kind of talk scared you?"

"It terrifies me. Oh, Bonita Kaye, it was so lovely and uncomplicated before we tapped that black gold. We had fun falling in love, but then everything got tangled up." She tipped back her head to accept the caress of a breeze. "All this is a holdover from my years with my father. He spent money like it grew on trees. When Houston started talking about all the things he was going to do with the money we'd make, it brought back all the uncertainty I lived with when I was growing up. Mother and I never knew from one day to another if we'd have enough money to pay the bills. We were mortgaged up to our eyeballs." She laughed, but it had an insincere ring to it. "We lived in a mansion, but our checks bounced. It was a weird, chaotic life, and I don't want to repeat it."

"You know that sister-in-law and brother I told you about? The ones who visited once and won't come back?"

"Yes," Faith said, confused.

"They're rolling in money, but they're as tight as the bark on the log. Do you know that they have a luxury condo in Miami and they *pick fruit* along the way from Corpus Christi to Miami to pay their car fare and expenses?" Bonita Kaye laughed incredulously, then clicked her tongue. "They've got as much money as me and Mac, but they're afraid to spend a dime."

"Yes, but—"

"So I guess there's extremes in any situation," Bonita Kaye finished, turning serious eyes on Faith. "The trick is to find a happy medium. Something you *both* can live with. Of course, that means you've got to compromise. Sometimes you've got to bend just short of breaking."

Faith eyed Bonita Kaye with a growing awareness, then laughed softly as she realized she'd walked right into the other woman's trap. "It might be too late," she said, sighing. "When Houston left I got the feeling that he wanted to end our partnership."

"And you believed that?" Bonita Kaye asked, giving her a chastising frown. "We all say things we don't mean, honey." She set her chair to rocking back and forth, and it made a creaking noise that carried across the plain. "Let me tell you about Texans. Texas men are like this land. They need wide-open spaces to roam in, and they've got hearts as big as the prairie." The rocker sang its high-pitched song for a few moments before Bonita Kaye broke in. "Take my Mac, for instance. Every so often I have to put my foot down to his free-hearted giving, but I wouldn't have him any other way. I wasn't too thrilled with him spending all that money on that car for Nita's girl, but then I saw the smile on his face when Nita's daughter saw that hunk of gold metal, and it was worth it. Mac's got a great smile."

"Yes, he sure does." Faith said, seeing Houston's smile in her mind and longing to be with him.

"As for me and Mac accepting Houston's offer of percentages, we won't, but we'll be grateful for the feelings behind it."

Seized with remorse, Faith covered her face in her hands. "I feel like such a shrew!"

"There, there, honey," Bonita Kaye said soothingly. "I'm not pointing a finger at you. I just want you to realize that Houston is generous, but he's not foolhardy. It sounds like he was riding high the other day and was talking off the top of his head. I know that young man, and he'll pay off his debts before he spends a nickel on himself."

"I know he will."

"Now don't be too hard on yourself," Bonita Kaye said, halting the motion of the rocker. "You're right in wanting him to talk things over with you. Sounds like he's been alone for so long that he's in the habit of doing what he wants, when he wants, with no regard for anybody else."

"He's not that thoughtless...." She smiled, realizing that she was defending him, but what Bonita Kaye had said struck a chord of understanding within her. "I know how difficult it is to consider someone else after years of doing exactly what I want to do." She laced her hands around one knee and focused on the twinkling starfire. "Independence is a heady thing. I like not having to notify someone if I'm going to be later than usual coming home, and I like not having to confer with someone else before I make plans for the weekend." She sighed wistfully, and a helpless smile tugged at her lips. "On the other hand, I'd love to have someone worry about me if I was late coming home, and I think it would be wonderful if someone planned his week-ends with me in mind.'' She laughed and glanced at Bonita Kaye. "I'm a mass of contradictions!"

"Aren't we all?" said Bonita Kaye, joining in her laughter. "What you have to do is decide what you want most."

"Him." Meeting the older woman's gentle gaze, Faith shrugged helplessly and spread out her hands to emphasize her point. "I love him."

"Why, of course you do!" Bonita Kaye squeezed her hand and laughed. "Anybody could see that! He loves you, too. Why, honey, he's nuts about you."

"You think so?"

"You *know* it, and if he hasn't told you yet, then he needs his tail kicked." She winked. "You send him to me and I'll give him a good swift one." She waved a shooing hand. "Now, go on. He'll be home soon, and you two have a lot to clear up."

Faith rose from the chair and bent over to kiss Bonita Kaye's rosy cheek. "Thanks, friend. What would I do without you?"

"You'd get by, I imagine. Y'all stop by when you've got things settled and we'll celebrate."

"It's a date," Faith assured her, then ran to her car.

Driving through the veil of night, she went over all the things she would say to Houston, but the words fled from her mind when she saw his pickup parked outside the trailer. He was home!

She wanted to run to the trailer and burst through the door, but she reined in her enthusiasm. She didn't know what mood he'd be in, and she didn't want to make a complete fool of herself. Moving with restraint, she climbed the steps outside and opened the door. Houston was sitting in the recliner, the television tuned to an old western. The Apaches were spilling over the hill, and the cavalry was ready for them. Before the first shot was fired, Faith fired one of her own.

"You just missed Odessa."

He didn't look at her. "No, I didn't. I ran into her in Pecos. She and Peewee were having lunch when I stopped by his place for gas."

"Lunch?" Faith moved inside and closed the door. "I fed her lunch."

"You did?" This brought him around to face her, and she could see how tired he looked. "I'm surprised that you didn't string her up."

"So am I." She laughed, turned off the television and sat on the floor in front of his chair. "She has a way of slipping the noose." Looking up into his face, she asked, "How did it go? With Odessa, I mean."

"I told her that I was hopping mad at her for what she did and that I'd never trust her again."

"And?"

"And she said that I was a sight for sore eyes and got better-looking with every breath I took. Then she gave me a kiss and told me that she loved me."

Faith tipped her head to one side and winked at him. "Works every time." She rose up on her knees and rested her hands on his arms when a look of self-reproach passed across his face. "Don't, Houston."

"Don't what"?

"Don't regret giving in to her. I don't." She leaned forward between his knees. "She's not malicious."

"No, she's like a long, hard winter. Nothing you can do about it except endure it." He lifted his hands and slid them down the sides of her hair as a gentle smile formed on his lips. "Where have you been?"

"Here."

"I meant tonight."

"The MacQuays. They invited me over for dinner." She pushed herself up to her feet. "You look positively beat."

"I am."

"Anderson's men have been swarming all over this place. We've even had visits from neighbors I didn't know existed. Everybody is happy for us."

"That pump is a pretty sight." He ran his hands up and down his face in a way that transmitted the weariness he felt.

"I've got some cold milk in the refrigerator and some of Bonita Kay's pecan pralines just for you." She grasped his hands and helped pull him to his feet. "Right this way, oilman." She pushed him into one of the kitchen chairs and poured him a glass of milk. His eyes widened hungrily when she took the foil-covered pralines from her purse and placed them beside the milk.

Sitting next to him, she propped her chin in her hands and gazed at him with open adoration. "Why did you tell Bill McCormick that you were just a legman and that I made all the decisions? Was that a barbed message to me?" She reached out and plucked a loose thread from the sleeve of his blue shirt, and Houston smiled at the familiar gesture.

"I was licking my wounds," he said, giving her a crooked grin. "You know you have a way of cutting a man to the bone with that sharp tongue of yours."

"Me?" She placed a hand over her heart in feigned shock. "What about you? You left here with instructions for me to find a new partner."

"Did you?"

Mischief bubbled within her, and she had trouble keeping it from curving her mouth into a grin. "Well, as a matter of fact, Odessa and I had a long talk about men and the trouble they can cause. I was thinking that Odessa would be an easy person to work with, and—"

"Do you really think I'm buying this?" Houston asked, his brows lifting over shining eyes. "You and Odessa? Give me a break."

"You know why she took off with Peewee, don't you?"

"Because he's breathing," Houston said with heavy sarcasm.

Faith giggled and shook her head. "I let it slip that we owed Peewee a one percent override."

"Faith, I'm ashamed of you! That's like siccing a dog on a defenseless kitten!"

"Peewee seemed to be enjoying the attack," Faith noted. She smiled when he bit into one of the pralines, then fell back in the chair in a mock swoon.

"Yes, sirree. He was soaking up Odessa's flattery like a dry sponge when I broke in on them," Houston said when he'd recovered enough to speak. "What's this?" he asked, glancing at some papers Bill McCormick had left earlier.

"Anderson's projections," Faith said, grinning when he sucked in his breath. "Not bad, huh? Do you think we can live with that, or should we run to the bank and beg for money?"

"Five hundred barrels a day!" He swallowed hard. "That sounds like a winner to me."

"Like us," Faith added with a happy smile.

"Like us," he agreed.

The low timbre of his voice drew her gaze to his, and her heart skipped a beat. His tawny eyes glinted attractively, carving a tunnel to her soul. He popped the rest of the praline into his mouth and washed it down with the rest of the milk. Lacing his fingers on top of his stomach, he looked at her with a serious expression.

"So, what will it be? Shall we remain partners?"

"Yes. Is that okay with you?"

"Fine with me. I just want you to be happy."

"I am." She sighed with bliss and propped her chin in her hands to soak in the rugged beauty of him. His hair, light gold and attractively mussed, grew like a lion's mane back from his wide forehead. His eyes, earthy and warm, held hers in an hypnotic embrace. His face, weather-beaten and deeply tanned, was perfect, flawed only by the scar on his chin. "Isn't this nice?" Faith asked. "I like doing business with you, Mr. Traynor."

"I was thinking that we've made a lot of decisions sitting at this table."

Faith laughed softly in agreement. "It's not a kitchen table; it's a conference table."

"Or confrontation table, depending on what we happen to be discussing."

"Oh, well. What's life without a little confrontation from time to time?"

"Does that mean that I'm forgiven?"

"Forgiven?" She ran her hands along his arms to his elbows and held on. "What about me? I was out of line when I blew up about offering Mac and Bonita Kay an override. They deserve it."

"But I should have asked your opinion before I blurted it out."

She narrowed her eyes thoughtfully. "You've been thinking about this, haven't you?"

"I've been miserable. I thought that you might have packed up and left a forwarding address."

"You actually thought that the same woman who tracked you down in Mentone and begged you to come home would surrender so easily?"

"Well, I hadn't thought of it in those terms. Now that you mention it, I should have known better. All alone in my motel room I kept thinking of how my life has changed since you came into it." His hands cupped her elbows, and his thumbs made lazy circles against her skin. "I could understand how you might think that I'd gone off the deep end after we struck oil. You said I was just like your dad, and—"

"You're not. I was wrong," Faith hurried to correct him. "Besides, there are worse things than being overly generous. I know that you were delirious—so was I. I just came back down to earth before you did."

"You brought me down to earth with a thump, lady." He chuckled, shaking his head in a bewildered way. "Who would have thought that a level-headed, cultured lady like you would take up with an impulsive roughneck like me?"

"Stranger things have happened," she allowed, then smiled as she moved from the chair to Houston's lap. He wrapped his arms around her waist, and Faith nestled closer to him. "Are you positive that you don't want to abandon this venture? I want you to be happy, too."

He stood up, moving slowly and deliberately as he gathered her into his arms and kissed her hungrily. "I think we'd be crazy to abandon it." His lips danced upon hers, sliding and dipping and swooping. "This isn't a shallow pocket. It's a major discovery."

Overjoyed, she laughed and matched him kiss for kiss. He lifted her into his arms and took her into the bedroom, where the laboring air conditioner was having trouble keeping the room cool. When he set her on her feet, she wasted no time in removing his shirt so that she could drop tiny, nibbling kisses on his moist skin.

"That feels wonderful," he murmured as his own fingers released the buttons on her shirt. "Is it warm in here, or am I having a hot flash?"

She laughed and unfastened his jeans. Slowly pushing them down his legs, she dropped to her knees before him and kissed the skin just above the nest of crisp hair. He gathered handfuls of her hair, and his legs trembled.

"*We're* having a hot flash," she whispered as her hands moved up to explore his arousal. "Look what we have here," she murmured playfully, but she could see that he was in no mood for teasing. He was barely breathing, as if he were trying desperately to maintain a thread of self-control. She kissed him and ran her tongue up and down before taking him fully.

"Faith!" His voice broke on the word, and in one swift move he lifted her from her knees and onto the bed. "You're wicked, Faith," he teased. "Wicked and wonderful."

"I'm just a woman who knows what she wants, and I want you." She ran her hands across his shoulders and along his waist and he undressed her and threw her clothes all over the room.

A moan filled the room and shook the windowpanes, and Faith realized that it wasn't Houston who had released the mournful sound as the wind moaned again and beat against the trailer, bringing an end to the still, sultry heat.

Tuning out the other elements, Faith listened to the hammering of her heart as Houston moved purposefully on top of her. His hands seemed to be everywhere; on her breasts, her legs, her waist, her shoulders. His mouth hungered for hers, and she drank in his kisses as if they were sweet wine.

Touching him was a soul-stirring experience. Faith couldn't get enough of the taste of his lips, the swift caresses of his tongue and the gentle brush of his hands across her moist skin. Arching upward, she took him into her, and her entire being welcomed him home. She held his face between her hands, and her fingers traced the contours of his high cheekbones, lean cheeks, short chin and deep-set eyes. He turned his head to kiss her fingertips, his eyes closed in gentle submission.

"Nothing has ever felt as right as this," he whispered against her palm. "I wish I could tell you...could find the words..."

She curled her fingers against his cheeks and ran her thumbs across his lips. Raising her head off the pillow, she brushed her mouth against his, her lips parting to accept his probing tongue. The sensuous movement of his body told her all she needed to know. With an ease she had come to expect from him, he brought her to the height of passion again and again until she was begging him to join her in the exquisite experience.

When his body shuddered into hers, Faith felt as if he had forged a union that could never be broken. No words, not even holy ones, could bind them any closer than they were at that moment, when their shared ecstasy wedded them for all time.

His lips nuzzled the side of her neck as he slipped out of her. A chuckle escaped him, and he lifted his head to look at her.

"All good things must come to an end," he said, grinning. "I never thought I'd be attracted to a brazen woman, but here I am—bewitched, bothered and bewildered, as the old song goes."

"Brazen woman?" Faith felt her eyes widen. "Me?"

"Well, you aren't shy, honey."

"Not as shy as you, but I have my moments. Remember that night when I taunted you about LaQuita until you kissed me?

"Mm-hmm," he responded as his tongue traced the curve of her ear. "One of my favorite memories."

"Well, I was shaking inside," she admitted, recalling the mixture of fear and fascination. "I wanted you to kiss me, but I was beginning to think that you never would!"

"I was scared."

"Of what?"

He looked down into her face, and his lips brushed across the tip of her nose. "Of what your reaction might be if I tried to kiss you. I couldn't imagine a woman like you taking up with a wildcatter like me."

"There was a time, not so long ago, when I couldn't imagine such a thing, either." Her hands slipped up his spine to the solidity of his shoulders. "That was before I was bowled over by a Texas tornado called Houston Traynor."

He smiled, obviously delighted with her description of him. "You played me right down the line, didn't you?" He laughed lightly at her confused expression. "Teasing me about LaQuita until I was out of my mind with the need to kiss you." He moistened his lips, then touched them to hers. "You're good for me."

"I hope so...."

"No hoping about it," he said, rolling onto his back with a contented sigh. "You bring out the best in me."

Faith propped herself up on one elbow and caressed him with loving eyes. She let her fingers lift the hair off his forehead and smooth it back so that she could kiss his wide forehead.

"Listen to that wind," he said, turning his head to meet her gaze. "It's kicking up out there."

"In here, too," she said with a wicked grin. "Glad to be home?"

"I'm glad to be with you again." He held one of her hands and placed it on his chest. "I saw a piece of land in Muleshoe that looks real promising. I know you don't believe in surface geology, but I swear I could see an oil structure. I walked it off, and I felt the same way about it that I felt about this spot."

Running her fingers through the crisp hair on his chest, Faith smiled at the excitement that coursed through his voice. "Is this a proposition?"

"Well, I thought we might mosey over to Muleshoe and check it out. You could run tests to confirm my hunch about the place."

"We make a good team, don't we?" she asked, suddenly feeling as if a verbal commitment were in order. He had done everything except ask her to marry him, and the omission bothered her and made her feel vulnerable.

He squeezed her hand and dropped a kiss on her lips. "We sure do. What do you think about Muleshoe?"

"Muleshoe," she repeated with a little laugh. "Sounds...romantic."

"There's a lot of oil around there," Houston said, capturing her hand and squeezing it. "You like being a wildcatter, don't you?"

"I like being a wildcatter with you," she amended, her gaze caught by the hand that held hers. "I never thought that taking risks could be so much fun."

"Well, hell! It's only money."

She laughed with him and gave him a smacking kiss. "And all it takes to make money is more money."

"And we've got that now," he agreed. "I still can hardly believe it." His eyes took on a faraway glimmer. "We've struck oil, Faith! Everybody said we were nuts, but we showed them."

"We sure did." A tingle raced up her spine when her thoughts veered to the future. "Do you think we could do it again?"

"Don't see why not." His thumb moved to caress the inside of her wrist. "I'm willing if you are."

"Well, I—"

"Shhh." He kissed her lips, silencing her. "Listen to that."

"What?" She cocked her head to one side and heard a soft tapping. "What is it?"

He looked at her, his face breaking into a smile.

"If I remember right, that is the sound of rain!"

"Rain?" She sat up, straining her ears. "Here? Impossible."

Houston bounded out of bed and grabbed up his underwear and jeans. "Hot damn, it's been ages since we've had a good rain. We've got to see this with our own eyes, honey. Hurry up! Get dressed and let's go take a look-see."

Faith scrambled from the bed and pushed her arms into a brushed cotton robe. She raced from the room as she tied the sash at her waist. Looking over her shoulder, she laughed at the sight of Houston, hopping on one foot as he struggled to pull up his jeans.

When she opened the door, raindrops splashed onto her face. Holding up her hands, she let the water pool in her palms as her laughter mingled with the sound of the rain.

"You're right!"

Houston pushed her outside and followed her. "Right as rain," he said, lifting his face to the downpour. "I'd forgotten how good this feels."

"Does it rain in Muleshoe?"

"Yes." He turned in a slow circle, and water ran in rivulets down his face. "It rains oil *and* water." He looked at her with passion-darkened eyes. "Come here, woman." His hand caught hers and yanked her to his chest. His mouth was warm and wet. "You're so beautiful," he murmured as his thumbs moved across her cheekbones. "Sometimes when I look at you, I'm afraid that you're just a vision and that you'll float away from me."

Faith swallowed hard as her gaze moved over his rain-spattered face. The need for a deep commitment was strong within her, but she battled it. He had called her "brazen", but he would be surprised to know that she felt like a shrinking violet at this moment. Remembering his earlier vow not to be tied down until he was ready and able, Faith ground her teeth together to keep from begging him to marry her.

Marriage! The word exploded in her mind. She used to think that marriage was a distant dream and something she could live without, but Houston had changed all of that. Couldn't he sense how much she wanted him—not just physically and emotionally, but legally as well? She wanted to be bound to him in every way possible.

His hands tightened on her shoulders, and he stepped back so that he could look at her. His gaze moved from her face down to her toes and back up again.

"I like that robe, but I *love* it now that it's wet." His fingertips moved down to the thrusting crests of her breasts showing through the soaked material. "You're not going to drift away from me, are you? I mean, we *are* partners, aren't we?"

"You want a guarantee?" Faith murmured through trembling lips.

"Am I asking too much?" Houston countered as he filled his hands with her pliant breasts.

Faith closed her eyes for a moment as the touch of him made her dizzy. "Houston, I need a guarantee, too." Her hands captured his, and she shivered.

"Let's go inside before you get cold," he said, starting to move away, but her hands held him fast. "What's wrong?"

"You're drifting away from me," she said, oblivious of the cold rain that had plastered her hair to her head and had begun to make her shiver. "I don't want to corner you or...or make you feel as if I'm forcing you to say things that you don't feel...."

He tipped his head to one side for a careful scrutiny. "Faith, what are you getting at?"

"Don't you know?"

"I'm not sure...."

She let go of him as her courage deserted her. "Never mind." She rushed past him into the trailer. A deep shudder passed through her, but she knew that it had nothing to do with the cold rain. She didn't turn around when she heard the door close. She couldn't face him. She couldn't let him see her disappointment.

Houston stared at her and smiled. The robe clung to all the right places. He couldn't help himself—he stepped closer and cupped her hips in his hands. She didn't move a muscle, so he bent his head and kissed the side of her neck.

"Let's make love again," he murmured.

"No. Not yet."

The thread of pain in her voice brought his head up and sharpened his senses. He spun her around and saw the glitter of tears in her eyes. "What's this?" he asked. "Are you having second thoughts about getting tangled up with a wildcatter?"

"No." She looked down at his chest, unable to meet his eyes. "Houston, can I ask you something without you taking it the wrong way?"

"Ask."

"Do you...well, love me?"

"Let me think..." He smiled, feeling lighthearted and giddy, but her answering frown dampened his amusement. "Hey, hey!" He crooked a finger under her chin and lifted it until her eyes met his. "Are you serious?"

"Of course I'm serious!" she snapped, jerking her head and backing away from him. Tears filled her eyes, and she clenched her fists at her sides. "I need to know!"

He spread his hands out in a helpless gesture. "Well, hell, Faith! I thought that went without saying."

She gave him an incredulous glare and was speechless for a few moments. "Without saying?" she finally managed. "Don't you want to know if I love you?"

He shrugged and shook his head. "I never questioned it."

"Never...questioned..." she sputtered, then planted her fists at her waist. "Well, *I* question it! You've been stringing me along all this time and—"

"Hold on a minute," he interrupted. "How have I been stringing you along?"

"Do you remember the first time we made love?"

He rolled his eyes in exasperation. "Of course! Do you think I'm so unfeeling that I'd forget *that*?"

"You don't want me to answer that question," she said, folding her arms across her breasts and moving out of the puddle she'd made on the carpet. "You told me that you couldn't make a commitment until you were financially stable...or something to that effect. Well, how financially stable do you have to be? A millionaire? A multimillionaire? I mean, how long am I expected to wait?"

Understanding dawned in his eyes, and he plowed his fingers through his wet hair and chuckled. "Okay, okay. I'm beginning to see where you're headed. You're feeling uncertain about my intentions, is that it?"

"I just want to know if you love me," Faith said, finally able to blurt it out without stammering.

"Honey, I've told you I love you a hundred times. I've said it every time I looked at you; every time I touched you; every time I made love to you." He reached out a hand and ran his fingertips down the length of her robe's damp sleeve. "If you want to hear the words, then listen carefully—I love you, Faith Hutton. I love you when you're soft and cuddly and when you're foul tempered and sharp-tongued and even when you're soaking wet." He glanced toward the bedroom. "Now let's go in there and I'll prove it."

She smiled warmly but moved out of his reach. "In a minute," she promised.

"Now what?" he asked, his voice rising with exasperation.

"Well, for one thing, I should tell you that I love you."

"I already knew that."

Her brows lifted. "What an ego! How could you have known—"

"You wouldn't have gone to bed with me if you didn't love me," he said, smiling smugly.

"I beg your pardon! I'm a—"

"Oh, I know, you're a modern woman and all that, but deep down you're an old-fashioned girl." He grinned at her startled gasp. "That's right. Old-fashioned. When it comes to loving, you're not the sort to take risks. I knew you loved me after that first night. I just wasn't sure if your love would last."

"Are you sure now?"

"As sure as I can be." He held out his hand and looked at her beseechingly. "Now come on, honey. Let's quit talking and—"

"No." She shook her head and ignored his sigh of frustration. "We were talking about guarantees earlier."

He propped his hands at his hips. "Yes?"

She stared at him, her mind screaming at him to propose. When he stood his ground, she gave in to her overwhelming frustration and stamped her foot angrily. "Damn it, Houston! Don't make me ask you!"

"Ask me?" He blinked his eyes in utter confusion. "Ask me—" His lips pressed together and his blue eyes widened, then narrowed to glittering slits. "Miss Hutton, are you by any chance waiting for a proposal of marriage?"

"No," she said sarcastically. "I'm waiting for my clothes to dry!"

He grinned and closed the distance between them in one long stride. His arms enfolded her, and he laughed softly.

"It's not funny," she said, her lower lip inching out into a pout.

"I'm sorry," he replied, grinning, "I just didn't realize you were *that* old-fashioned!"

"It's not old-fashioned. It's common sense. If two people love each other and—"

"How does honeymooning in Muleshoe sound to you?"

Her head jerked back and her lips parted in surprise. "Honeymoon?"

"I guess I'm putting the cart before the horse. Will you marry me, Faith?" He shook a finger in her face, his lips slanting into a rakish grin. "Now, don't you dare turn me down after putting me through all this."

"Did I force you into this, Houston? If you don't want—"

"Just answer the question," he cut in.

"Yes, if you're sure." Her heart hammered against her ribs as she brought her hands up to the back of his neck. "I don't want you to feel cornered."

"Cornered?" He threw back his head and laughed. "Honey, marrying you would be a dream come true. I just didn't want to rush you into it. I know you're a careful woman when it comes to matters of the heart."

"Not where you're concerned," she admitted, letting her lips brush against the crisp hair on his chest. The rain tasted good on him. "I want to be your wife, Houston. I want to grow old with you and have children with you and do all those other things that people in love do." She laughed softly and rested her cheek against his chest. "I never thought I'd say those things, but I mean them. I really do." A long sigh escaped her. "Oh, Houston Traynor, I love you so much!"

"Does that mean you'll marry me?"

"Only if you take me to Muleshoe. I'm itching to call up some more dinosaurs."

He kissed the top of her head. "You sound like a wildcatter."

"I *am* a wildcatter, and damn proud of it!" She tipped back her head to share the moment with him. "I guess I'm my father's daughter. He should have worked in the oilfields instead of being stuck behind a desk."

"He'd be proud of you, Faith," Houston whispered as his lips claimed the last drops of rain from her face. "Do you think he'd approve of me as his son-in-law?"

"He'd be tickled pink," Faith said, leaning her head to one side so that Houston's mouth could nuzzle her neck. "Let's name the next well we bring in after him."

"Fine with me." He leaned back in her arms and smiled. "I owe him a lot. He gave me you. I hope you're making the right decision. Wildcatting is a risky way to make a living, Faith. Sometimes you're rich and sometimes..." He shrugged off the last of the thought.

"Houston, you're looking at a rich woman," she said as her love for him filled her heart. "And it has nothing to do with money. As long as I have you, I've got everything."

His smile was tender, and his lips trembled slightly with a burst of sentimentality. "Oh, Faith," he whispered hoarsely. "Do you mean that?"

"With all my heart," she vowed to the man who had come to mean the world to her.

He smiled and untied the sash at her waist. His hands moved inside, warm and welcome. "We've got it all, darlin'." He placed a sweet kiss on her lips, then let out a joyous whoop. "Muleshoe, here we come!"

Silhouette Special Edition

COMING NEXT MONTH

BIRD IN FLIGHT
Sondra Stanford

Andrea had worked non-stop to become one of the most acclaimed reporters. It had cost her marriage as she felt she couldn't be the wife Bill needed. A crisis brought them together and the magic suddenly came to life. But were they building false hopes or a new beginning?

TRANSER OF LOYALITIES
Roslyn MacDonald

Adrienne was dedicated to her work but she hadn't counted on her responsiveness to Jared. It was tempting to reveal the passionate side of herself but could she afford the risk. Was it time for a transfer of loyalties?

AS TIME GOES BY
Brooke Hastings

Dr Sarah Byers forced herself to look past Jonathan the man and concentrate on the investor. He was interested in her project but he was a man who spent most of his time negotiating deals. And Sarah would have to barter for everything she wanted — except his love.

COMING NEXT MONTH

LOVE'S HAUNTING REFRAIN
Ada Steward

Amelia had come to Oklahoma as a young bride
following King Stockton into a world of open
spaces. Their passion survived the years, but the
sharing that should have brought them closer was
kept at bay by a secret King dared not reveal.

MY HEART'S UNDOING
Phyllis Halldorson

Collen had been in love with Erik for as long as she
could remember and now he was getting married.
But when he was jilted Collen was there to pick up
the pieces. Could Erik learn to return her love? . . .

SURPRISE OFFER
Carole Halston

Dana was part owner of a cleaning service but her
heart had always belonged to football. So when one
of her clients walked·in to find her watching football
on his T.V. Dana had some explaining to do . . .

MAY TITLES

RETURN TO PARADISE
Jennifer West

REFLECTIONS OF YESTERDAY
Debbie Macomber

VEIN OF GOLD
Elaine Camp

SUMMER WINE
Freda Vasilos

DREAM GIRL
Tracy Sinclair

SECOND NATURE
Nora Roberts